MW00783313

Masques of Darkover
Darkover® Anthology 17

Edited by
Deborah J. Ross

The Marion Zimmer Bradley Literary Works Trust
PO Box 193473
San Francisco, CA 94119
www.mzbworks.com

Contents

INTRODUCTION

by Deborah J. Ross

When I read the submissions to each past Darkover anthology, I felt as if I was unwrapping a stack of holiday gifts. This year, in part because of the title, the "unwrapping" also felt like "opening night" or "special VIP dress rehearsal." Discovering what these authors have created out of their own superb imaginations and their love for the world of the Bloody Sun is a privilege, and this first reading is like a private performance for my delight. But just as a play or concert or opera—and Marion adored opera—ought not to be limited to an audience of one, so this anthology fulfills its promise by entertaining the widest possible readership: Darkover's devoted fans, old and new.

The masque originated in the late Middle Ages as a folk tradition in which masked players would entertain nobility with dancing, music, and gifts, often to celebrate a special occasion. We're all familiar with the play-within-a-play, "Pyramus and Thisbe," as a wedding entertainment in William Shakespeare's *A Midsummer Night's Dream*. In the literary version of a masque, here is a procession of revels to delight your reading hours. Some are humorous, others dark, some gritty, others whimsical, all reflecting the richness and breadth of adventures to be had on the world of the Bloody Sun. Here you will find tales by authors featured in previous Darkover anthologies, as well as others who have returned from an absence or are making their "Darkover debut" but are seasoned professionals nonetheless.

We begin our festivities with the setting of the scene: an arrival on Darkover as Jane M. H. Bigelow escorts us on "Duvin's Grand Tour." Every anthology I've edited has presented me with "variations on a theme," also a technique in musical composition. *Masques of Darkover* is no exception, so we will see other, very different arrivals, with equally diverse consequences. People come to Darkover for many reasons: personal, professional, even religious as in Meg Mac Donald's "Upon this Rock," that offers a new dialog between Darkover's *cristoforo* sect and its Terran Christian cousins. Travelers find mysteries and sometimes answers, love and loss, and always Darkover's special magic. Sometimes, as the protagonist of "Where You're Planted," by Rebecca Fox, they find themselves, a theme featured in a number of Marion Zimmer Bradley's early Darkover novels. The stories by Robin Wayne Bailey ("The Mountains of Light"), Ty Nolan ("Dark Comfort"), and Leslie Roy Carter and Margaret L. Carter ("Believing") show other ways talented authors interpret the simple premise of "a Terran arrives on Darkover..."

Traveling to Darkover's distant past to the generations following Landfall, Rosemary Edghill examines the transformation of those early settlers to become truly Darkovan. What do they gain, and what must they surrender? In "The Wind," Shariann Lewitt takes us a little further forward in time, but still within the years when Darkovans—sometimes aristocrats, sometimes ordinary people—explored the psychic Gifts called *laran*. In a subsequent time, the use of *laran* led also to the creation of weapons of horrendous power, as Marella Sands depicts in her chilling tale, "Bone of My Bone."

One of my favorite "variations" in these stories involves innovative uses of *laran*. Some of the previously-mentioned stories involve new twists on psychic abilities, both in Darkovan and alien peoples. In *Hawkmistress*, Marion portrayed the mental bond between woman and hawk, and now Evey Brett explores that link (in this case, between boy and horse) in "Only Men Dance." The dangers of the powers of the mind, carelessly invoked, drive Steven Harper's "Sight Unseen." And, finally, India Edghill offers equal parts unsettling tale and humor in "The Price of Stars."

On that note, our *divertissement* draws to a close, with the hope that you have not only been amused but come away with something of lasting value.

DUVIN'S GRAND TOUR

by Jane M. H. Bigelow

Jane M. H. Bigelow celebrated her first professional publication in *Free Amazons of Darkover*. Since then, she has published a fantasy novel, *Talisman*, as well as short stories and short nonfiction on such topics as gardening in Ancient Egypt. Her short story, "The Golden Ruse" appeared in *Luxor: Gods, Grit and Glory*, and she is currently working on a mystery set in 17th century France. Jane is a retired reference librarian, a job which encouraged her to go on being curious about everything and exposed her to a rich variety of people. She lives in Denver, CO with her husband and two spoiled cats.

Jane brings her curiosity and humor to Darkover. Her story "Snow Dancing" (*Realms of Darkover*) introduced cross-country skiing to the world of many snows. Here she presents us with a most unlikely hero, one who reminds us that competence comes in many varieties, and even on Darkover it is best to not judge a book by its cover or a tourist by his costume.

Just on the other side of that scarred beige door, Darkover began. Well, technically I'd have to get out of the spaceport and embassy area first, but still. I hoisted my luggage.

"Excuse me, sir," someone chirped. "I was to meet Mr. Duvin Wrothesley here?" A weedy young man dressed in loose trousers, shirt, and tunic, all in some scratchy-looking fabric, smiled at me.

"Yes, I'm he." I didn't remember Fensey, my IPA, arranging for a greeter. Fellow looked respectable enough, though, from what I'd been able to learn of clothing standards on Cottman IV. Darkover. I must start calling it Darkover.

"I'm Istvan MacAndra, here to help you find the Hotel Universe, sir. Our *Terranan* guests find their first few days a challenge without their electronics." A stocky man with a hand cart trotted up.

It didn't seem wise to leave with strangers. How could I ask for ID without sounding fussy?

"Ah," said Istvan, and produced a small card. It had his picture on it, and the logo for Hotel Universe. He was evidently one of their welcome committee. No chip to scan, but then, I hadn't anything to scan with.

"Thank you," I said, and we left the building.

Walking into the red sunlight felt like going through a magic curtain. Even the other Terran Standard spaceport buildings looked eerie. We had to stand around again while a guard checked our papers, but I had something great to look at.

My Aunt Amelia hadn't believed the pix. "No place is really that dramatic," she'd said. "Pixglam gone wild," she'd sneered.

She was wrong.

Comyn Castle stood on the other side of a wide valley. A gap in the clouds let big streaks of light down onto it like a scene in a historomance—not that I ever watched them, really, but sometimes one couldn't get out of it without being rude to one's sisters' friends. I did think it would be great fun to wear a cape.

The tops of the castle towers gleamed. One could picture lords and ladies out of old legends strolling up there. I squinted a bit—yes, that was definitely a battlement. Too far to tell if there were people on it. I'd read Comyn Castle was still a functioning government building *and* a residence for some of the—

Telepathic rulers. Had Istvan read my mind? He wasn't royalty—not even noble, so far as I knew. Mustn't be paranoid. He'd read my body language. Yes, that was it.

I've always thought myself to be good at direction-finding, but wayfinding without being able to check a wayfinder program of any sort was different. Once we left the spaceport, there didn't seem to be a simple crossways intersection anywhere. The hotel stood at the edge of the Trade City; long before we got there, my feet ached. Good thing we had a porter. He hauled my luggage upstairs, too. My room looked like a child's fairy story file with carved wooden furniture and embroidered textiles. It had no view through its tiny window, but I decided I didn't care.

As I spread tips about, Istvan said, "I'm leading an orientation tour tomorrow, if you'd care to join us?"

I opened my mouth to refuse.

"I've obtained official permission for us to go inside Comyn Castle."

Oh, ah.

"I've an office here. You can let me know tomorrow morning, if you like."

I wasn't going to be on my own nearly as much as I'd hoped, was I? Still, it had been a totally closed planet until quite recently.

My first sight of Istvan's tour group made me glad I'd decided to go solo. One married couple pointedly not speaking to each other, one other married couple chattering away madly, a ferociously fit woman with short dark hair who reminded me of the woman I was engaged to before Emma, though she hadn't had freckles, and one amiable old duffer who kept trying to tell her a story. Istvan introduced us all. Freckles's name was Francine Salazar; the duffer was Cao Jin. I forgot the rest immediately.

We went into the public courtyard of Comyn Castle, up the grand staircase, and into an entrance hall. I wasn't impressed. When we have a public day at home, we don't keep people standing on the doorstep.

I'd met Emma on one of our public days. Her friends had gone on without her, and the poor girl was wandering in circles trying to find her way out. She was so tired, and so embarrassed when I told her that Uncle's study was not part of our tour that I took her down to the kitchen for a bit of tea and cake, and it all went on from there.

So far this trip was not doing much to take my mind off Emma.

"Now, as I told you, we're here by special permission." Istvan was one of those professionally cheery fellows, but right now he looked a bit tense. "Please do not ask the guards to pose with you; they are at work."

I don't believe I would've tried to chat with those guards anyway. The younger one looked at us as if he'd seen Landarian slime molds oozing across the cobbles. The balding one stared straight ahead, hand on his sword.

Looking at him, I missed a step and staggered up two. The

younger guard muttered something to the older one. It doesn't take any psychic powers to tell when you're being laughed at. Was it my fault those stairs were worn in the middle?

An awful lot of feet must have crossed them, to wear them down so.

We trooped in through a small door let into a large one. Translucent panels of stone let light into the foyer's upper reaches where brightly colored banners hung. A red-haired man whose name I didn't catch began explaining, in detail, who and what several of them represented.

Rooms and corridors opened off the foyer. The castle must be as much of a maze as my uncle's place, and maybe worse. From where I stood, it looked as though some rooms opened straight into other rooms.

All that stone sent sound bouncing around like tennis balls. Somewhere, someone was playing a tune on some kind of woodwind. My toes twitched as I listened. The music stopped, and started again, repeating a phrase. I could hear someone say, "Again!"

That was one of the first words I learned on the long voyage here, along with please and thank you. As soon as people find out you speak any of their language they start chatting away as if you'd spoken it all your life and words get lost. Happens everywhere I've been.

The music stopped, and a woman's laughter rang out, musical as the tune. Maybe more so. Odd, how much laughs vary; Emma's always had an edge to it.

"*Damisela* Ginevra! Show them how," said Teacher-Voice.

Could I get Istvan to find me a dance class? I'm rather good at dancing, though you wouldn't think it to see me stumble up those steps. Takes real talent to fall upstairs. Could I see, through that doorway—

Right behind me, Istvan cleared his throat. "Mr. Wrothesley? Please stay with us."

"Oh! Ah, sorry." I could feel myself blush.

The music stopped. A tall, skinny man in worn velvet came into the foyer and stared down at us. Suddenly I was standing alone.

Apologizing's the second thing I learn in a new language. It doesn't usually come in handy quite *this* fast. "Sir, I regret my intrusion."

The man blinked. "Your apology is accepted, young sir."

I'm pretty sure that calling me "*young* sir" was not entirely respectful, but I wasn't about to make a fuss. Istvan gathered us up and led us out into rain that couldn't decide whether to be snow. The air wasn't any chillier than the other tourists' faces.

I could hear someone murmur, "Do you think he's quite safe to be on a trip like this alone?"

Istvan half-jogged up beside me. "You speak good *casta*." It sounded almost like a question, and not entirely approving.

I shrugged in what I hoped was a nonchalant way. "Thanks. Languages come easily to me. It always seems to me as if other travelers must not be trying much." I'm certainly not the brightest light in the harbor. Languages aren't that hard unless you're dealing with something like Nahouendari, with its three kinds of "r" and its weird gutturals.

I found a Trade City shop for capes all on my own that afternoon, and bought a splendid one in a subtle green and brown plaid. On my way back, I caught a glimpse of a local non-human sentient, a *kyrri* I think. It was a little gray simian sort that stared at me a moment with great green eyes and slipped off down another street.

I also caught sight of Istvan and the group, too late to avoid them. He tried to interest me in their plans for tomorrow. "The rest of Old Thendara's much harder to navigate than the road to the castle," he warned.

I told him I had a printed map; he said they were seldom accurate. The conversation went on like that until I said I'd consider it.

Next morning, I woke before the hotel was stirring. I don't for a moment admit that Istvan had any right to tell me what to do—not as though I were part of his group, after all—but I hate arguing. Better to slip off quietly, leaving a hand-printed text at the front desk. I missed Fensey so much! He would have taken care of communications for me.

Getting into Old Thendara alone was easy. No identity checks, no questions, no officials at all. The narrow streets were full of men and women in wool and leather, blithely ignoring the chilly mist.

Shops spilled out onto the cobblestones. Anyone who sold food had put out a bench or two. All up and down the street were wooden houses and signs. How big *were* their forests here?

Each food place had its own wonderful smell. Sausages! Since I'd scarpered before anyone else was awake, I'd missed breakfast. Here it was. The proprietor took one of the coins I held out and folded my hand firmly over the rest. "That's plenty, lad," she said as she handed me a plate of sizzling food. "Take care, now. We're honest here, but there's places down the hill as aren't, eh?"

I nodded. "Thank you," *what should I call her,* "Mestra." Must've been the right honorific; she smiled again. I set to my sausages. Fatty, salty, spicy, they were everything we were warned against back home. I ate an entire plateful, plus a chunk of nut-bread, washed down with some local tea.

Ah, there was a meal to set a man up for a day's exploring! The local populace looked at me out of the corners of their eyes a bit, but when I polished off breakfast the man next to me said, "Best in Thendara, Alicia's sausages."

"I can believe that." We did the usual my-name-is bit, and then he asked quite bluntly what I was doing here. I explained. Felt a bit sillier with each word.

"You mean," he said slowly, "You came all the way here from Terra just to walk around and look at things?"

"Well, not Terra itself, actually," I began.

"Must be nice," said a voice in the shadows. "Some people have to earn a living."

"It is nice," I agreed, with more cheer than I really felt. Thing is, there isn't really much work for me to do at home. Aunt thought maybe they should ship me off to Cousin Algy after the problems with Emma, but Uncle said I was too much to inflict on any businessman, let alone one beset with contract negotiations with the Arghinian Collective. Uncle does not want any help running the estate. So, I exist beautifully.

It seemed like time to move along. My new cape swirled around nicely when I turned.

I stopped so quickly that the cape slapped my legs. The most beautiful woman I'd ever seen made her way up the street, turning and darting as if it had been a dance floor. Was it the light, or did her blond hair have red lights in it? She laughed, and pushed spirals of hair back into her hood. The hair popped back out.

A curly-haired man loomed out from behind a cluster of other shoppers. I couldn't quite hear his words, but the meaning was clear: Hey, wait for me!

Things were a bit slippy underfoot, but not too bad until the mist thickened to snow. An animal that looked like a cross between a horse and a stag shook its horns at me as I skidded by. It made a peculiar high-pitched bleat and lowered its head.

I leaped aside like a ballet dancer. Wish I'd landed like one. Instead I crashed into the beautiful curly-top.

"Stranger, you are standing on my foot!"

I stepped away. "Oh, ah," I said. "I am so sorry," *Mestra? Damisela? Domna?* Better use the most important one. "Oh, *domna*, I am sorry! Are you injured?"

She flexed her foot. Nice trick, standing on one foot in the snow. I offered my arm, but she waved me away.

How anyone could look so alluring wearing that big bundle of wool with a long cape over it, I didn't know, but she managed. Oh blast, *could* they read minds? Womanly, that was the word I wanted. Womanly.

I tried to look anywhere but at the beautiful woman. She had green eyes, tilted up at the ends... How was I supposed to not think about how attractive she was? The old children's trick of singing, "La la la, I can't hear you," came to mind, but this would have to be "La la la, you can't hear me." Would it work any better?

She giggled.

The man who'd been following loomed up beside her. "Ginevra," he said, in a voice like doom. I was dashed glad she hadn't taken my arm.

She shook her head. "Oh, Alastair, (something). He barely looked at me."

Husband? Brother? I hoped it was brother. Not that it mattered, really, after Emma.

I smiled at them both. People have told me I've a nice smile.

Her giant friend drew himself even taller. "Ginevra. You are—"

Lady Ginevra wrapped both hands around his forearm. "Alastair. Come on, we're already late for this morning's dance practice."

Alastair made a low grumbling noise, rather like a bulldog my Aunt Amelia used to have, and let Lady Ginevra lead him away. Whew.

Istvan pounced the moment I stepped through the door of the hotel. "Ah, good, you're back. We wouldn't want to be late for tonight's cultural evening, would we, Mr. Wrothesley?"

I had hoped to miss it entirely. It sounded dreadful. I strongly suspected there would be a performance by school children involved. Also, what does one say to people at these things? A man can't very well just stand there grinning foolishly. Or rather, he can—I have, lots of times—but it isn't much liked.

As it turned out, they had enough questions to keep me positively chatty. Quite refreshing, being among people who actually thought I knew something! My throat did begin to get dry from talking so much.

The room smelled of beeswax, hot wine, spices, woodsmoke, and lots of people. There was a refreshments table, away at the other end of the room from me. It—the room, I mean, not the table—stretched from front to back of the house. Candles flickered in polished stone sconces all along the way.

They flickered in the red-gold curls of a woman in dark green. "*Damisela* Ginevra, how lovely to see you," cried one of the other ladies. Punch could wait.

Damisela. Damisela. That meant she wasn't married. Not that I cared about that, really. I wasn't looking for a romance. I swore off all that after Emma let Uncle persuade her to go away. I think money may have been involved. Not going to think about that right now.

"Ginevra, Mr. Wrothesley was telling us about hunts on Herschel V. Imagine, they chase a machine!"

She opened her eyes wide. "And does it prey on machines that make *Terranan* cloth?"

"No," I began, and saw the joke in time to change my words. I laughed. "It's only a game."

A man loomed up beside her. "Hunts are real enough here. Ginevra, isn't this the man who ogled you in the market?"

"This is Mr. Wrothesley, brother, and he's taken the trouble to learn *casta* quite well."

The G.B. looked elsewhere.

"Mr. Wrothesley, *Dom* Alastair Lindir-Delleray. Alastair, he's been telling us all about hunts on Herschel V. Imagine, they chase machines."

Dom Alastair frowned. "Why?"

It did sound a bit silly, I suppose. But we haven't herds to protect, not with the vats turning out perfectly good protein without anything having to suffer. And we can have the thrill of the chase without actually hurting anything, which is rather nice. I was still trying to explain this when there was a stir by the street door.

"Oh, look," said Ginevra. "Here come our young dancers!"

It wasn't half bad, actually. Then we strangers were allowed to try for ourselves—only ring-dances, though. No chance to dance with Ginevra.

If I'd told the group about my plans to find a dancing-master then at least half of them would have wanted to come along, so I didn't.

The hotelier's directions were not all that they might have been. I never did find the dance master. Once I was well away from our hotel, rain started coming in sideways. My cloak was gaining weight by the minute and whacking against my legs hard enough to sting through my trousers. When I spotted a *jaco* place, I dived for it.

The cup I got was clean. The place itself could have used a scrub and polish; I wedged myself into a seat against one wall where the light wasn't too good. Sometimes one really doesn't want to know. It was away from the doorway, also a good thing.

The windows let in light, and a blurry glimpse of colors moving about. Two blurs moved towards the shop; two women, one tall and one short, blew through the door in a flurry of skirts. The shorter woman put back her hood and looked around at the crowd.

I wish I were a poet. I can put words together in several languages, but I can't tell you how those copper-gold curls shone in the dark room.

The man behind the counter grinned at them. "Fruit buns with your *jaco*, ladies?"

Were they regulars here? They were almost the only women, but no one looked surprised to see them.

The only tables were by the door. I rose and edged out of my corner, waving at the bench. If they sat close together they could both squeeze in. *Damisela* Ginevra hesitated.

Oh, no. Was it dreadfully rude? I just wanted to offer them a seat.

They buzzed together a bit and headed towards me. Sitting near me must be more-or-less acceptable.

The taller woman didn't sit down. "Oh, *Damisela*, I'm so sorry! I've left the cheese for the buns." And she zipped back across the room.

Where she stayed. In fact, I could see a small pot of soft cheese on the tray she'd plunked down.

I began to feel a bit uneasy.

"I suppose I ought to discourage Marja from flirting with Ethan, but it really does seem harmless," Ginevra said.

Ah. I stretched out a bit, trying to look casual. My trousers rode up, and my heart sank. I'd put on socks of two different colors. *Way to impress a lady, Duv. I wish I could've brought Fensey with me.*

"Who's Fensey?" Ginevra asked. Then she blushed. "Oh, Mr. Wrothesley, I'm sorry! I don't think you meant me to hear that. Shall I pretend I didn't?"

"No, no ... it's okay. I just wish I knew how to—I mean, that one's nothing embarrassing, but sometimes—" *Not going to think about that.*

Ginevra waited for me to fight my way through the tangle of words. "Anyhow," I continued, "Fensey's my IPA. My integrated personal attendant, I mean. He kept my clothing straight, so I didn't do things like wear mismatched socks, and he managed my calendar, and, and," I shrugged. "He kept things organized. Will again, when I go home."

"Why couldn't you bring him? I bring my maid with me whenever I travel. I'd be lost without her."

"Because you still ban most of our technology."

She looked blank.

"Fensey isn't a person. He's a," I paused. There didn't seem to be any word in *casta*. Not surprising, I suppose; if they don't have it then they don't need a word for it.

Ginevra tilted her head to one side, frowning. "You mean, like *kyrri*?"

Okay, try again. "He's *makina*," No, wrong language, "A machine. He's integrated with the rest of the infosphere."

She drew away from me on the bench. "A machine? Your body servant is a machine?"

"Yours isn't?"

"Oh, really, Mr. Wrothesley!"

There it was, the what-kind-of-idiot-is-this tone. *Of course, the tall woman flirting with the jaco seller must be Ginevra's maid. Whew. Sounded like a language exercise—possessives, genders, fancy verb tenses and all. Congrats, Duv, you've convinced a beautiful woman on yet another planet that you're a complete goof.* "Sorry. Istvan says you can send each other messages without communicators, and all sorts of things, so it didn't occur to me..." Guide writers had been hesitant to say for certain about psionics, but not Istvan.

She giggled then, and touched the back of my hand so lightly that I wasn't sure she'd done so. "We can do many things with *laran*, but it would be silly to use it for socks when people can sort those so easily. And I don't think I'd care for having my hair brushed by *laran* at all."

"Doesn't it feel awkward having a person do something so, well, personal?"

"Doesn't it feel awkward having some machine that can talk to other machines knowing all about your clothing?" Now she blushed for real, a hot pink flooding face and as much of her neck as I could see, which wasn't much.

Would she be upset if I patted her hand, a very respectful sort of pat to say 'there, there'?

She patted mine. Hm.

Ginevra set her *jaco* cup down with a thunk. Words came rushing out of her; I strained to keep up. "I can't hear most of your thoughts, Mr. Wrothesley,"

"Oh, please, call me Duvin."

"Duvin, unless you're holding them very clearly on the surface of your mind. Even then I'd need my starstone to be certain."

Her what? But she'd gone on speaking.

"—Not great except for hearing surface thoughts, and *that* so-called gift is the reason I might go into a Tower, even though some of what I catch does make me laugh."

I hoped that didn't include my thoughts.

"People there know how to shield, but it means being shut away from the world so much. I love to dance, and laugh, and you don't do much of that in a Tower—not Dalereuth Tower, anyway."

This jolly girl, closed away, gone all serious? What a waste! I said so.

She glared at her cup as though it had done her an injury. "And I don't want to get married and start bearing babies either, not yet! Not before I've had a little fun, and there's always been some reason for 'Not this year, Ginevra'."

What was I supposed to say to that? And didn't it bother her that the other customers could hear? Maybe not, when you were used to people hearing your thoughts.

I didn't blame her, though. I don't know much about what women go through having babies—one doesn't ask, after all, and that's the sort of conversation that always stops dead as soon as a man comes near. Then they all glare at you as if you, personally, did something horrible to them. "No," I said, "You ought to have fun, and dances, and lots of reasons to laugh."

She laughed then. "But what am I thinking of, to speak so to a stranger? You must think me very bold."

"No need to apologize, *Damisela*. Truly. I, well, ah," I'd better get this said before she got going again. "I'm honored." And I was. Women don't usually tell me things like that. It made me feel quite special. "And I don't think you bold, not at all."

The room must've warmed up some. Even the breeze through the open door of the *jaco* seller's didn't make me shiver.

"For what it's worth, not a married man myself, but on Herschel V marriage isn't so grim. M'sister Julia still seems to laugh a lot, even though teaching at the University and keeping up with her family does keep her busy."

Ginevra looked thoughtful.

"Ginevra!"

Oh ye gods. It was her giant brother again. Now I did feel cold.

"Ginevra Lindir-Delleray!"

Ginevra sat very straight. "Speak a little louder, Alastair. There may be a few people at the other side of this room who haven't heard my name."

He gulped like my Aunt Amelia's bulldog the time it stole the chop, and lowered his voice. A vein jumped on one side of his forehead. "Sitting in a public *jaco* house—"

"It's hardly a den of depravity," Ginevra said.

Alastair gripped his hair. Never actually seen anyone do that, tear their hair. He'd have some out by its roots if he didn't ease off.

"You are not now in Dalereuth Tower, Ginevra! This is Thendara. Please, my sister, I have left the choice up to you. Have I even tried to force your steps either way?"

"That's as well."

"But you must choose."

The maid scurried over from the counter, keeping to the wall until she reached us. She plunked herself down beside Ginevra, who said, "That took you long enough!"

"I'm sorry, Mistress. I, well..." she glanced at the G.B.

The G.B. spared a glare for her. "And you, Marja, I'll deal with you later." Marja edged closer to Ginevra.

Ginevra reached up to pat her shoulder. "If my maid requires correction, which I do not by any means think to be the case, but *if* she should do so then I will see to it. Not you." Very crisp, every consonant perfectly enunciated. She could do learning files for the language people. Alastair had the sense to keep quiet, aside from breathing heavily.

Could I slip away while they were having this family chat? Probably. But there are things a gentleman simply doesn't do. Besides, I didn't want to abandon Ginevra to such an angry brother.

Alastair turned his glare on me. "You, *Terranan*, leave my sister alone. Stop following her, stop—"

"I'm not following her!" Nasty thing to say. He made me sound like some kind of stalker.

"He isn't following me, Alastair. Truly he isn't."

Ginevra sounded worried. Suddenly I was glad Darkovans don't carry guns.

Alastair touched something at his side; a long line shifted under his cloak. Oh, ah. They *did* carry swords. He saw me looking, and smiled.

Ginevra spoke quickly. "He was already here when Marja and I ran in to get out of that—" (Something I didn't understand. Rain, I supposed.)

The G.B. shook his head and sighed. He spoke slowly now. "Ginevra, I think it's time we went back to the town house."

She slid a glance at me and grimaced. "Thank you, Duvin Wrothesley," she said as she stood, "for the pleasure of your company."

I stood up myself. It seemed the thing to do. "Thank you, *Damisela*. The pleasure has been mine."

The G.B. didn't move. "Leave my sister alone."

It was all so blasted unfair. Why shouldn't a girl have a cup of *jaco* and a chat, if she wanted them? Why shouldn't I have a few words? "Nothing that passed between us could not have been said in the presence of the lady's own mother." It sounds pompous in Terran Standard, but positively stately in *casta*. And it was mostly true.

"That's good to hear, *Terranan*." He didn't look impressed. Or convinced, either.

"His name's Duvin Wrothesley." Ginevra smiled sweetly. Oh lord, was she winding him up just as he'd gone off the boil? Not that you can wind up a pot of water, I mean, but...

The G.B. sighed like an actor who wants to be heard in the last row. "We are going back to the town house. Now."

We all waited to see what Ginevra would do. The G.B. glared, but he didn't touch her. That was good. I mean, I would have had to defend her, wouldn't I? And I doubted purity of heart would win against a sword.

Ginevra swept out ahead of him, followed by the maid, who sniffed loudly. I almost felt sorry for the man. Not quite, though.

Late that afternoon, I was summoned to the Terran administration building. Istvan came with me, looking worried and not chirping once the whole time. I tried to tell him he needn't, but he insisted that he did.

The Cultural Assistant to the Planetary Administrator's office could have been anywhere in the known universe—beige and gray, scuffed furniture, and a visitor's chair the seemed to have been constructed for someone at least 15 centimeters taller than I. Istvan stood. Sensible man.

After Darkover, the air in here felt dry. I sneezed; the C.A. leaned back in his chair. "We have a complaint from Lord Alastair Lindir-Delleray concerning your frequent contact with his sister, Lady Ginevra."

But not from Ginevra herself? I couldn't keep from smiling.

"This is serious, Mr. Wrothesley." He certainly looked serious. Those little lines between the brows are never a good sign.

It was awfully quiet. Oh, I was supposed to say something here. "I'm sorry, but really, I haven't been following her around or anything."

"Three meetings in three days, Mr. Wrothesley?"

"Oh, ah." Couldn't argue with that, could I? But it wasn't—I mean, I wasn't pursuing Ginevra. I couldn't have known she'd come into the *jaco* shop. She'd come to the cultural evening after I did. I tried to say so.

The CA folded his hands tightly on the desk. "Personally, I was against opening the planet to tourism. Local customs are hard enough for Terrans to understand, even when we get the training sessions for working here. This is one of the things I worried about. Cross-cultural romance here has almost never—"

"Oh, no, really! It isn't a romance!" She was such a jolly girl, and it was so restful being with a woman who didn't try to uplift me. I had a sudden image of Ginevra's face if someone said, "This is serious" to her in that tone of voice.

Now, there was a thought. "Has anyone asked *Damisela* Ginevra how she feels about this?"

The C.A. drew a sigh up from his toes, by the sound of it. "Mr. Wrothesley," he said, and paused.

"Oh, call me Duvin, please." Then he would tell me to call him by whatever his first name was, and we'd be much friendlier.

His jaw muscles bunched. "Mr. Wrothesley, by local custom, a lady's nearest adult male relative may oversee her behavior unless she is resident within one of the Towers which their *leroni* manage and supervise. We have had and we have given grief enough by ignoring local custom in the past that none of us, and I'm sure that includes you, wishes to repeat that mistake, which makes your and my personal opinions of the custom irrelevant." He took a deep breath, and after that statement I'll bet he needed one.

"In any case, you'll be leaving tomorrow morning for your expedition to Carcosa and Lake Hali."

Wait, what? I glared at Istvan. "When did I sign up for that?"

"No charge," he chirped.

"So you're not charging me for kidnapping me?"

"Oh, hardly that."

The CA raised his voice. "Not that at all. It's this, or you leave on the next ship—which is a freighter. Yes, Mr. Wrothesley, we can do that. I'll be happy to send you a copy of the regs, which you can read on your way to Hali or on the freighter, at your choice.

"You won't run into *Damisela* Ginevra on the trip to Hali. *Dom* Alastair should calm down when he doesn't see you for awhile. Please don't contact the lady before you leave. By the time you return, there will be only a short time remaining in your visit. You should be able to stay out of trouble that long."

Well, that sorted it all out, didn't it? I shifted position in the too-tall visitor's chair.

He looked at me, and his jaw unclenched. "It really isn't kind to the girl to persist, Mr. Wrothesley. They can be rather unforgiving here."

My stomach twisted. "What do you mean? This isn't one of those places with, with, honor killings, is it?" They didn't seem like that sort. Had I put her in danger? Oh, God, why didn't somebody warn me? I'm a bit slow sometimes, but I don't mean any harm.

The corners of the CA's mouth twitched. "It's tempting to let you think so! Only in the Dry Towns, but here in the Domains she needs a good reputation to make a good marriage or to go into most Towers. She's from a minor family anyway, no prestige and not much money. An intrigue with one of us wouldn't help her."

Istvan nodded silently. On our way out, I realized that the CA had never answered my question. I thought I knew why. No one had talked to Ginevra, at least, no one on the Terran side. Whoever else might be upset with me, Ginevra wasn't.

Our transportation awaited us, noisily. When a hovercar isn't hovering, it doesn't shuffle its feet or shake its harness till the air rings with the sound—well, it can't, of course, because it hasn't any harness, but you know what I mean. Besides the horses harnessed to the carriages, there were several spares fidgeting about.

The carriages looked more like wagons to me, and not terribly well-sprung wagons at that. For a miracle, the sun was shining. "I can ride," I told Istvan.

He was quiet, in the long, looking-at-the-ground way that chappies do when they're wondering how to ask a possibly impertinent question.

"I don't ride to hounds with my Aunt Amelia, mind you; those foxbots lead the horses over hill, dale, and ha-has, but I can stick on well enough for ordinary rides."

"Hm-phm," said Istvan. He got me a horse, though, an amiable gray beast who tended to stop and graze if I didn't nudge him now and then.

With the carriages, we couldn't move all that fast. My horse and I ambled along through rolling green hills. Dark forests began not far off the road. Mountains beyond them simply shot upwards. Had I really considered adding a jaunt to Caer Donn to my trip? The distance didn't look like much in the guide, but with terrain like that...

It had been awhile since I rode, and my thighs told me so. Carcosa was a welcome sight even though it wasn't much of a place. It did have a goodish-sized inn, with chimneys sticking up here and there, all of them smoking. The inn yard was already full of everything from dray wagons to somebody's rather elegant-looking carriage, with two bay horses that made all of ours look sad. A man was leading them tenderly off to a side yard.

Francine leaned out of the carriage. "Isn't it kind of early to stop?"

"Oh, we're only stopping for lunch," Istvan said. "Our camp's being set up in some lovely meadows a little way from the lake, very secluded and peaceful." He turned to me, "I'm afraid you've got the longest walk, Mr. Wrothesley; we didn't know to expect you."

"How should you?" And I meant it to sting.

Just then three young men rode in on chervines. The travel writers don't say that chervines can bleat at a pitch that operatic sopranos might envy. The first man shouted over their calls, "Hey, there, innkeeper! Food for man and beast, aye?"

Istvan winced. "Much more peaceful than here, *Damisela* Francine," he said as he helped her down from the carriage, nimbly avoiding a steaming pile of droppings.

He turned and shouted to us all, "But the lunch, my friends! The Crowing Cock's known throughout the Domains for its chickens! I've bespoke plenty of them, and the wine and ale of the valley."

A yelp came from the second carriage. "We're camping out? Nobody said anything about camping out!"

Cao Jin leaned over. "I think that must be the 'authentic Darkovan rustic accommodations'."

The lunch would have pacified a barbarian horde. Fat chickens smelling of fire smoke and herbs arrived as we sat down. Bread with some kind of fruit and nuts in it, ale and wine, and big bowls of something resembling mangel-wurzels with butter melting on them followed. The innkeeper didn't seem to believe in green vegetables much, but I didn't mind. We'd a short walk around town afterwards to settle it all. It also gave us all time to buy some local crafts.

I'm not an imaginative man as a rule. Dusk on Darkover, though— the light gets even dimmer, and the shadows look as if anything might be in there. Beyond the gentle grumbling of the wagon passengers, I could hear all sorts of rustling and strange cries from the forest. Blasted if I can see why people say the country's so relaxing.

It was quite a nice camp, actually. There was a rough circle of tents, all sitting on sturdy wooden platforms. Appetizing smoke rose from one long, low stone building in the middle. I had my own tent, with walls made out of some thick cloth that barely stirred in the wind off the nearby mountains.

A large bundle along one wall turned out to be a clever sort of oiled cloth tub; two servants brought warm water for a bath before dinner. My muscles slowly unclenched. Only extreme hunger made me lever myself out, that and cooling water.

We were not a chatty group at dinner; I gather that riding in the wagons was at least as tiring as riding a horse had been. In the short time it took us to wreak havoc among the roasts and pudding, our good weather left. One of the local staff came and lit the way for me through wind, rain, and darkness with a torch the size of a young tree.

At least the tent was warm. Coals glowed in a clever sort of stone pot that sat inside a box of sand. Well-tipped, the staffer set off into the night whistling. Now for the pyjamas and the deep sleep, rainstorm or no.

Suddenly the tent flaps were pulled apart enough for a gust of cold wind and rain to come in. A young woman came in with them. A very wet young woman.

"Ginevra?"

She yanked back the hood of her cloak and stared at me open-mouthed. "Oh, no. Duvin, I didn't know—I just ran into the first tent I saw." Her lips were blue.

"Here, come over by the fire." I took her hand; it was ice cold. She flinched back from me. "Sorry. But you're freezing, please come get warm."

She limped slightly as she came over to the fire box; her hands shook as she stretched them out to the heat. Steam rose from her garments. Even when a beautiful woman's wearing it, wet wool doesn't smell good.

Ginevra giggled. It got louder; she clapped both hands over her mouth and made fizzing noises like a champagne bottle that's about to pop its cork.

I'd imagined the two of us alone together, but this wasn't what I had in mind.

The noises trailed off. "I'm sorry; I must sound deranged. But you see, Alastair was taking me back home to get me away from you. And here you are."

I gasped, and choked on some bit of local insect life. When I could speak, I told her, "Our Cultural Affairs man insisted that I go on the excursion to Hali so that I wouldn't see you again."

It occurred to me that if having _jaco_ with Ginevra was a problem, then having her found in my tent might well be a disaster for us both. This time it wasn't the breeze that made me shiver. But how could I smuggle her out, and to where?

Suddenly she squeaked and dived for the back of the tent.

"Wha—" Then I heard the footsteps. I also heard scrabbling sounds. There was barely time to assist her in tipping the bath tub over herself, dumping some residual water onto my trouser leg, before her giant brother strode in. The ties of the tent flaps didn't even slow him down.

"Where is she? Where have you taken her?"

I must not look in the direction of the bath tub. Not even think about it. Perhaps he could read my mind and just hadn't bothered to try yet. Too bad that left me with nowhere to look except right at the bright red G.B., and nothing to think about but whether his head really did brush the tent roof. Mustn't shiver, either, in spite of the cold bath water all down one leg.

"Where is who?" I asked.

"My sister. Who else would I be looking for in a storm like this?"

"I haven't taken her anywhere." Which was technically true. My throat still felt tight.

The G.B. yanked at his hair as he paced back and forth in front of the tent's doorway. "If you're telling the truth, which I suppose you might be—" He did the hair-tearing thing again. He was going to be bald before he was thirty if he kept this up. "I hope you're lying. I hope she isn't out there in that storm. There are three ways from Carcosa to Alicante and in this weather I don't know which of them's the most dangerous. "

I felt a complete heel not telling him that his sister was in fact curled up under my bath tub. It didn't take any psychic powers to see that he was really worried. But I could hardly betray Ginevra, could I?

"She's headed towards Alicante, I'm sure of it. In good weather it would be a few hours walk from Carcosa, even if she took the hunters' way, and Aunt Mirella's halfway to being a Renunciate herself. She'd shelter Ginevra."

I held my tongue. "What's a Renunciate?" was probably not a good question to ask.

"Idiot."

I made allowances for his mental state, but insults didn't help.

"Idiot fool of a girl! I would never force her to marry someone she didn't care for." He spun around and faced me, arms flung out. "And it isn't *possible* to force someone into a Tower. There was no need for her to take off like the persecuted heroine of an old song."

There was a loud dampish splat as the bath tub landed on its side, and Ginevra was among us. "Well, I wish I'd known *that* earlier today!"

Alastair had gone dark red now, breathing like Aunt Amelia's favorite Peke. A corpse in the tent wasn't going to help us. "*Dom* Alastair, are you quite all right?"

"I'm well, but you won't be." He flung back his cape and drew his sword.

"Alastair, no!" Ginevra tried to lunge forward, but several meters of wet wool tangled around her legs. I didn't know the words she used as she unwound her skirts.

He didn't even look at her. "I'll deal with you later. How could you run to this damned *Terranan?* Ginevra, in the name of modesty!" She'd tucked up her skirts somehow. Still didn't show much above the ankle.

He turned to me. "How did you do it, you damned sneaking seducer?"

"What? I—we never—" I hadn't even kissed the girl!

He made a disgusted sound. "You don't even have a sword, do you?"

Maybe you couldn't skewer unarmed people? A small hope sprouted.

He flung back his cloak on the other side and pulled out a smaller sword. Then, he tossed the longer one onto my camp bed. "Take it. Take it! Will you not even defend yourself?"

The small hope shriveled. I hauled in air to yell for help.

It was closer than I'd thought. Ginevra pushed between us. "No," she said.

He jumped back. "Are you out of your mind? Never, never rush up to a bared blade like that!"

She shrugged. "I knew you wouldn't hurt me. Alastair, he's done me no harm."

"No harm? No harm, when I find you in his bedroom—Ginnie,

I'm warning you, get out of my way." She didn't.

"Duvin," she said over her shoulder, "Take that sword—" her voice shook. "Alastair, only to first blood, promise me! If he fights you, honor's satisfied; you don't have to kill him."

Why did everyone want me to take a sword? I didn't want a sword. I didn't know how to use it. I didn't want to know how to use it. There wasn't any need for this, even by their standards

"Listen, please," I said in the calmest voice I could manage. "There's a perfectly blameless explanation—"

"I know my sister's blameless. You, on the other hand," Alastair tried to push Ginevra out of the way. She swayed slightly without moving. He leaned around her. "Take the sword, you coward!"

He still had the smaller sword in one hand. Couldn't he put that damn thing away until we got Ginevra out of the middle of this?

"Ginevra," I shouted. "Will *you* listen to me?"

She looked over her shoulder. "I'm listening."

"I don't want you to fight for me."

"What?" Her eyebrows snapped into a frown.

Alastair grunted and stared at me with narrowed eyes. He still didn't put the sword away.

Ginevra spun all the way around to face me. "I'm not fighting for you! I'm trying to save you from being killed by my idiot brother!" Oh dear lord. Wildly flailing arms, how close had she come to that blade with those arms I loved? Loved? Did I?

First I needed to get her away from that blade.

"And I really appreciate that! But please, I can't stand seeing you so close to his sword." She stayed where she was. "Ginevra, I love you! Please don't get yourself skewered."

For a moment they both stared at me in silence. It was almost restful, or would have been except for the bared sword in his hand, and another one lying on the bed.

Alastair coughed. "I won't skewer her, I promise. It doesn't happen accidentally, you know. Or do you?"

"You could put it away." It seemed such an obvious thing to do.

Alastair rolled his eyes. "A sword drawn for honor must not be sheathed until honor is satisfied." he recited. "And talk of love's very pretty, but I haven't heard anything about marriage."

"I was getting to that. You might give a man time to speak."

He stood there with his mouth open. So did she.

My love shook her head. "Oh, no, this is ridiculous. Duvin, you don't have to offer me marriage."

"Yes, he does," said Alastair.

"Is it," I paused to swallow hard. "Is it such an awful thought?" If Alastair laughed, I, well, I might have to find out if I *could* skewer someone. I sneaked a quick glance down. Yes, great long shiny sword, still lying there.

She wrung her hands. "It ... it isn't a awful thought at all. Duvin, I love you."

I could swear there were birds singing. Couldn't possibly be, of course, because I could hear rain still bucketing down. She loved me.

Then she went on speaking. "But Duvin, we've met, what, four times? You can't possibly wish to marry someone you've met only four times!"

"Yes, I can." I had to stop and swallow hard. "I do."

I suppose it was too much to hope that Alastair could have kept quiet. "This is just the brother-in-law I've always wanted, a head-blind stranger with no visible means of support." He did, finally, sheath the sword. Either honor was satisfied by my offer, or he was tired of holding a metal bar out at the end of his arm. He retrieved the longer sword as well.

For once I thought of the clever thing while I was still in the room. "How did you think I got all the way out here, mere charm of manner?" Ginevra laughed.

I gazed at her, rumpled and half-soaked, and smiled. "D'you know, I heard you laugh before I ever saw you. I thought then what a beautiful laugh it is."

"When was that?"

Alastair trampled what might have been a beautiful moment. "Is there any way that I can check on this?"

"Stop it! Stop it, both of you! Stop arranging it all for me!" She gripped her hands together so hard that the knuckles turned white. "You bade me choose, Alastair. I choose to accept Duvin Wrothesley's offer of marriage."

Why didn't she look happier? "You don't have to do this," I made myself say. "You certainly don't have to do it right away."

There didn't seem to be any air in the room.

Then she smiled, and I breathed again. "I want to do this." She looked over at Alastair. "I'll admit, I never imagined being proposed to while my brother stood waving a sword. May I be alone a moment with my affianced husband, please?"

"No, you may not! It's still pouring out there."

Damn.

"May a brother ask one thing?"

"Ask, surely."

"Will you two please not rush the wedding? Give it a little time?"

"Many a Comyn bride has gone to her wedding with less acquaintance with her husband than this."

Alastair winced. "True. But then, their parents had a chance to ask questions, probably knew each others' families already."

My turn, I thought. "You can vet me through the Terran Embassy. I'm from a good family, by the way. I do have an income, and expectations—no, Ginevra, it's reasonable for him to ask. If Darkovan women don't have careers after marriage, then," I shrugged.

"You're not asking much about me," she pointed out.

"Oh, I can find that out while he vets me. I think I might need to ask you many questions." We sat down side by side on the sword-free bed.

Were we all three going to try to sleep in here? How was that going to work? Ginevra would have the bed, of course ... maybe we could shove the bath tub out the door, but the floor was probably damp there.

Alastair must have had the same thought. He drew aside one tent flap to see just how bad the rain was. "Zandru's teeth."

Ginevra peered around him. "Oh, no!"

I bounced from side to side behind them, trying to see. Ginevra retreated into the tent, and much became clear. Istvan, Francine, and Cao stood huddled under the rain-flaps at the front of the tent.

"Sorry," said Istvan, "But you could be heard even over the rain. People were worried."

Not worried enough to come in, I noticed.

Ginevra shivered in the breeze through the open flaps. "Come to my tent," said Francine. "Didn't Duvin even offer you a hot drink?"

No, I hadn't. She'd stood there dripping wet and I hadn't the wit to find a cup of tea for her. In fairness, it's hard to be a good host while someone waves a sword at you. "I'm sorry, Ginevra! It was just all so, so—"

"It's all right, Duvin. There really wasn't time for tea, was there?"

"We can squeeze Alastair into my tent," said Istvan. "And you should both get into something dry." Looking at Alastair, he frowned.

Cao chimed in, "I brought a robe that might help."

"I have coffee brewed in my tent," added Francine.

I hate to shout, but—"Could we have just a few minutes alone, please?"

We got them, with Alastair waiting stoically just outside the tent.

Ginevra dodged my attempt at a kiss. "No, let me say this! I mean it about not holding you to this. We can divorce later. A cousin of mine was divorced on Vainwal and she said it was simple."

Oh no. Were we really going to do all that again? Maybe this wasn't the splendid idea it had seemed.

Heartache's real, did you know? Mine felt as though it had swollen up to block my throat. Had I just hauled us all into a horrible mistake?

Ginevra finally turned her head to look at me, and I knew. Love or telepathy, I knew. "I don't want a divorce. I want marriage. And I'll say it again as many times as you need to hear it."

She smiled then. "That's a rash promise." The smile changed to a long considering look. "But you keep your promises, beloved. So do I." And the smile was back.

Beloved! I could feel a completely goofy grin spreading across my face. "Beloved. And let's not waste any more of however few minutes Alastair's willing to give us."

Finally, we kissed.

GENERATIONS

by Rosemary Edghill

Rosemary Edghill describes herself as the keeper of the Eddystone Light, corny as Kansas in August, normal as blueberry pie, and only a paper moon. She says she was found floating down the Amazon in a hatbox, and, because criminals are a cowardly and superstitious lot, she became a creature of the night (black, terrible). She began her professional career working as a time-traveling vampire killer and has never looked back. She's also a New York Times Bestselling Writer and hangs out on Facebook a lot.

Here Rosemary "fills in the gap" of the time period between the arrival of Terran colonists, castaways on a planet they are ill-prepared to comprehend, let alone survive, (*Darkover Landfall*) and the rise of *laran*-Gifted Comyn in the Ages of Chaos. What do they gain by adapting to their new world ... and what must they ultimately surrender?

Round and around they dance, torches trailing comet tails of sparks, laughing, grasping and losing hands clutched in the dark, circling the Tower on its high place, circling the rock, as the sweet soft winds of Midsummer blow over their bodies...

+20 TSY (Terran Standard Year):

Eloise Asturias climbed the last of the winding steps to the top floor of New Skye Tower, and leaned out the open window to gaze over the foothills of the Wall Around The World. She'd been a communications technician on *Gagarin*; now she was a meteorologist. On a planet where the weather could kill without warning, it was a vital skill.

Those skills hadn't come to her from Earth Expeditionary, or even from Camilla Del Rey's patient teaching, but because of what this place had made of her. Something about the planet of the red sun and the four moons had opened the castaways' most primitive senses, those gifts and powers labeled as "psionics" and long-thought to be mythical. But it was the starstones that shaped those flickering hints of telepathy, precognition, clairvoyance into something they could use. MacAran had been the first to find them, and Camilla Del Rey had named them, but it had been Lori Lovat—Judy's changeling child—who taught them how to use them.

Now Eloise drew the small leather bag out from beneath her tunic and teased it open. Inside lay a blue gem about the size of her thumbnail. It was all very well to be able to sense a change in the weather, but it never hurt to be sure. She concentrated on the stone in her hand. Its brilliance increased as she gazed into it, the silver lights in its depths waking to life and beginning to dance...

Suddenly, as if in a waking dream, New Skye Tower was gone, replaced by an impression of alpine meadows miles to the north and a thousand feet higher, and a warm greeting. *:Is it well with you, sister?:* Fiona asked.

Eloise did not see Fiona MacMorair in any conventional sense, just as she did not hear her voice—it was more as if she was aware of the idea of Fiona; clever hands and open mind. Emotions, not words, crossed the link, Eloise knew, but she put her question into words anyway.

:Well enough, sister. And the weather?:

She could sense Fiona's laughter, though she could not hear it. One of the greatest barriers to using these new/old powers was in believing in them in the first place. The Terran need for proof, its belief in only what one could see and touch and prove, had handicapped even some of the neo-ruralist communards.

:It will be clear and dry through Midsummer—and you know what that means!:

The brief contact faded, and once more Eloise was alone in her own mind. *Yes, I know what it means,* she thought darkly. *Time to get indoors and shutter the windows.* When the Ghost Winds—warm winds freighted with hallucinogenic, psychotropic pollen—blew, you acted on your deepest uncensored desires and instincts.

Ones you might not even know you possessed.

She'd been twenty-six years old when she first stepped from the wreckage of the Earth Expeditionary Ship *Gagarin* (named for an old folk hero). That had made her one of the youngest survivors. For the first few (Terran) weeks after the crash, the castaways—or at least the crew—had hoped *Gagarin* could be repaired, and they could continue on their way to Phi Delta Coronis. When the Ghost Winds first blew that hope had been put to rest, but they'd hoped at least to be able to build upon the heritage of knowledge they'd brought from Earth ... until that too had proven impossible. Since then, everyone had reconciled themselves to the thought that there was no hope of accidental rescue: the prankish winds of space that had destroyed *Gagarin* had also swept the ship to the far edge of the galactic spiral arm, and they had no way to launch any of the *Gagarin*'s surviving distress beacons.

Years ago, they'd programmed the three they'd been able to salvage and started them transmitting. There was no reason not to; the beacons' atomic batteries would keep them calling out their forlorn message for the next thousand years or more. But here on the planet's surface they were useless, their signal degraded by atmospheric interference and the solar wind from the great red sun. Only in vacuum would a beacon's tiny thrusters engage, driving it out to the edge of the system, far from electromagnetic interference, where its plaintive call might perhaps be heard.

It would be easy enough to get one into the upper atmosphere. Even their primitive ancestors had been able to build hydrogen-lift balloons: separating water into oxygen and hydrogen was simple enough. That would carry the beacon almost 200,000 feet up—but the lowest orbital point was over 500,000 feet up. Impossible.

"Hello the tower!"

A shout from below made her hurry to the window and lean out, pushing the shutters open as she did. She smiled at what she saw.

"If it isn't Aindreas Kerr, howling like a lovesick banshee! Too lazy to come up here and great me properly?"

"Too smart!" her husband called back. "Are you done talking to the walls? There's work to be done, even for ancients like us!"

"I can out work you any day, old man! Outrun you, too!"

He gazed up at her, smiling as he leaned on his cane. Frostbite had taken three toes on his left foot sometime around Year Seven. "Heartless! Come down here and say that!" the father of three of her surviving children said.

She laughed, turning away from the window. She took one last look around the tower, making certain that the precious things were safely stored. Once she left the tower, they'd be behind three locked doors that could only be unlocked by solving elaborate puzzles—something the castaways had learned was unlikely anyone caught in the Ghost Winds would do. The beacons were too precious to lose. Maybe someday they'd find a way to launch them.

Perhaps my great-great grandchildren can go home someday, even if I can't.

The foundations of the keep-to-come span the whole of the rock, a swirling mandala spreading from the skirts of An Dara Tower. The chain of dancers use them as a guide, turning the chain back on itself, coiling and uncoiling to the high wild song of pipes and strings, and the insistent heartbeat of the drums.

And as they dance the power grows, rising from the night and the music and their own bodies like an insubstantial silvery fog...

+35 TSY (Terran Standard Year):

They'd come down out of the foothills of the Wall, down from the village and crofts of New Skye, across the plain they'd christened *A'meadhanan*, The Midlands, where the land was gentle and soft. Here they would build a city, *An Dara*, Second One, the second true settlement on this wild, savage, beautiful planet they had never been meant to see.

It had been thirty-five years as reckoned by the salvaged ship's chronometer the castaways and their children kept with the rest of the precious salvage at New Skye Tower; less than thirty as reckoned by the movement of the planet of the red sun and the four moons. Time enough to birth three generations and bury nearly half the infants before they took their first breath, time enough to bury another third of the survivors of *Gagarin's* crash.

But they'd kept their foothold on their strange new world, and begun to thrive.

Beathag Asturias stood in the doorway of the new longhouse and gazed up at An Dara Ràth. It would be a fine large thing when it was done—enough to hold not only the folk, but their flocks, when winter snows grew deep—and that might be as soon as next summer. For the last four years they'd been able to keep a herders' camp here over the winter; the south was fertile and mild, better for the horses and sheep. Nothing that had come with them to this world really flourished here: the people in charge of livestock said it would take at least a score of generations for the Terran animals to acclimate—if they ever did.

The sound of axes and hammers echoed across the valley; it was Midsummer, and they had only a few more weeks (there were five-and-a-bit Terran weeks to the local month, which was awkward) to work on the new settlement before they had to pack up and head home. There was plenty to do back in New Skye before the first snows fell and as always, never enough hands to do it, though the population was growing steadily. It was said that in another two or three generations, women would no longer risk a fatal miscarriage every time they quickened. Beathag wondered if that were true—though she knew those who told her that believed it; how could she not? Just as she knew that though Mama Eloise loved her dearly, each of Mama's pregnancies had brought her close to despair.

There were many things the First Generation said and thought that their children and grandchildren didn't understand. Mama Eloise had often spoken bitterly of once having had more use than as an incubator for endless children, something that made little sense to her daughters. Children meant life for all of them, meant the colony would survive. How could anyone not want that?

When Beathag had been a child, she'd begged Mama for tales of that unimaginable land where the sun was bright as flame and the sky as blue as a starstone and snow never fell. But far too soon, Mama had stopped telling such stories. *"Wanting what you can't have will eat your heart,"* she'd say.

When she was a child, Beathag had raged against that deliberate withholding of knowledge, just as she'd raged against the willful destruction of all the information that had come from Earth. But now that she had children of her own—blessedly, after five miscarriages there'd been a living child, followed by two more—she wondered if Mama had been right. What good would it do them to yearn over all the wonders of a planet they would never see?

But if we could launch the beacon ... if it worked ... if we're found ... if we're rescued...

She shook her head. That was impossible, though it didn't stop the arguments about whether they should or they shouldn't. It was partly so she wouldn't have to hear them all summer that she'd begged her husband to bring her south with the work parties this year. Every time the "discussion" started up again she thought of what Mama Eloise had said when Beathag'd begged for stories of Terra.

Was it right for them to spend their lives, generation after generation, yearning for a rescue that might, when all was said and done, be nothing but a false hope? She picked up the yoke and buckets and began to walk toward the river, but her mind would not quiet itself.

How can it matter one way or the other? Say that Lucas and Jason are right. Say there is a way to get the beacon into orbit. We'll go on as we are, anyway, won't we?

But what if they launched it and that wasn't what happened? For a brief moment she imagined a world they could not make their own because they had not given it their whole heart. Because their thoughts were fixed on the dim and distant stars; because memories of a homeworld none of them had ever seen poisoned their minds and souls. And it was hardly certain that rescue would ever come, even with one of the beacons—or all three—transmitting.

But what if it did? What if her daughter or her granddaughter was there to see the day? Four generations, three born on this world, all irrevocably changed by it, with as little in common with their rescuers as with their ancestors. Unable to go home again, unable to stay here, because they'd be whisked away as soon as Terra discovered there were native sentients...

She reached the riverside and began to fill her buckets.

Is it better to have hope, or to accept that this is the only world we and our children will ever know?

With full water buckets, Beathag walked the curving path to the top of the crag. An Dara Tower had been the first structure to be completed; they'd hung the doors and shutters this spring, but the keep itself would be building for years to come. An Dara Ràth would be immense when it was finished—large enough to shelter every soul in the colony, and all their animals, from winter's terrible storms. From the tower, you'd be able to gaze down on the whole of the valley. Useful for spotting both lost animals and changing weather. (It was another thing to argue about, the spending of resources to build a second settlement instead of using them to somehow launch the beacons, and the arguments were passionate and endless.)

She passed to and fro among the toiling workers, stopping to let them fill their cups or flasks from her buckets. When she'd reached the top of the outcropping, and the buckets were nearly empty, she poured out the dregs into a cask set against the sheltering wall of An Dara tower, and began her trek to the stream again.

Mama said once that on Terra you could get all the water you wanted for no more than the press of a button...

Fire and music and the rising tide; the energy of the dance and the memory of the Ghost Winds ... the stars of the heavens shone, not in the sky, but in the starstones they wore. This was their world ... they wanted no other...

+50 TSY (Terran Standard Year):

"I am pregnant, Donal Arascain, not crippled!" Ailios Asturias skipped lithely away from her husband, still clutching the basket of apples she was bringing from the latest supply wagon to the kitchen.

"You are my own, my beloved, my true heart's compass north!" Donal cried laughingly, the casks he carried in constant peril of falling as he followed after her. "My darling, my dove, I am pledged to share your life's burdens—"

Ailios continued walking as Donal capered around her playing the fool, even though he'd been up since dawn hauling blocks of stone for An Dara. Work had stopped early today because of the Festival.

And because of the launch.

It was a lovely day, bright and warm, though she missed the

bracing air of New Skye and its mountains. Even on summer days like this, her grandparents' generation bundled up: Ailios wondered what the planet they'd come from had been like. She had only the vaguest notions, for *Neanaidh* Eloise had forbidden anyone to speak of it in her hearing.

Soon enough, Neanaidh *won't be able to forbid anything,* Ailios thought sadly. And when she was gone, what stories would die with her?

"Where are you, my love?" Donal asked softly into her silence.

"Woolgathering," she said with a smile, shifting the basket higher on her hip. "And on such a grand day as this. We're to launch the beacon tonight, you know."

"I know," he said, taking her hand gently. "And we've all agreed to it."

"We have," she said, sensing his unease. The arguments had raged since before she was born—but ten years ago, the impossible had become the possible. So they'd done what had become customary for the colony, and voted on what they would do. Technically the vote had been secret. In reality, everyone had known who cast what vote, though they pretended they didn't. The knowing and the pretense of not knowing was normal for her, just as it was for her mother, and she couldn't imagine what it would be like not to live constantly in touch with the thoughts and feelings of everyone around you.

But that was how Terrans lived. When they came, as the children of the crew swore was inevitable, suddenly they would be the normal ones, and the castaways would be ... different.

"We'll give it a grand party to see it off," she said rallyingly. Donal pretended to believe her, and they walked on without saying anything more.

At the longhouse kitchens, Ailios surrendered her basket and Donal his casks, and they stepped aside so that others could take their places. The kitchen was filled with good smells from the ovens, and the open hearths held sheep and deer that had been cooking all day.

"I'd best be getting the old girl warmed up if I'm to play for the dancing," Donal said. "And you'll be wanting to change into your best dress. Can't dance in work boots."

Ailios smiled gently. "In a while," she said. "I'm going to go for a walk. If I can't shake this mood, at least I can keep from spoiling everyone else's."

"Come back to me soon," he said, raising her fingertips to his lips. Even though she was pregnant with their first child, his ardent desire for her made her cheeks flush and her heart beat faster.

"Soon," she promised, hurrying away.

It was only a little past noon, but already people were drifting back from the worksite. Ailios hurried onward. It was easy enough to find solitude, even here; the Venzia Valley had been densely wooded when they'd first come here; now only the trees covering the far hills still stood. By the time she reached the top of the nearest, the noise and the clamor—psychic and mundane—of An Dara had faded completely, and she might as well be standing in primal woodland.

Now that she was certain her emotions could not be sensed by others, she allowed the worry and the fear to come into the open— things she should have settled in her mind long before the vote. *But it seemed meaningless, something that couldn't affect me. Or any of us. No one ever thought this day would come!*

Those who had argued on behalf of the launch said it was their heritage as children of Terra, even while saying that nothing would happen for centuries. And so those who were against launching the beacon, or even merely undecided, had held their tongues and shielded their thoughts when the vote was decided in favor.

But what if it does? What about Lori?

Lori Lovat was one of the first children conceived here and still looked young enough to pass for Ailios's sister. She'd come to Lori with her problems for as long as she could remember: Why had her kitten died? Why did adults always fight? Why was Papa always gone? Who should be the father of her first child? Even when Lori didn't answer in words, somehow things were always clearer in her presence. She wished she could talk her now.

The trouble was, Lori wasn't here. She'd disappeared from New Skye as soon as spring came. Lori spent half the year wandering the forests, and the other half telling her friends what she'd seen and done and learned. If she ever encountered her father's people, that was something she didn't speak of.

Everyone in Ailios's generation knew Lori's father was one of the Beautiful Ones; the unseen sentients to whom this planet truly belonged. Lori, their changeling child, had taught her siblings and cousins all that had allowed them to flourish here. She'd made them welcome on her father's behalf. And Lori had children of her own, and someday *they* would have children, and what would happen when the Terrans came back? Would they leave them here?

Would they leave *any* of them here, once they heard about the Beautiful Ones?

She knew the answer to that. If *Neanaidh's* generation had become reluctant to talk about Terra, that reluctance hadn't extended to the ethics and mechanics of colonizing new planets. If a planet had an indigenous native species, it was off-limits. Forever.

If we were "indigenous," too, that would solve all our problems!

But they weren't and they couldn't pretend they were. Even if three generations knew no other home ... they still remembered they were immigrants.

Ailios blinked back rueful tears, one hand sheltering the child growing in her womb. They'd always want to go home. Or at least to *know* home. That was just how it was. You couldn't just turn your back on where you came from, even if it would solve all your problems.

The hand that did not rest upon her unborn child went to cover the starstone Ailios wore around her neck. Lori had made a game of it when they were children: looking into the flashing lights, courting their wordless knowledge. Almost everyone wore them now, but very few of them could make it work as Lori did.

But some of us can—like Jason—and that's the trouble!

She knelt down on the soft cool moss and cupped her starstone in her bare hands, gazing into its soothing blue glow.

Perhaps just trying to reach Lori with it will stop making me feel as if I'm going to burst apart into a million pieces, she thought. *It isn't as if there's anything anybody can do to change things...*

She didn't call out to Lori—starstones weren't one of those "long distance communicators" that her grandparents' generation so mourned the loss of. Instead, Ailios Asturias let her mind sink into the dancing silver lights, let them grow until she sank down into their midst, and then filled them with all her worries and realizations.

It seemed to her that the clearing filled with evening fog, though the air was still warm. And as the fog swirled around her, it revealed and concealed two pathways she hadn't seen before. They glinted like silver in the strange light, and suddenly she knew she wasn't alone here.

:*You're right*,: something that might be Lori's voice whispered to her. :*We have to choose. We've tried to follow the right path. But choosing is hard. We need help.*:

"Lori?" Ailios whispered aloud. Her answer was a silvery ripple of joy washing over her thoughts.

:*The Shining Ones saw this day coming long ago. But they told me they couldn't help unless you chose this path yourselves. All of you.*:

:*But we can't!*: Ailios wailed silently. :*We don't all agree, and, and we already voted and there's no time to send to New Skye, and—*:

:*Trust me, Ailios,*: Lori's thoughts whispered in her mind. :*We can help ourselves. It's not too late. You'll know what to do when the time comes...*:

The mental voice faded, but Lori's presence did not. For a long time, Ailios stayed in the strange dream: it was as if she inspected every future decision, sorting them into right and wrong, best and worst. When she finally roused, she retained that sense of doing and judging, but she remembered nothing more.

The launch team was gathered atop An Dara Tower. Last night, Lucas Leicester had tested the battery pack for charge. This morning he'd hooked it up to the fragile and unwieldy apparatus that would separate oxygen from hydrogen. The balloon was nearly-full now, and straining against the ropes that held it down. The dozen members of the team watched impatiently

Hell of a view, he thought absently, looking out over the valley. The evening clouds were already rolling in from the east, but they should be able to launch before the rain started. After that, it was up to Jason.

"Will it work?" Jason Stuart asked, kneeling down beside the crate to open it. Inside lay one of *Gagarin's* distress beacons, swaddled in straw for the trip to An Dara despite the fact it had been designed to withstand the rigors of a space disaster. Its makers wouldn't have recognized it now, the thing that was a strange fusion of old technology and new. The blunt, torpedo-shaped beacon was garlanded in a web of starstones—the largest they'd been able to mine—held in place by a netting of irreplaceable copper wire. He lifted it out gently, running his hands over the webbing as if petting a cat before he began the process of attaching it to the balloon.

"*My* half will," Lucas answered rather sharply. He took a breath. "Sorry," he said. "Nerves."

Jason gave him a crooked smile. "Me, too," he said. "I know I can throw something that weighs twice as much as this over five miles—"

"Horizontally, not vertically. And be flat on your back with migraine for the next three days," Mateo Castillo interrupted. Mateo was their engineer. He was the one who'd done the calculations that made it all work. Tonight, with a mixture of Old World science and New World sorcery, the castaway Terrans would do as their ancestors had done, and launch a manmade object into space. Mankind had reached for the stars ever since it had first looked skyward and seen them—and if there weren't many to see in their new home's night sky, spaceflight was still their heritage.

"Just carry me in out of the rain afterward, beloved," Jason said lightly. "That's all I ask. But as I was saying—"

Lucas let their familiar bickering wash over him, soothing his nerves. When they'd discovered that Jason was an apporter (not a teleport, since he couldn't move himself) Lucas had realized his grandfather's plan had finally found its missing piece. At first he'd hoped Jason could do all of it. But "up" was apparently harder than sideways, and tossing something the weight of the beacon straight up for even half the distance it needed to go was ... risky.

So they'd send the beacon as high as they could by balloon, and Jason would teleport it the rest of the way—into orbit. It seemed utterly mad, desperate, even. But desperation fueled so many of the things they did to survive here. And apportation *worked*.

Whether it reaches orbit—whether our message gets out—or not—we may never know. But knowing that we tried, that there's a chance of going home again, will give us hope.

The balloon was straining tautly at its ropes now. Lucas did a final check of the cables that bound the beacon to the balloon. Mateo was talking quietly to Jason, preparing him for the work to come.

"Give her some line," Lucas said. The launch crew untied the ropes from the moorings and played them out slowly until the balloon took the weight of the beacon as well.

Now or never. Grandfather, wherever you are, I hope you're proud of us.

Lucas looked to Mateo. "Ready?"

"Ready," Mateo answered.

"Ready," Jason echoed.

"Let 'er go!"

At Lucas's command, the riggers dropped the ropes. The balloon bounced upward, bobbled, skittered perilously close to the edge of the tower's roof, and then began to rise steadily, carrying its payload aloft. As it rose, it caught the last rays of the setting sun, and its pale surface was touched with fiery gold. They'd timed it perfectly, launching in the brief windless moment before the evening clouds rolled in, and the ascent was swift and nearly vertical. Jason rose to his feet, staring skyward fists clenched, as if he were pushing it higher by his will alone. Mateo crouched over their precious and irreplaceable chronometer, the only accurate timing equipment they had left. It would take an hour for the balloon to reach its projected jump-off point—if they waited any longer it might begin to sink or simply burst.

The moment stretched. To keep himself from infecting Jason with his worry, Lucas gazed out over the valley again, steadfastly blanking his mind. He could hear music as the musicians warmed up for the dancing, and there was the scent of wood smoke and cooked meat on the air. The midsummer celebrations would go on all night—a celebration of survival, of endurance, of triumph.

And this year they would have more to celebrate than ever.

The bonfires were lit in New Skye as they had been for forty Midsummers. Beathag Asturias laughed as she was pulled into a ring dance about the fire. Not so old as all that, she thought, giving herself over to the music. Each time she faced New Skye Tower, she glanced up at it, wondering about its counterpart in the south.

Ailios Asturias laughed, flinging her arms around her husband's neck as he sheltered himself and his fiddle from the brief evening rain. "And you, lovely man of mine, I expect you to get our babe a fine crop of brothers and sisters this night!"

"Look!" he said, pointing.

On the top of An Dara Tower, the signal fire blazed.

It was done.

There was food and drink, dancing and blazing bonfires. The night wore on, and the celebration became wilder and more abandoned, the dancing more vigorous, until the celebrants all across An Dara seemed to become extensions of one mind and one will. When one of the sword-dancers snatched up a torch and began to run, whooping, everyone, young and old, followed.

Across the camp and up the crag. Nine times around the tower, skipping and leaping over the half-finished foundations, and down again, laughing and cheering and staggering with exhaustion, falling and rising to dance again, a complicated hypnotic dance whose steps they had never known before and never would again.

And as they danced, every mind was open to every other, reaching out to friends, family, kin, in the hills they'd left. Reaching, and joining, and celebrating the home that they loved, the world that was in their blood, their bone, their hearts.

And it seemed to them, that night, they were all gathered together as one being, with one mind and one thought to fill it. And in every heart the question was asked and answered.

Will you choose this world and forsake the other, for yourselves and your children unborn?

Will you?

Eloise Asturias lay in her bed in New Skye listening to the music of the festival. *Too old for dancing,* she thought in rueful good humor, and seemed to hear, as if from far away, her daughter's answer: *Not so old as all that!*

She closed her eyes, smiling as she drifted off. It seemed to her that she dreamed, that someone she could not see asked her a question.

"Will you forget Terra? Will you give yourself to this world forever?"

Why yes, she answered, feeling vaguely surprised. *That's the answer, isn't it? It will solve the problem...*

And the voice answered her: *"Yes, my darling, it will. Thank you. Sleep well and deeply. Your children will call Darkover their home forever."*

When her family discovered her body, Eloise was still smiling, as if death had kissed her and whispered a wonderful secret in her ear. Her children gathered around her to wash her and wake her, and when the solemn joyous leave-taking was done, they buried her in the little cemetery on the far side of the hill beside her husband and her lovers and her children who had gone before her.

None of them remembered what the memorial in its center stood for, nor why it had been built, nor that Eloise Asturias had once walked among the stars and called another planet her home.

The beacon drifted until it reached the edge of the system. There, century after century, it sent out its signal, receiving no response. Nor would it have gotten a reply even if it had reached its system of origin, for the Dark Years had come to Terra, and Sol III's inhabitants would not return to space again for centuries to come.

A thousand years later, a comet on a long elliptical orbit passed by the beacon. Several of the chunks of ice in the comet's train struck it, thrusting the beacon into the orbit of one of the rocky balls of ice at the edge of the system. After another century, the beacon's new orbit decayed, and it crashed to the surface, there to be slowly buried in methane snow. Over the next three centuries its song wavered and weakened and at last died to silence.

And no one cared.

UPON THIS ROCK

by Meg Mac Donald

After a number of years away from writing, Meg Mac Donald set pen to page again in 2011. Delightful chaos ensued. She shares her home in Michigan with her husband, children, a Norwegian Elkhound, and a clowder of cats (yes, she assures us, it actually is bigger on the inside). She would like to own horses again and has sadly never been to the Moon. Meg has sold stories to two previous Darkover anthologies (when she was very young but no less silly).

Darkover's version of Christianity, the *cristoforo* tradition, diverged from its origins, in no small part due to the personal tragedy of Father Valentine Neville (see *Darkover Landfall* for his story, and *The Heritage of Hastur* and *Hastur Lord* for its devastating effects on future generations). It is easy to stereotype a tradition by its strictures, at the risk of ignoring the fact that any faith capable of enduring for millennia must be deeply meaningful to its followers. Meg has highlighted the parallels—and the differences—between Terran and Darkovan traditions, as seen through the eyes of a devout traveler. Surely, on a world like Darkover, the possibility of miraculous is ever-present.

"Father? Father Dolenz, can you hear me?"

Hear him? How could I not? Peter always spoke too loud, sang too loud, whispered silent devotionals too loud. Could I hear him? Ha! Even over the drone in my aching head, I could not help but hear him.

"Father?"

An obscene montage of light and color flashed across my closed eyelids. Dear God, but it was cold in that old bucket of trans-stellar bolts we had been saddled with for the last leg of our journey.

"Father..."

"I hear you, Peter. I heard you the first time," I told him, bracing myself for the harsh, artificial light of the ship's interior. Instead, I saw only a cast of dim rose on grey walls around me, and frost. The environmental systems were clearly on the fritz again.

Warm, sweet tones like those from archaic hand bells reminded me of long ago childhood, of summers spent with my great-grandmother, walking each evening to the old part of town to attend vespers at the ancient Catholic church. Eyes still heavy with sleep closed as I concentrated on the sweet whisper of comfortable dreams. *Wake me when we get there,* I wanted to tell Peter. *Better yet, wake me when this awful trip is over.*

The bells continued to ring up and down the lovely melody until a seed of a thought bloomed: I had brought no such recordings on our trip. Still half a day from Cottman IV in a broken down excuse for a shuttle and I was hallucinating about my childhood. Cottman IV, that forbidding planet under the fabled—I looked up toward the light-kissed window—red sun. Somehow, I had missed our descent. Last I remembered, I had gone to my cramped quarters to sleep under the pretext of studying my sermon. I had been doing a lot of that. Sleeping, that is.

Bell song continued to fill the air, low ringing and high tinkling like angelic voices; my temples throbbed.

"I must be space sick, Peter," I said, closing my eyes again. Rediscovered darkness gave some small comfort. "I hear bells."

"You hit your head, Father. Thank God you're awake now."

Good Peter, always concerned about this old priest.

"Yes, thank God," I growled, touching my hand to a pulsing, swollen brow.

Thank God that Pius St. Pierre V had chosen to send me off on a spaceship farther from Earth than I had ever imagined even Heaven would be. *Me*, of all people! An appointment of great importance, I'd been told after a copy of the petition arrived. A small handful of lonely research and exploration teams on a distant planet wanted a clergyman to come for Christmas. Any clergyman would do, since none had accepted the invitation to *live* on that awful planet, and the petition was turned over to the Pope. Clerical bureaucracy should have held it up at least a year before foisting the honor on someone with something to gain from such a misadventure. Not that time.

"I've been worried, you know. You've been in and out all night," Peter said, fussing around me with blankets and an extra parka.

He had not stopped talking, even as I slid into self pity, reliving my anxieties about a trip I wanted none of. Peter, on the other hand, was a young deacon with enough energy for three people and had jumped at the chance to accompany me.

"How do you feel? Are you warm enough? The Brothers are gathering wood. Would you like to study the..."

"Stop twittering, Peter," I said, struggling to comprehend what he was saying. "Brothers? Whose brothers?"

I tried to sit up again, regretted it, and groaned instead. Peter leaned closer, his large brown eyes as concerned as a faithful herding dog's. Tiny bits of frost clung to his twisted blond moustache.

"From the monastery. They found the crash site yesterday." Peter smiled slightly, showing the unnaturally perfect teeth modern orthodontics had provided him with when genetics hadn't. I knew. I'd known him from boyhood on, had pulled him from the rubble of a war-torn city. Now ... I blinked. One of his front teeth was chipped badly. "They saw the fire as we..."

Truth told, he had lost me when he said "monastery." His broken tooth had merely been a distraction. I waved him to silence. This time Peter came to my aid, steadying me as I looked around what should have been familiar surroundings.

Jesu...

The dimly lit hull was a nightmare of wreckage and tumbled equipment. How Peter had gotten me from my quarters through the crushed doorway behind him, I couldn't tell. His eyes met mine, but he didn't speak, only allowed me full silence to absorb the shock. I could see no casualties, though from the crimson stains on one wall it was obvious there had been at least one.

Through a shattered portal I glimpsed a snow-covered wasteland dotted with stunted trees. Beyond the tree line, almost directly below the ledge we evidently had slid to a stop on, stood the tiny stone and mortar suggestions of distant buildings.

Monastic dwellings, I thought, pressing my nose against the frosty pane. Eighteenth century. No ... like a monastery wall of far more antiquity, void of excess decoration—save one shamefully beautiful stained glass window that flickered and glimmered across the snow-covered landscape. My fingers dug into the smooth thermal quilt Peter had drawn over my shoulders. I felt my skull beginning to pulse again from the strain. Sleep had distinct advantages.

Peter broke the silence. "We crashed."

"And this is where errant priests dwell for eternity," I guessed, the words coming out a mere whisper. Fire I had never really expected, but cold, marrow-chilling, frost-biting cold. Here we were.

"You might better lie down, Father."

"I might better know where I am!" I snapped, rubbing my hands together as the truth became painfully clear. I looked at the blood again. "The pilots?"

Peter shook his head.

"Did you...?"

"Of course, Father. And I've started letters to their families."

"He is better now?"

The new voice was strange—heavily accented Terran Standard. A balding man stepped through the dented escape hatch, moving quickly so as not to let the blowing snow in with him. It occurred to me the bells had stopped ringing and I heard chanting.

The tones were as clear and sweet as any I had ever heard, singing in ... Latin? Like none I'd ever heard, certainly, yet Latin it seemed to the part of me deep inside that had struggled so hard to learn it decades earlier. Young voices joined in lovely harmony. Most young men had long since stopped pursuing the priesthood on Earth, and young women too. Some, yes, some always would. Vatican V had encouraged a few, and young people still wanted to escape, to learn and to teach and to take the message of our faith to the stars. But what were these angelic singers doing out in a blizzard?

"Father, are you sure you're well enough to stand?"

I hadn't realized I was up, or that I had escaped from Peter to travel toward the sound of the voices.

"I'm fine. Hungry." *Cold.* I wondered if I had remembered to pack the thermal mittens I was given by the parish. Peter would know; he kept track of all the little things. Now he was keeping close track of me, too. I looked at the stranger in brown monkish robes, then to Peter in his black thermal trousers, high-collared wool shirt, and thermal vest. They in turn looked at me as if I were a crazy man.

I must be, I thought.

"You are certain you aren't hurt?" The stranger was younger than I had first thought, closer to Peter's age than my own, what remained of his auburn hair trimmed short. His brows were bushy, red slashes over deeply set, grey-blue eyes that twinkled with vitality.

"Father Dolenz is a bit in shock," Peter said on my behalf. I supposed he was correct in his assessment.

"We'll have soup soon," the newcomer said, struggling with the words, to make himself understood no doubt. "We will need it tonight, even those of us not used to luxuries." He paused, smiling. "Petra said you were going to the *Terranan* city?"

Petra? I blinked at the name, finding my tongue at last. "Yes, to celebrate Christmas Mass for—what day is it, Peter?" He hesitated just long enough for me to guess the bad news before he could deliver it.

"Wednesday, Father."

Wednesday! Christmas Eve was Friday night. I stifled a groan. All of this just to miss our only reason for coming to this forsaken chunk of snowy rock? *Ah, St. Pierre, you've really done it to me this time.*

"How far are we—?"

"The *Terranan* city? I know of it," he said gently, extending a strong arm for me to lean on, "but it is too far to walk in a snowstorm. You're so much better already! Yesterday I would not have thought it."

I smiled, still listening to the singing. After a flight spent with Peter's ill-sung harmonies, the voices were like angels to my ears. "The Lord is my strength, Brother."

I was surprised when he did not reply.

"Brother Raffe and the others saw the ship crash," Peter explained. "The locals have been hiding in the mountains because of civil unrest. I'm not sure I understand it all. It wasn't in the briefing. The Brothers and a few students were coming back from leaving medicine with someone when ... Father Chris? Father Christopher, where are you going?"

"Out," I said, moving slowly away from the monk to push open the door.

Snow swirled around the glade where several small buildings stood, the remains of another cast to rubble beside a missing airship wing. They had the look of ancient European Earth about them, thatch roofs fallen to disrepair in winter. In the center of the field stood a handful of boys, most dressed in the barest of raiment, many with bare feet. Their voices raised in the dulcet tones of what might have been an *Ave Maria* though the words, so strange in this dialect, escaped me.

Instinct or curiosity, I'm not sure which, drove me forward, clutching the thermal blanket I had yet to release. I peered over the shoulder of a shivering red-haired lad to see what they were gathered around. One by one the boys approached the statue in homage before I heard Peter's hushed voice say my name. Too late, I stepped closer, shielding my eyes from the snow, staring at a child kissing the feet of a statue the likes of which I had never seen in any Church anywhere.

"I tried to warn you."

I waved Peter away, concentrating on the bowl of greasy onion soup cupped in my numb hands. Outside, the chanting had ceased and whatever came next to this brotherhood was being conducted. Whatever it was, I was not sure I wanted to know.

"They did save our lives, Father; we should be thankful." Ever the diplomat, Peter tried again to appease what he interpreted as anger.

I finished my soup without answering. I could think only of the beautiful, grossly disfigured statue, a statue that looked like the personification of madness. And they had worshipped before it, bending knees and kissing the feet as if ... the thought made me shudder.

Three ill-clad boys brought firewood for a makeshift fire pit into which snow had been falling through a tear in the roof all morning. The littlest one, a redhead of perhaps eleven, shivered under his stiff robe, tugging a complicated twist of green and black tartan closer.

"Have you eaten?" I asked, pitying their pink little feet and feeling all the colder for looking at their bluish lips. "Hmm? Have you?"

"We've each had a cup," the oldest one answered in Terran Standard less accented than Brother Raffe's had been. He brushed snow from the kindling as it was placed expertly into the shallow storage tub we hoped would contain a fire without becoming too hot itself. If the hole in the roof proved sufficient, we might not choke to death of smoke either.

"One cup?" I mused.

"Yes, sir."

I snorted and they all looked at me in surprise. A smile inched across the little one's face, and as quickly was replaced with the solemn, pious expression of a monastic statue. Grey eyes continued to twinkle. Some things never changed.

"What's your name?" I asked the leader. He was tall and gaunt, perhaps sixteen and by the look of his feet, still growing. And he needed more than a single cup of soup.

"Dewin, sir." He paused for a moment. "You haven't had enough, sir?"

"I have had several cups, am wrapped in blankets, and still am near to freezing to death. You say each boy has had one and one only? How do you expect to stay warm and keep your strength out there?"

"The body makes unnecessary demands," he said, glancing down at the little boy half-dressed in tartan, "for more food or warmth than are required. I'm not cold, sir."

"You may not be," I told him, drawing my blankets closer, "but the little fellow next to you is shivering so badly I can hear his bones rattling all the way over here."

Dewin scowled and I felt vaguely guilty for having drawn such attention to the youngster.

"We all have lessons to learn. He'll be all right, sir, he's just been pampered before coming to Nevarsin. He still is," Dewin said, flicking an edge of the handsome dark tartan as he pushed the little boy back toward the door. "Excuse us, but we've more wood to gather before nightfall. A bad storm is coming."

The sky was clear come morning, the red cast of the sun like blood on the ice. I walked around the camp, a blanket fastened over my thermal coat, trying not to think about the nagging need to urinate. It was too cold.

Christmas Eve tomorrow. I shook my head. Had I not been a priest I would have damned the circumstances. To be truthful, I think I did anyway.

"Father, don't go too far. We don't know what might be out there."

Peter trudged through knee-deep snow after me, rubbing his makeshift mittens together. After the burials of the only two crew members we could find, he had scavenged through the wreckage with several of the boys and found limited supplies still within the battered hull—blankets, parkas, food provisions, and extra clothing, all of which he distributed to our rescuers. His mittens used to be fine wool socks; mine, I think.

"The storm's still coming."

Dark clouds hung over the mountains, the high reaches almost totally obscured. I could feel the wind howling down from what the natives referred to as the Hellers. A most fitting name.

"Brother Raffe went back up there with some of the boys to get help," I told him, gesturing toward a path in the forest. Blowing wind had effectively erased their footprints already. I shook my head, icy droplets spilling onto the crusty white earth. "They'll freeze to death in this snow before they get back."

Peter nodded, rubbing the dark blue socks together again. I left my hands, also wrapped in socks, in the deep pockets of my parka. Before us, the panorama of Darkovan cliffs and the monastery, far below and unreachable from this direction, was almost enough to make me forget I was cold. Almost.

"Petra! Petra!"

I recognized the child as the ginger-topped lad from the day before. Minor alterations had rendered my thermal mittens into slippers for his little feet, but his flapping robe and Celtic style plaid still looked awfully drafty. He rushed up to us yelling in his native language, his checks as flushed with color as his wavy locks.

"Slow down, slow... Oh, never mind, here, give me your hand," I told him. "Show us."

"Dear God."

My thoughts echoed Peter's words when we found Dewin, the tall youth with all the answers, lying in the snow beyond the tree line north of camp, bloodied and quite dead. I administered last rites, but even as I spoke I noticed a severed arm, stiff fingers reaching grotesquely from a trail of blood. A quick intake of breath told me Peter had seen the same thing.

We carried Dewin's body as far from camp as we dared, covering it with a light dusting of snow and pine boughs. A cold grave, I thought, looking down at a corner of the poor boy's robe. He had not been cold in life, I told myself. Neither would he be cold in death, even buried in snow.

"No one saw or heard anything," Peter told me as we walked back.

I didn't see how that was possible, given the extent of the injuries or the condition of the unidentified arm, but I accepted his words.

A group of bewildered boys waited at the forest's edge, wringing their hands, looking as cold as I felt. I had to smile when Peter caught the hands of the two youngest as we made our way through the snow. Always quick to win the trust of children, I thought.

"Brother Raffe took Dewin with him," one of the boys said.

"Where are the others?" another asked, a tremble in his voice. "Should we search for them?"

I thought of the arm we had seen, the crimson stains on the white snow.

"No. No, we were to wait here. I don't think we should go looking," I told them. What I didn't say was that I did not think we would find anyone. Not alive.

"It's going to be a long night, Father Chris," Peter said. "But we might live a lot longer if we all stay in the ship. Together."

I nodded. It had already been a long life, but I was fond of it.

"Oh Holy Night, the stars are brightly shining, this is the night of our dear Savior's birth..."

I would have told Peter to put a damper on it the following
night had I not loved that old song so much. The four lads Brother
Raffe had left behind seemed grateful to weather the storm with us.
I suspected not a one of them was accustomed to the extreme cold
or hunger their lives seemed filled with. Bastian and Alamir, clearly
kin, had flame-red hair. Aerin was blond and eager with questions.
The last was Delaney, a brooding little fellow with a cap of straight,
dark locks. All of them had sharp grey eyes. Bright eyes that stared
at me expectantly. Perhaps they thought I would provide answers
to unspoken questions, some reassurance that we were not doomed
to either freeze to death in this alien, metallic hull of a space-craft
or be torn to pieces outside by some unseen menace. Children,
looking for an adult's guidance. Perhaps mistreated children. Dear
God, why were they here and not with their families? I did not
understand and, once more, wasn't sure I wanted to. I turned
toward the smoky fire, wishing they'd stare at Peter instead. After
all, he was the one singing the loveliest of Christmas songs out of
tune.

The ship creaked and newly-fallen snow sifted through pinprick
holes in the frame like salt. I shook a smattering of it from my
head. The blond-haired boy giggled. My favorite, little red-headed
Bastian, jabbed him with an elbow. They all drew closer to the fire
as the night deepened and the wind howled and Peter's singing got
worse.

"Peter," I said at last, "look again to see if anyone is coming."

He sighed. "Father, I couldn't see even to the trees last night,
and earlier today the storm was only worse. Soup anyone?"

I looked around at flushed faces, red noses. I had looked like
that on Chirstmases of my youth, I thought. But cold from
sledding and snowball fights, not because our fire was smoky from
damp wood and inadequate ventilation and the only food left was
onion soup and dehydrated liver no one had shown a particular
interest in. A cup of herbal tea with a twist of cinnamon would
have been a blessing just then.

"Father Dolenz, look!"

Outside the portal behind me, snow had piled up, blown into a
mound against the side of the ship to obscure what light had
filtered in earlier. Behind the cracked plasti-glass I detected

movement.

Tap.

Tap. Tap.

"Peter...?" We glanced at one another. I wondered if I looked as anxious as he did. The tapping came again, like nails on a tin can.

"Sweet God," he said at last, "what is it?"

"Brother Raffe?" I chanced, getting up on numb toes to investigate.

The escape hatch groaned but would not budge, even as I put my shoulder against it. Aged I was. Decrepit I was not. I shoved again and again to no avail. Peter joined me and we threw ourselves against the door.

"I think it's buried," Peter said, rubbing at the glass.

"Already?" I rapped loudly and called once again, listening for a reply.

Bastian's piercing cry nearly turned me inside out. Snow tumbled into our already smoldering fire, embers and ash and white fluff scattering out of the fire-tub.

"Brother Raffe?" Peter called, his voice lower and louder than mine. "Brother Raffe, is it you?"

Tap.

Tap. Tap.

Just as mittened fingers of my youth had cleared the snow from frosted panes, now fingertips outside the ship rubbed the shattered portal clean in small, circular strokes. Huge, hairy fingers poked and pried at the cracked surface. Peter said, "*Sweet God*" again, but I was more explicit as I dragged him toward the rough wood and metal remnant of a table we'd rigged to stand last night. Even tipped on its side it was far too small to shield four shivering boys, a tone-deaf deacon, and one thoroughly frightened priest.

The tapping came again, then something more than a tap. A thud. On the roof. I remembered an old song about "*the prancing and pawing of each little hoof,*" but it did little more than amuse me for a moment.

"Alamir," Bastian whispered to his cousin. "What is it?"

"Is it one of the Ya-men?" Aerin asked.

Delaney gave him a withering look. "Don't you know anything?"

"No," Alamir said softly, taking a step forward. His angular features looked even sharper as his pale eyes narrowed. He ran a hand through his collar-length mane of flaming red hair. For the first time, I noticed he had six fingers. "There are things far worse than Ya-men."

I did not want to know how he came by such knowledge.

As one, we looked up when we heard more thumping on the sturdy roof, as if something was jumping up and down. I motioned for Peter to help me pry two twisted metal legs off the table. If whatever it was wanted to get in and the door was blocked, that left...

"Look!" Bastian cried. "More snow!"

Indeed, a smattering of white flakes cascaded onto smoldering embers, and thick smoke wound through the ship. What a way for an old priest to die, I thought, motioning for the boys to lie on the floor where the air was clearer as Peter and I moved toward the fire, brandishing our makeshift swords.

"No way to close this off, huh?"

"Not at the moment. Maybe if we keep the fire going we can scare it away."

I looked at him, incredulous.

"Well, I wouldn't want to land on it," he muttered.

Using the table leg, I poked the wood furiously, stirring hot coals until a little fire flickered again. *Dear God*, I prayed, *please, please...*

I give myself credit for not being the first one to scream. Of course, I screamed too when that—that *arm* reached into the ship from above, gnarled hairy fingers snatching for whatever was near enough. As it turned out, that was Peter, swatted across the room like a ragdoll to crash amid a tangle of electrical cable spilled from a ruptured wall. The boys scattered when a second hand shot down though the hole, gripping the back of my coat, then my arm. The table leg I had been holding clattered to the floor as I struggled against the force pulling me up and over the fire.

"Father Dolenz!" Bastian squealed.

"Don't get too close, boy!" I shouted, struggling with the mitten on my free hand, with a frozen coat zipper and ice-cold fasteners and—

"Father Chris, I—"

"Just hit the dogged thing, Peter!"

"Alamir!" one of the boys cried. "Alamir, do something!"

"Move, Bastian, move!"

Alamir's voice, I thought, unable to see as my parka was yanked over my face, the rest of me still trapped though I wiggled and twisted to pull my arms free. Above, obscured in smoke, I could hear the excited sounds of a killer reeling in its prey.

Me.

Below, children yelled, and I felt hands on my ankles tugging me clear of the fire. As I spun, I glimpsed Alamir stepping forward, one hand extended, six fingers spread wide, the other at his throat as he uttered a name:

"Aldones, Lord of Light..."

A blast of pale blue light, brighter than the blizzard of snow had been, surged from his fingers, igniting the smoldering wood into a leaping white flame that licked past me. The hairy arm withered before my eyes, a cry of terror from whatever was left filling the ship's hull.

"Sweet God!"

It was my turn to use Peter's phrase as I fell. I narrowly missed landing in the embers, falling hard on my backside, Bastian tumbling down on top of me. Behind him, his face grey with soot, Alamir drew ragged breaths. In the makeshift fire pit, a natural-looking fire now burned freely, and the monstrous arm was gone.

"He needs to eat," Bastian said after a little while, his little mitten-encased feet scuffing against the floor. He tugged at my sleeve, struggling with Terran Standard and I with the formal language of his people. "My uncle is at a Tower—I've heard about it. He has to eat. And you're bleeding."

I know I was gaping at him like a stunned carp, but I accepted the child's words as law.

"Peter, warm some soup for Alamir." Feeding a sick boy liver was too great a sin.

We heard no more sounds from outside, neither from Brother Raffe's party nor from the thing on the roof. Night had come quickly during our brief encounter with the Darkovan nonhuman, cloaking the land in blackness accentuated by the fact that we were trapped. I glanced at the wall portal. Snow had blown up around it almost entirely, and my impression was that it was still snowing. I glanced around. The boys were watching me again.

"Delany, Aerin? Come sit near Alamir and keep him warm. When the soup is ready, help him drink it."

The boys scurried to do my bidding, robes and blankets rustling, stocking feet skidding on the cold floor. I wrapped my torn coat around poor, shivering Alamir, not sure I wanted to inspect my wounds too closely. My arm hurt, but we had more pressing problems. I bent to knock the embers of our dwindling fire apart, searching the compartment for a way to seal the gaping hole in the roof.

"We can use the top of the table to cover it," Peter said, gesturing to where we could slip the flat piece between ruptured hoses and failed wiring in the ceiling.

"Maybe." And maybe the fire was the only thing keeping those things away from us. I stared at the flames, cradling my aching wrist. The hole above was large enough for whatever it was to get through, if it really wanted to. If it really wanted us. I nodded at last, giving Peter a boost up to secure the patchwork as he suggested. My arm throbbed all the more, but I wasn't the only one hurting just then.

"Did you get any briefing about things like that?" I asked, rolling up my sleeve to check my arm. The skin was broken, but not the bones. I glanced around the room. Already it was darker, colder. Peter was busy rummaging for another emergency lamp; it cast a warm, red glow over our chilly quarters. He was a long time before answering my question.

"All I got was a map of the facilities in the city and eight weeks of intensive language and so-called custom studies." He glanced at Alamir, lifted an eyebrow, then just shook his head. So little rendered Peter at a loss for words.

"That's more than I got," I muttered, feeling the last of the fire's warmth dissipate.

He wrapped a blanket around my shoulders. "Sit down, Father, you're pale as a ghost."

Soon I will give even that up, Peter, I thought, complying nonetheless. I leaned against the smooth, cold wall under the portal, thinking of nothing, my eyes tracing the tortured features of the ugly little statue I'd allowed Bastian to drag in the day before. Lined to each side of it were the hand bells, glinting like upturned gold goblets in the dim light.

"Father," it was Bastian. He offered me a cup of soup which I accepted gratefully. Like Alamir, he had six fingers. Why hadn't I noticed before?

He hunkered down in front of me, gazing at the chain and medallions that lay on my breast. "These are *Terranan* symbols?"

I nodded, fumbling with each in turn. He didn't look twice at the crucifix and I had no intention of explaining its significance just then, but the silver St. Christopher medal sparked his interest.

"Ah, my patron saint," I told him, kissing the medal my grandfather had presented to my parents at my birth. "My Christian name is Christopher."

Christopher, patron saint of travelers, have mercy.

"*Cristoforo?*"

I blinked at him, at his curious, innocent face. Yes. Yes, that was it. I sat forward, looking across the room at the strange, twisted statue, then at Alamir drinking soup slowly. *A bent figure, struggling, persevering...*

Tap.

Bastian looked up. I swallowed deeply.

Cristoforo...

"Here, you're cold, aren't you?" I drew Bastian down beside me, motioning for the others to come closer. Wanting to protect them, I gathered them like a shepherd gathers his sheep.

Tap.

We clung together, all of us and I prayed. First silently, then, when the tapping and clanging and thudding became more insistent, I prayed out loud, over and over and over. Curse the edict against vain repetition—this wasn't vain, this was desperation! The sounds stopped.

"Father? Who is Jesu?"

I opened my eyes, hardly aware that I had closed them. Four children sat around me, Alamir looking stronger already. Rosy cheeks like the cheeks of a thousand children on a thousand

Christmas Eves past glowed in the dim lamplight.

Tap.

"Was he a *Terranan?*" Alamir asked softly.

"A space traveler?" asked Aerin.

Dark-haired Delany snorted, as if speaking of space travel was some sort of nonsense not to be tolerated. Then he met my eyes, glanced briefly at Peter, and shuddered.

"Something like that," Peter admitted, taking the place closest to the door.

Out of the corner of my eye I kept watching to see if snow was falling around the table top covering our now-useless chimney.

Tap.

"He came to Terra," I found myself saying, struggling for words to mask our fear. "He came from—from far away to live among us, to teach us, to save us ... to return someday to reclaim us."

"Like Aldones, Son of Hastur, Lord of Light," Bastian said smartly. One of the others made a rude noise.

"On Christmas Eve, tonight," I said quickly, realizing I'd never spoken a Christmas Mass or even spoken of the scriptures to a more naïve group, "we celebrate His birth. Born of a virgin in a little town..." Lost. A town lost a galaxy away, burned and pillaged, windswept and buried, ruined ages ago. Bethlehem. Oh, Holy Night!

"A virgin?" Aerin piped up, eyes wide.

"Was she a Keeper?" Delaney asked suspiciously.

"*Shhh.* She was a *Terranan,*" Alamir stressed the word, then frowned. "How did a virgin conceive a child?"

"The Holy Spirit overshadowed her and," I gazed up at the roof when I heard sounds like clacking jaws, "in due time, He issued forth from her womb like ... light." *Sweet God. Sweet, sweet Jesus...*

"It is," someone whispered, in the dim light, "the Son of Hastur."

"The Son of God," Peter said gently.

Tap.

"But, what about Cristoforo?" Bastian asked, fingering the St. Christopher medal. "Cristoforo, on your medal. Did he make the virgin pregnant?"

"No, he..." They were all looking at me, leaning forward,

hanging on the question, waiting for my answer. The battery-powered light on the floor glimmered like a mass of tangled Christmas lights.

Tap.

"A legend," I said finally, fingers caressing the medal as I tried to remember the story, ashamed in part that I could not.

But legends had a way of mutating. What I had heard as a child was not what children heard today, just as what my grandfather had heard was probably slightly different from what I had heard. I was thankful when Peter began to translate the story slowly. Eyes moved from me to him, eager, so very eager.

"A legend of a righteous man, a traveler, who, having come to a river, found a small child there crying, for he could not get across. And so Christopher lifted the lad, thinking little of it, for the boy was tiny, and he put him on his shoulder. But as he crossed the river, Christopher grew weary and his steps grew heavier until he thought he could not go on. In the middle of the river he stopped, unable to move his feet against the rising water. But he trusted the Lord for his strength, and finally he reached the opposite side. There he put the child down safely, and saw ... saw in his tiny hands the scars by which our Savior is known."

"Here, and here," I said, showing the boys the spots I meant on my own wrists. I lifted the crucifix then. "Scars from nails that held him to a cross when the world crucified him. And Christopher realized that he had carried the Christ Child across the river, and the heaviness he felt was the weight of the world's sin which is Christ's burden. For a short time he bore the Child on his shoulders, and with Him the burden of all the world." And later he was martyred. Tradition? Truth? Did it really matter?

They stared at me, even Peter who had heard the story a hundred times. They stared at me and I at them until my eyes grew too weary in the dim light and I leaned my head back, wishing I could clear the red haze away. Bastian stirred first, rising to cross to where the *cristoforo* statue hunched in front of the main hatch, flanked by bells that might have made that holy night bearable were it not for the danger outside. At long last, he bent to lift the figure reverently, holding it at arm's length.

"I made it wrong," he said softly. "The Bearer of Burdens

carries nothing. But he should, shouldn't he?"

Before I could answer, a splintering crash shattered the unsteady peace of the night. Bastian dropped the wooden statue as he scurried into our midst. As one we pressed against the bulkwork, Peter and I shielding our young charges, dreading the hour of our deaths. The door I'd been unable to budge earlier dropped inward with a resounding clang, and the hinges snapped wide open. The statue exploded into slivers and sawdust, the bells clanging and rolling across the floor.

We crouched in anticipation of the creature's attack. But nothing came. Filling the space where the door had been stood a glistening wall of ice and snow, the delicate crystalline pattern like closely packed stars flickering in the dim light. Each tiny crystal pattern sparkled in the red light, unique and perfect in its frigid beauty. Above the ship I could hear nothing. Or, just maybe, it was the song the shepherds had heard so very long ago.

"Father Dolenz? Father Christopher Dolenz, are you in there?"

I ignored the dream in favor of sleep and what little warmth the six of us shared in our nest of parkas and thermal blankets. Again, the muffled sound of my name, like someone calling down into the grave. A third time someone said my name. I struggled awake, sitting up in time to see part of the wall of snow that filled the hatch cave into the ship. A hooded figure in a steel-grey thermal suit and goggles crawled through with a collapsible shovel.

"They're here!" he hollered back down the tunnel. He grinned at us. "Ric MacKenna, from Search and Recovery, Father. Sorry about the delay. We had to rescue a party of Brothers from Nevarsin last night, they were..." I guess he just then noticed the four *cristoforo* novices and students dressed in their mixture of native and Terran costume. "Uh... Merry Christmas."

"Merry Christmas, Ric," I told him, brushing frost from my sweater. Peter bent to pick up the glowing red lamp. I lifted sleepy Bastian to his feet, then into my arms, ignoring the strain in my wounds. "Now, how about getting us out of here?"

The sea stretched away from us for miles, a rolling pool reflected darkly under the red sun. The ship cast a shadow against the waves and I found myself concentrating on it, watching it shimmer and bend in the light. Alamir's strange magic came to mind, that blinding light. Darkover's red sun's reflection on the ship's hull became too bright for my eyes and I sat back. Beside me, Peter was strangely quiet.

"Penny for your thoughts, Peter."

"Hmm? Oh, Father Chris, I'm sorry. I was just thinking..."

"About something pleasant, I hope. No? What's wrong, Peter?"

He looked past me at the clouds, blushed and burnt under the star I had become fond of. Alamir's family had sent for both boys as soon as news of our exploits reached them. For whatever reason, the family had removed them both from the monastery. Something smelled of political intrigue and war. The authorities at the Terran City told us the planet was rife with it.

"What do you think He thinks of what has happened here?" Peter asked.

"I wouldn't presume to know God's mind," I told him," "but Christianity has manifested itself in stranger ways."

I knew my history well enough to know the brothers at Nevarsin were not so unlike other expressions of faith that had come and gone on the time scale of many worlds humankind had touched down on.

"Oh, but Father..."

"Well, then, what do you think, *Petra?*"

He squirmed under the name. True, it had sounded better from the lips of the native children, but it was part of him now, just as this place would forever be part of both of us. He sat up straight, his fingers playing with the shoulder harness for a moment before straying to the gold cross on his neck. "It is fascinating, but they've forgotten Christ..."

"Have they?"

I thought of the children. I thought of the broken statue of St. Valentine-of-the-Snows and young Bastian's words: *I made it wrong ... the Bearer of Burdens carries nothing. But he should, shouldn't he?*

Yes, I thought. *He should.* And Valentine, like St. Christopher, had struggled under some great burden, something terrible and weighted with sin to give his brow that saddened twist.

I glanced back out the window. Darkover was receding.

"It's remarkable," Peter said at last. "They've kept their faith for centuries."

"And apparently the Comyn have kept theirs." Not that I understood it.

"But, Father! The Lord of Light—doesn't that sound—"

"Careful," I said, raising my hand to still rash words. "I don't know, Peter. They base it on legend and history, just like the *cristoforos*. Who are we to judge what these legends are when they don't even know themselves? How are we to know His will in this when much of our own faith is based in history and tradition?" *And legend.*

"Like the story of St. Christopher?" he asked. "Father, your medal…"

It had taken him a long time to notice my saint's medallion was gone.

"I left it with Bastian," I explained. "I would have left him and Alamir a Bible as well, but the only one that we found at the crash site was the Greek and I told them we hadn't enough time to teach them that."

"I could teach them," he said slowly. "Were I to return after I'm ordained."

For almost three years he had been a deacon in my parish—the boy I'd pulled from the rubble and later helped through seminary. His time to move on had come.

"You could indeed, *Petra*," I told him softly, doing my best with Darkovan dialect flavored with tongues my ancestors had forgotten. "You might even find out what you want to know, given time."

"You could come with me," he said, dark eyes flashing with mischief. "The Pope could—"

A glance was warning enough. It was the Pope who had gotten us into this mess to begin with. And yet, I wanted to believe something beautiful might come of all the tragedy.

"Staying crossed my mind," I admitted, "but I might try to convert them; I'm not sure that's wise right now." *I'm not sure I know how.*

Let Peter plant the seeds. Let Bastian lead the children to a new understanding just as he had created a new statue. Such a wonderful talent for one so young! I had been permitted a glimpse before I left, my heart warmed to see a Bearer of Burdens with the familiar visage of a tired priest whom I often encountered in the mirror. A Bearer of Burdens shouldering a serenely smiling child who bore a striking resemblance to young Bastian Alton.

ONLY MEN DANCE

by Evey Brett

The love of horses runs deep in the Domains, although it remains somewhat of a mystery how they happened to be on Darkover before Rediscovery and the "modern" period. Marion often said she never let details (like geography or, in this case, the history of livestock importation on Darkover) interfere with a good story, and so featured the stallion Sunstar in *Hawkmistress*. With a sensitivity and knowledge rising from her own experience with horses, Evey Brett creates an adventure based on the special magic of horse and rider, one that on Darkover runs far deeper than elsewhere, perhaps into the very soul of each.

While this is her first sale to a Darkover anthology, Evey Brett is no stranger to magic, especially when it comes to horses—just ask her Lipizzan mare, Carrma, who has a habit of arranging the universe to her liking. Carrma not only insisted that Evey move to southern Arizona to coddle her during her retirement, but she was also the inspiration for Evey's books, *Capriole, Levade,* and *Passage,* as well as an anthology featuring supernatural horses. "None of those are based on real life," Evey says. "Nope, not one."

"The carrion birds are circling around something. There's probably a dead horse on the road," Pirro announced when he walked into the barn.

Calum didn't even bother to look up from his mucking. Being only ten, his half-brother was notorious for crafting fanciful tales. The grander they were, the more attention he got.

"Please, Calum. I want to go see."

And Calum was tempted to tell him to just go, but then he'd get a beating for letting the younger boy travel the hills alone. "I have chores to finish. You could help," he suggested hopefully, but of course Pirro didn't so much as lift a rake.

"It won't take long. I just want to look. Please?"

Canissa, Calum's elderly mare, snorted and began to lick and chew. Pirro noticed and said delightedly, "See? She wants to go too!"

"You're not helping," Calum told his mare as he rubbed her between the ears and let his mind sink into hers just enough to feel her surge of pleasure. To Pirro he said, "You know I don't like to take her out in winter. The wolves—"

"You're always scared of any animal that isn't *her*. They're nightmares, Calum. You can't actually become a wolf!"

But he could, and he had, and if he hadn't managed to latch on to Canissa's mind he might still be trapped inside a wolf andrunning wild. The distorted memories of the night the wolves had attacked the herd had bled into his dreams, waking both him and Pirro when they got bad. On those nights, he went to the barn and joined his mind to Canissa's. She was his security, his calm amidst a sea of unhappiness and guilt.

He'd almost lost her, too. After the attack, his stepfather Ranald had decided to get rid of all the horses after so many had ended up broken and useless. Now they bred *chervines*, the little stag-ponies travelers used to ride and haul supplies through the jagged trails of the Hellers. *Chervines* might be easier to take care of, but they lacked the personality of the horses. Canissa was the last horse, and she, too, would have been sold if Calum hadn't doubled his chores in order to pay for her keep. *Unnatural*, Ranald had said about his relationship with the mare. *Ought to be finding yourself a nice girl to bring home, otherwise people will think you're a sandal-wearer, like those monks.*

And from the way Pirro glared at him, he shared his father's low opinion. "Coward. I knew you wouldn't take me."

"I just—"

Canissa nosed the gate to her pen, a sure sign that she was ready for an adventure.

Calum sighed. He could never win against his mare. "Fine. We'll go."

Pirro was right. The raucous voices of the *kyorebni* echoed up the trail, alerting Calum that they had indeed found a meal. Canissa swiveled her ears, focusing on the sound, and headed down the trail. Calum dropped his consciousness into the mare's so he could share her senses. All at once the colors and sounds became sharper, and if she sensed any danger, he would know at once. The wolves were out there, somewhere, ready to come after them and—

He choked, remembering too clearly the feral intensity of *being* a wolf and the taste of a mare's blood in his mouth. The blame for the horse's death lay squarely on him. He'd been feverish and ill to the point of hallucinating that night, but if he hadn't lost control, if he'd managed to drive the wolves away, she wouldn't have died and so many others wouldn't have been injured.

"I won't lose control again, *carya*. I'll keep you safe, no matter what," he said, too softly for Pirro to hear. That was why he let his mind merge with hers as much as he did; they depended on each other for protection.

He couldn't, however, protect her from everything. Being mountain-bred, she had a thick coat and sure feet, but her later years were plagued by the same aches and pains humans felt as they aged. Calum let Pirro ride since he was lighter, to spare the horse as much as he could.

The morning was brisk and chill, and snow had fallen overnight, leaving the trails white and untouched. Calum had met a few of the Nevarsin monks during the yearly festival and wished dearly for their discipline in mastering their body's response to cold so the bitter wind would not cut so badly. Pirro, too, shivered in the saddle even while wrapped in a thick fur coat.

"There!" Pirro's mittened hand shot out. "See?"

Calum *did* see, and was dismayed by the form lying at the base of a steep slope, half in, half out of the drifts. Canissa snorted and shared her unease. She, too, disapproved of dead beasts on the roadside.

Between the snow, ice and loose rock, it took a long time to find a way down. Pirro clung to the saddle, stiff with fright, which only made Canissa's job harder. Calum felt her concentration as she focused on her balance, and adopted her calm as he picked out his own footing.

Once they'd made it, Calum shooed the *kyorebni* away, grateful that the wolves hadn't found the corpses yet, and scraped the remaining snow from the bodies. Even frozen, it was easy to see that the fall had killed both horse and rider and Calum guessed they'd been here no more than a day, two at most. The man lay off to the side, likely thrown from the saddle, with a large gash in his head which had left blood and brains frozen to the ground. The horse, whose neck and foreleg were broken, was a gelding, far more suited to the lowlands than the harsh weather here in the mountains. He'd been a fine beast, however, sleek and sturdy, and still wore a handsome bridle, saddle and bags. The latter, which Calum pulled free and searched, proved to be full of both supplies and letters.

"It's a messenger," he called to Pirro. There was no chance of hauling either horse or rider out. The animal was too heavy, and he wasn't going to pain Canissa with the burden of a frozen corpse. He searched the rider for anything of use and found a gold ring emblazoned with the messenger's seal, a leather purse full of coin probably meant to aid him in his journey, and another packet of letters wrapped in waxed paper and tucked into the man's coat. These he took, figuring they must be important since the messenger had gone to such lengths to protect them. He showed them to Pirro. "We'll hold onto these for safekeeping. Someone might come looking for him."

Pirro gripped the saddle, looking a bit pale despite his cold-reddened cheeks. Calum pitied the child somewhat, but it was Pirro's fault they were out here in the first place. Canissa pawed the snow, impatient to leave, and Calum winced at the pain the trip downhill had caused her. "We'll be home soon, and I'll give you a good rub down and some warm mash in thanks."

She snorted and set out determinedly for home.

Later, in the little room he shared with Pirro, Calum stared at a letter meant for Aldaran, turning it over and over in front of the candle, trying to see anything through the thick envelope. He'd slipped the ring onto his finger for safekeeping, and while it felt odd to wear a dead man's token, it fit rather well.

It also made him tingle. On closer inspection, he noticed the stone set into the gold. Staring at it made his head spin, and when he looked away he had the odd sensation that he could see Aldaran and *know* the safest route to reach it.

A matrix stone. A tiny one, but powerful enough to project a sense of urgency along with the message's destination.

For the first time in years, Calum felt a sense of hope. A messenger was bound to his vows to deliver letters and packages as swiftly as he could, and if he couldn't, he was beholden to find someone to carry on his mission.

This is my chance. Ranald had no use for him outside of chores, and when he died the farm would pass to Pirro, not Calum. He had a horse; there was no reason he couldn't deliver the letters. Perhaps those at Aldaran would be so grateful they would give him work, or maybe he'd meet with one of the official couriers along the way.

The only catch was that Canissa was elderly, and while her heart was as large as the mountains, her body soon wouldn't be able to keep up. A short trip, even to the city, might be her last.

But we can't stay here. The ring thrummed in his mind, urging him out the door toward the road.Once those messages were delivered he could make sure Canissa was safe and happy. She deserved a comfortable life in a city, far away from wolves and with better feed and other horses to keep her company. So Calum packed the saddle bags that he and Pirro had gone through. Besides letters and small parcels, they held a set of knives and flint and a packet of dried meat. Calum rolled up his blanket and shoved his spare set of clothes into one of the bags.

Pirro rolled over to stare at him. "You have to stay and look after the *chervines.*"

"It's your turn to look after them." And he didn't feel bad about it in the least.

"I hope the wolves eat you and your stupid horse."

"Maybe they'll eat you first." Gods willing, he wouldn't meet any wolves at all. He shouldered the saddlebags and gazed at his little brother one last time. "I have a letter to deliver."

Calum took nothing that wasn't his. He didn't want Ranald coming after him for thievery. So he took his blanket, his bow and arrows, the knife he'd been given when he'd grown into manhood, the saddlebags and Canissa's tack.

She gave him a questioning look when he saddled her. "We're going to Aldaran. What do you think of that?"

Canissa gave him a withering look. He didn't blame her. Spending days in the cold wouldn't be much fun for either of them, but he had to see the messages delivered.

The mare must have sensed his need for haste, because she let him saddle and load her with a minimum of fuss, and when they headed down the road she was full of her usual energy. If it weren't for her sagging back, one would hardly know she was nearing thirty. She'd had the usual bites and bruises from other horses and then the *chervines,* along with the occasional muscle strain, but overall she'd been remarkably healthy. Only once had she been truly ill, and Calum had been aware the second her belly had started to pain her. Soon he too was rolling on the ground in agony.

That night, he'd seen fear in Ranald's eyes. "You're making it up," he'd told Calum, and cuffed him in an effort to break him out of the illness. It hadn't worked, and for once, Ranald had bestirred himself to force Canissa to walk and trot in order to coax her guts into moving. When the pain had ended at last, Calum had been too exhausted to leave the barn, and Ranald had left him alone. After that, there'd been no mention of selling Canissa despite every other horse going to market. If he didn't mention the bond, it didn't exist.

And now neither of them would have any fear of such a confrontation again. The weather held, save for the bitter winds blasting them both. Canissa walked, head down, determinedly plodding forward. A few times Calum dismounted and led her through the snow, feeling the way so she didn't put a foot wrong and slip. Like the messenger, he'd put the most important letters in his jacket lest something terrible happen and he lose both Canissa and the saddlebags.

For the first day, they took it easy, stopping to rest often and making camp under a sheltered outcrop that afforded enough dry tinder that Calum could make Canissa a bowl of hot mash.

On the second, they reached the little town of Deadfall, so named because the residents earned a living collecting and selling wood. It was a ramshackle place, no more than a few log houses and a two-room inn that was little more than a waystation.

When Calum tried to explain his mission, the innkeeper scoffed at him. "I bet the messengers don't even know we're here. Best you keep riding, boy, all the way to Aldaran."

Which would be another three days, four if the trails were bad. He traded one of the messenger's coins for a bit of bread and meat for himself and whatever hay and bran the innkeeper could spare.

He let the ring guide him, amazed by his certainty of direction even when the trails were covered with snow and impossible to see. But three days later, Canissa jerked her head up and pointed her ears forward, and the alert tingled through Calum's body. Something was out there. Something bad.

A moment later, he heard what she had: the eerie, wailing cry that had terrified him since childhood.

"Go, *carya*, go!" Calum readied his bow even as he nudged Canissa onward. With luck, they could outrun the wolves. If not, they would have to stand and fight and pray to all the gods that there wasn't an entire pack out there.

Canissa skidded to a halt, nearly throwing Calum from the saddle. There were two of the wolves. No—three. They cocked their heads and sniffed the air, bodies stiff and poised to attack

He stared at the beasts, caught by how thin and rangy they were ... and how hungry.

As if the thought was a lure, Canissa's mind disappeared in a moment of utter disorientation. His vision shifted to black and white while other senses peaked—scent and sound and awareness, all complemented by the strength possessed by a compact, muscled body. This was what he'd felt before when he was no more than a child. He'd *known* this awful mix of predatory hunger and the need to attack anything.

No. Not again. Terror clung to him as he tried to grasp onto the wolf's mind and turn it awaybut the animal was too keen on its target to obey. There was no winning against that deep, predatory need, which meant Calum was as trapped and helpless as he had been on that terrible night years before. Canissa was going to die, and there was nothing he could do to stop it.

Yet the part of his mind that was still him, still Calum, rebelled against admitting such weakness. He was a man, now, not a sickly child, and a man didn't let his loved ones come to harm.In desperate fury he sent his mind lunging toward his mare. *I'll keep you safe*, carya, *but I need your help.*

There. He found her familiar presence, grabbed, pulled, and suddenly he was back in his own body just as Canissa let out a whinny of rage and stumbled to one side. He was too late. The wolves had already torn at the mare. Red scored her hindquarters, and both she and Calum cried out in shared pain.

She bucked and whirled, sending him tumbling into a snowbank. All three wolves descended on her, but she wasn't helpless. She kicked and bit, landing one blow squarely on a wolf's head and sending it flying backward with a crushed skull.

That left two, and one of them had sighted Calum.

His bow was gone, lost somewhere when Canissa had unseated him. Fast as he could, he pulled the knife from his belt, but it wasn't fast enough. The wolf dove at him, digging sharp teeth into the meaty flesh of his thigh. Agony tore through him, but Calum kept his head just long enough to drive the knife into the wolf's neck.

The animal staggered backward. Blood streamed from the wound, and within a few breaths it slumped into the snow and did not rise again.

Breathing hard from effort and fear, Calum lurched to his feet and headed toward Canissa. Long trails of blood smeared her flanks and legs and she was breathing as hard as he was. The second wolf lay crumpled in the ground at her feet, its body broken and smashed from the force of her hooves.

For his leg, he tore up his spare shirt and wrapped it as best he could. There was nothing he could do for Canissa's wounds besides bathe them in snow to slow the blood and clean it from her dappled hide. Calum couldn't help the tears streaking his cheeks. "I'm sorry, *carya*. I'm so sorry for losing control again. I didn't mean for you to get hurt."

Canissa whickered. She didn't want to move. He sensed that in every aching joint of her body, but if they stayed here, in the cold, they would die.

"Come on. Please, *carya*."

A huff of air was her only protest as he led her down the road, struggling to stay on his own two feet. His leg throbbed from the mauling, and his hips burned in sympathetic pain.

After a painful hour or so of walking, they rounded a curve which finally brought Aldaran into view. Calum took one look at it and leaned against his mare, unable to take one more step. Canissa whickered and nudged his arm. She knew as well as he did that towns meant people and food and shelter, and neither of them were going to get there if he couldn't walk. So, reluctantly, he hauled himself into the saddle and swung his stiff, swollen leg over her back.

If he'd thought someone in the town might help him, he was wrong.

Townsfolk eyed him but steered clear. Calum couldn't fault them; seeing a bloody young man riding a bloody horse would make him nervous, too.

Beneath him, Canissa swayed from exhaustion. He had to give his mare enough strength to keep going, so he willed the last of his energy into her and slumped in the saddle, overcome with fatigue and pain. Every step became more difficult than the last. Her legs hurt terribly, and her muscles ached with the weight of years. Her flanks burned from the ragged tears, yet she kept going. Once they reached the castle, surely there would be food and shelter, which were a courier's due.

The streets twisted and turned, and they were crowded with more people and carts than Calum had ever seen in one place. The ring led him onward, but the crowds wore on him and there seemed to be no easy way to reach their destination.

Then Canissa stumbled, and her heavy body landed hard against the cobbled streets. Calum only just managed to get his wounded leg out of the way in time to keep her from crushing it.

The mare gave a long, terrible wheeze. A sudden, bright agony grabbed his chest and clenched, cutting off his air. Calum gasped, hungry for breath, failing to find it. His heart pounded. Blood throbbed in his temples, making him sick and dizzy.

There came one last flare of burning pain in her chest, and he felt her tearing away from him.

NO!

He grabbed for her through the bond they shared, caught that last, fading bit of her essence, and drew it into himself.

I will keep you safe, carya. *Always.*

Voices reached his ear. Too loud, too harsh.

"What an idiot, to ride a horse to death in the center of town. Look at his clothes; he must be a peasant from one of the estates."

"Someone find a cart to haul this horse out of the road."

"Where do we haul *him*? Look at his leg. He's bleeding. Wolves got them, from the look of it."

Canissa. She was here, and so close he could feel her heart beat, but he couldn't *see* her. Something was wrong, so wrong. He groped at the icy cobbles, struggling to find purchase.

Someone yanked him to his feet—*two* feet—which felt awkward and off-balance, and a fiery slash of pain raced all the way to his hip. He tottered and threw his weight against his captor, eager to get free. When that failed, he whipped his head around and caught the man's arm between his teeth.

"Ow! Little brat!" The man shoved him to the ground. "Hold him. If he means to act the beast, I'll treat him like one!"

Rough hands grabbed his arms and legs. Someone jammed his head into the stone and he tasted grit and bitter ice between his teeth.

"He's a thief!" another man said triumphantly. "Look at this!"

Someone grabbed Calum's hand, which he managed to clench into a fist. The touch burned, ripping through him like an arrow, but instinct told him not to give up the ring.

"Bastard. This is a ring from one of the couriers employed by Lord Aldaran. What have you done to him? No doubt you're a thief *and* a murderer!"

Words pelted like hailstones as rage flowed to the surface. He redoubled his efforts, straining muscles in an attempt to break free. These dirty, angry men pawing at him meant to take him away and do something terrible. He couldn't let them hurt Canissa.

Where *was* Canissa?

He couldn't see her, yet she was there. It was her instinct that made him kick at his captors, lashing out with her feet and snapping at any hand that came too near.

"Enough!" cried an authoritative voice, female this time. "Step away from him, *mestre*. Can't you see you're scaring him more?"

"Him?" There was confusion in his voice, compounded by his leaking frustration, but at least he listened to the woman and left Calum alone. "A wild animal, more like. Look at it!"

"Let him go, lest you'd rather deal with my sword." The woman's quiet voice froze everyone. "I'm sure there's an explanation if you'd but give him room to breathe."

The men backed away, and Calum dragged in a deep breath. There came another touch, this time on his shoulder, and he flinched, expecting more pain. There wasn't any. The woman was calm and grounded as she crouched. "Tell me, how came you by the ring?"

He sniffed. The woman smelled of sweat and oiled leather, yet somehow instinct told him the woman could be trusted.

"Is the messenger dead? Is that why you carry the letters instead of him?" The woman stroked his head, putting him at ease so that when the woman sorted through his coat he didn't object. When the woman withdrew a packet, though, something snagged in his mind.

Mission. Have to get to Aldaran. Have to—

He tried to rise, but his body was awkward and off-balance. Everything felt *wrong*. Too small. Too tight. *Seeing* was wrong; he couldn't seem to focus.

"Stay down," the woman said, and forcefully kept him on the ground. The woman carefully pulled the ring from his finger and held both it and the packet of letters out to another, younger woman and told her, "Take these and ride to the castle, fast as you can, and bring back that *laranzu* that's staying there. We're going to need him. The boy is still caught in rapport."

The younger woman sped off through the crowd. The first eased him up, and he tottered this way and that as he tried to understand his surroundings.

"Don't look, *chiyu*. Close your eyes."

But it was too late. He saw the lifeless form that was both him and not him, and with that last, wrenching dissociation, his mind lost whatever tenuous hold it had left.

For a while, he was mad.

That was the only word he had for it, and one of the few that hadn't abandoned his mind completely. Otherwise, he lived a life made entirely of scent and sight and sound, watching the leather-clad women come and go. Sometimes they stopped to give him a bowl of food and change the bandages on his leg, but otherwise they left him alone in his stall, curled in the straw and wondering why his body wasn't working properly. It was thin and malformed, poorly suited to running and merely walking on four legs. So he stayed in the corner, waiting fearfully for what might happen.

One by one, words left him, though language had not. He could tell by tone and posture whether the women were happy, frustrated, or angry. He tried to communicate with the other horses in the stable, but again, his body failed him. His ears wouldn't move and his throat wouldn't make the proper sounds. So he paced and pawed the ground in frustration, and when he got tired, he slept, though his mind was full of terrible dreams. Fearsome wolves with sharp teeth and claws, the grief of his mother's death, the unfairness of another undeserved beating.

And every time he woke from such memories, he pushed them as far away as he could. They were strange, alien things. Not his at all.

Then out of the madness came song.

The buried part of himself, the little piece that was still human, followed the music. His mother had loved to sing, but since her death, he'd heard little music at all. He clung to it, relishing the sounds of a harp and the smooth tenor singing along.

That's it. This way.

It was the singer, speaking to him yet singing at the same time. There was a soothing, cool touch against his skin followed by a more intimate one, mind to mind. The touch was soothing and easy to follow, so he did.

Like this, bredu. *Unwind. Slowly. Come back to yourself.*

But he *was* himself, now more than ever. He spoke in a language of sight and scent and movement. He was centered and calm.

No. You're human. Two legs, two arms, ten fingers and toes. A physical touch accompanied each word, and Calum shuddered at the disorientation. This wasn't right. Someone was determined to rip away all things *horse* and stitch in everything *human.*

But he wouldn't. *Horse* meant more to him than anything. It was the only way he could keep on living.

Not the only way. I can show you another, the voice insisted, no matter how much he tried to push it away. *Unwind. Untwist. Let her go enjoy the pastures she's earned.*

But Calum clung fiercely to Canissa's soul. Through her, he'd found balance and ease, calm and the simple pleasures of safety and companionship. She'd protected him, and he'd promised to do the same. He'd failed.

Not failure. Never that. But your heart will break again and again, but so is life, bredu.

The last word caught him. *Bredu.* It meant "brother." Who was this voice, to call him such a thing?

I am a friend, and while we do not share blood, we are brothers in other ways, I think. And as such, I need you to let the great-hearted one go before you succumb to the madness of trying to exist as a beast when you are a man.

He'd never let her go. She was the only creature that truly cared for him, and he'd taken her on a journey and—

The realization hit with a sickening pang. *I killed her.*

The voice was sympathetic rather than shocked. *Were you the one that tore her with tooth and claw? I think not. She loved you. She sheltered you from worse harm and she carried you when you could walk no farther. Because of her, the peace accord reached Lord Aldaran before he sent his men to war. One day more and it would have been too late. Lord Aldaran is grateful for your efforts.*

Gratitude mattered little. Not now, not when he'd lost everything. There was no reason to return to life if she could not be there beside him.

No. I have seen minds lost to turmoil. I have borne witness to children dying of threshold sickness, lost to exhaustion and nightmares. Do not be one of them, my friend. I'm not of a mind to be grieving tonight.

The cooling touch came again, working through his energy like fingers. He enjoyed the feel despite his determination not to.

Only men laugh, only men weep, and only men dance, the voice said, quoting an old Darkovan proverb. *Come with me,* bredu, *and we will do all three together, but first you must let her go.*

She was already fading, slipping from his mind. The voice was right. She wouldn't have wanted him to hang on for so long nor understood his need. But it was hard, so hard, to let go of the only creature who'd truly known him.

Take all the time you need. There was a pause before the voice added, *Perhaps not too long. My teachers always told me I had a habit of overestimating my strength.*

There was something about this man, some sort of kinship and familiarity that Calum longed for. Loath as he was to give up Canissa, he thought this man might—just *might*—be worth the risk. Words remained a hardship, but he forced them out anyway. *I ... don't know how.*

Then let me show you the way, bredu.

When he woke, the first thing Calum noticed was the terrible, gaping emptiness inside him.

The second was the hand clasping his. Calum looked at it and followed the arm up to a shoulder and then to a man's face—a very *pretty* face.

Calum knew it was rude to stare, but he couldn't help it. He'd heard of the *chieri* and knew the legends about their ability to change gender and that a number of Darkovans were descended from them. Some of the monks at Nevarsin possessed both masculine and feminine traits, which rendered them sterile. This man was no doubt similar. He had the general sense of being male, yet his features lacked the usual roughness and thickness, and Calum found it easier to imagine those long, thin fingers more at home on a harp than a sword.

Suddenly embarrassed by his thoughts, he snatched his hand away. The man didn't seem to mind his interest. In fact, he seemed rather amused. "There you are, my brother. I was beginning to worry I'd gotten here too late. I was away when your *Comhi-Letzii* friend came to find me, and by the time I reached the Guild House you were near senseless in a stall with your leg swollen to twice its size."

So those crazed days when he'd found comfort in being Canissa hadn't been a dream, after all.

The man grasped his hand once more and squeezed. "I'm sorry. I know you loved her a great deal. You must have, to want to become her so badly."

Calum pursed his lips and turned his head away.

"Ah, *bredu*. I know you grieve, but there are things that must be said. Tell me, when you had threshold sickness, did your family ask for the help of a *leronis*?"

At that, he gazed at the pretty man, narrowed his eyes and gave a little shrug. The question was odd, since the only time he remembered being seriously ill was when he was thirteen, the night the wolves had attacked. For days afterward he'd been so feverish that he'd dreamed of becoming not only wolves, but horses, *chervines*, and a number of other creatures. He'd always managed to find his way back to the safety of Canissa's mind, though, and after that he'd always known when she was hungry or hurting, but—

Oh.

The realization hit him with the force of a kick. *Laran*. He'd had *laran* all these years and never realized it for what it was. All the stories he'd heard involved Keepers and Towers and relaying messages and speaking mind-to-mind with other humans—not animals.

"I take it that's a no," the man said dryly. "No wonder you fell into rapport so easily. You practically lived in it. Had there been a *leronis* nearby, they would have taught you how to make shields instead of trusting an animal to do it for you. It's something you must learn. Giselle—she's the one who rescued you from the crowd—did what she could while you were at the Guild House barn. Here, I am doing much of the work, because I do not want to see you slip into madness again. But you will, and you must, learn. Understand?"

Calum nodded, although all this talk of shields made little sense.

"I don't suppose you feel like talking, yet? This conversation is a little too one-sided for my taste."

He did. Sort of. His mind had to wrap around the idea of vocal communication and words came with difficulty. "Who are you?"

"Ah. Sorry. My name is Gethin. I'm the *laranzu* for Aldaran these past few months."

"I'm at Aldaran?" That explained the fine furnishings and stone walls.

"We thought it best. The Renunciates couldn't look after you for long, and after your efforts in delivering news of the peace accord, Lord Aldaran asked that I tend to you. Besides, with *laran* so strong and that red hair of yours, you must have Comyn in your blood somewhere. MacAran, probably. They're the ones known for rapport with animals."

"My mother never said."

"A pity," he said with real sympathy. "Now, I must check your wound and make sure it's healing properly."

Although the *laranzu* took care to preserve modesty, Calum blushed when Gethin raked up his nightshirt to expose the wound that ran from hip to knee. There was a twinkle in Gethin's eye. "I think no one's seen you so since your mother, eh?" Then, more seriously, he said, "It was a nasty gash, and I had to deal with the infection before I could think about bringing you out of your rapport. You should be able to bend your knee in a day or two. You'll have a scar, but that isn't such a bad thing. Something to brag about later. Not every man kills a wolf and lives to tell the tale."

But Canissa had killed two, and she was dead. His eyes stung and he blinked hard.

"Only men weep, *bredu*. There is no shame in that." Gethin righted the bedclothes and stood. "I'll fetch you something to eat."

The tears came as soon as Gethin had shut the door.

The next day, Gethin had him out of bed and hobbling around the castle on crutches. After three more, Calum had set them aside in favor of limping. Supportive and understanding as Gethin was about Calum's physical impairments, he was unyielding about the mental.

It didn't help that every time Gethin lowered his shields, even a little, Calum started to panic. He could sense *everything*, from the castle's servants to the cats hunting in the cellars, and it terrified him.

"What are you so afraid of?" Gethin asked.

Calum closed his eyes, recalling that time of sickness and nightmares. He'd been so aware of *everything*, from the chittering birds scouring the ground for seed to the herd of stag-ponies to the wilder, more frightening predators lurking in the mountains. He shook his head. "I saw things. And felt things. And I..." Here, the memory returned. Hard as he'd tried, he'd never been able to rid himself of the terror of losing control.

"Tell me."

He grasped for the calm he'd carried within him for so long, and found it gone. Of course it was. Without Canissa, he was only a shell, weak and fragile.

"The wolf? What about it?"

"I felt it before."

"When?"

"When I was ... ill."

"Can you tell me what happened?"

The words didn't come easily, simply because the experience had been entirely visceral. Yet he felt Gethin there, reliving the memories alongside him. "The wolves. I felt them. They were going after the horses. Vicious things. Hungry. I was inside them. They went after the yearlings. I was there, and I couldn't stop them." The coppery taste of remembered blood filled his mouth and he gagged. "I *killed* one of mares. The other horses went wild. It was chaos. They were all mad and would have trampled me if..."

"Your brave creature protected you, didn't she?"

"And I failed her. The wolf attacks were my fault. Don't you see? If I lose control, I hurt the ones I love." He was trembling, now.

"No, *bredu*. Never. You were a child, and a wild telepath besides. Whatever happened that night was not your fault, just as the wolf attack on your beautiful girl was not. That's why you are here, with me. I will teach you control. You need never be frightened so again."

To Calum's ears, Gethin sounded overly optimistic. "You're ... very kind. Not like other men I've known."

"My *laran* is for empathy. It wasn't easy being raised among men who favor swords and hunting." He smiled wryly. "No doubt we heard many of the same things."

"Like sandal-wearer." Ranald had been fond of that epithet.

"And *ombredin*." But he said it in such a way that the word wasn't demeaning at all. Instead, it was a secret shared between them, and Calum thrilled to sense it.

For the first time since he'd lost Canissa, he dared to smile.

"Only men laugh." Gethin chucked him gently under the chin. "One day, I think you will remember what that's like."

"This time, I'm going to take down all of my protections, and it will be up to you to raise your own shields. Think you're ready?" Gethin asked one afternoon. They were in Calum's room. Red-tinged sunlight had finally broken through the clouds and burst through the window to spill across the floor. Winter was losing its harsh grip, and both men welcomed the warmth.

After two weeks steady progression in being able to raise his shields with Gethin's support, Calum knew he'd better be able to manage alone. "Do it."

Gethin obeyed. Those in the background—the servants and animals within the castle—bothered him less than usual, but Calum was overwhelmed by *Gethin*, both the mixture of masculinity and femininity along with worry, anticipation and … something else. Something Calum didn't want to feel.

So he yanked up his shields. Too fast. A headache struck him and he ground the heels of his hands into his temples, cursing.

"Easy. Slow and steady, now. You can do it."

He thought of Canissa, how deliberate she'd always been and how she'd always conserved energy until it was needed. Everything she did had a purpose. So this time, he went slowly, building his shields little by little until Gethin disappeared and he felt … nothing at all. The silence was strange and eerie, as was being so terribly alone.

Gethin poked at Calum's mind, but the shields held. "Well done!" He clasped his hands together and grinned. "For that, I think you deserve a reward. The weather is fine; what do you say to a walk outside?"

Once Gethin had tracked down a spare coat and boots, they went out into the chilly air. It wasn't *quite* as frigid as usual, and the wind lacked its usual bite. Curious, he followed Gethin down a trail to an area surrounded by a stone fence. But when he saw what was inside, his heart sank, and he was grateful Gethin's lessons had taught him how to keep his emotions from leaking. Of all the places in the Hellers, this was the last he wanted to be at.

"Why bring me here?" he asked, and hoped Gethin would blame

the weather for his hoarse voice. There were several dozen animals inside, all of them fine, beautiful creatures and some of the best-bred mountain ponies he'd seen. The stallion was in a pen by himself, within sight and sound of the herd, but he couldn't reach them.

"Lord Aldaran knows of your sacrifice and wished you to have a mount of your choice. With the exception of the stallion, of course."

The offer might have been meant kindly, but to Calum it was a blow to the gut. "No one can replace Canissa. I'm not going to ride again. Ever." It didn't matter that this was a mixed group of geldings and mares; being near them was a painful reminder of all that he'd lost. He'd never go that deep with any creature—human or animal—again.

Beside him, Gethin flinched. *That's no way to live,* bredu.

But without Canissa to protect him, it was the only option he had. He clamped his shields tight so he felt nothing, not the horses, not Gethin or his disappointment. "Then maybe you should have let me die."

For a long time, Gethin didn't move. There was no sound other than the occasional footstep or snort from the ponies. "Maybe I should have," he said at last, and walked away.

Spring came early to the Hellers, and with it came the storms, flooding rivers already swollen from melting snow.

Calum watched the black clouds rolling through the sky. He didn't need his *laran* to feel the crackle of energy in the air or the ominous sense in the air. This storm was going to be bad.

Though it couldn't be much worse than the tension inside the castle since his spat with Gethin. The *laranzu* still came for lessons in the use of *laran*, but he was distant and coldly courteous. Calum missed their friendship, but he told himself he was better off without it. Now that he could manage his shields on his own, he wasn't going to take them down. Not for anyone.

Not even Gethin.

So it was a surprise when Gethin burst into Calum's room without knocking. He was red-faced and breathless from running. "We need you," Gethin said. "The herds are moved from one pasture to another in the spring, but the floods have come early. They're in a low-lying area and this storm has them spooked. If we don't get them out..."

He didn't need to finish. Calum had an image of floating, bloated bodies. Terrible as it was, he couldn't bring himself to do what Gethin expected of him. "I can't."

Gethin pursed his lips before looking away. "Please, *bredu*. If there's anything you can do—"

"*No*," Calum said, more firmly. The last thing he wanted was to lose the tenuous grasp on his shields. If he lost it now, he might never get it back. Better to be as cold and isolated as the Hellers themselves than to risk feeling all *that*.

"Coward," Gethin spat, and he was off, rushing outside.

Calum stayed where he was, back to the window, listening to the rumble of thunder and feeling the *snap* of lightning. When he finally dared look, a torrent of water rushed down the hillside—straight toward the pasture.

Get them out. He wanted to scream it, but nothing came out. He stood, frozen, watching the flood. Water sloshed off the edges. Branches, stones and other debris broke loose, filling the water with more hazards.

Calum squeezed his eyes shut. *I can't do it again. I don't dare. Not without....*

But the animals would die, and Gethin might die trying to save them. Calum looked for his friend and saw him out in the pasture among the panicking herd with about a dozen other men, all trying to urge the horses into the water. None would go. They reared and kicked and lashed out, and one poor man landed with a *splash* after a kick to the chest.

The herd looked out for each other. The herd protected each other. Canissa had given her life to spare his, and he was just standing here, watching, doing nothing—

She was dead and gone, but when he reached for her memory, she was there. At least, her essence was, and Calum bolted down the stairs and outside as fast as his healing leg would let him. Wind smashed droplets of rain against his face, but he didn't care.

Panicked whinnies drowned the shouting men. One foal, separated from its mother, had slipped from the island and struggled to keep afloat. Two men went after it, but between the swift-moving water and the dead trees, they were having difficulty reaching it.

There was no time left. Calum dropped the shields Gethin had so patiently taught him to build.

Panic/ run/ flee

The emotions slammed into him, doubled, tripled. He dropped to his knees, head in his hands, aching with cold and pain and fear. This wasn't like his bond with Canissa, who had been a single, albeit strong, mind. There were fifty, a hundred animals in this herd, geldings, mares, yearlings, and none of them gave a damn about him. Turning them toward safety was like trying to corral the water sluicing down from the mountaintop.

But they were herd animals. If he could turn the lead mare, he could turn them all.

He fought through the energy of the gathered ponies, touching each, soothing when he could and searching for a particular mind.

There. It belonged to a rather unassuming mare nearly the color of mud, but she had an air of authority the others lacked.

This way, Calum called to her, and tugged with his *laran. Through the water.*

She resisted, but Calum was used to such struggles with Canissa. Mares were bossy by nature, but they could be coaxed with treats and warmth and safety. The latter was what she wanted most right now, so he urged her with his *laran,* sending along images of a warm barn with the herd inside together.

Come. Please. This way, he begged.

It worked. The mare shouldered her way through the herd and stepped boldly into the water, calling after the others as she went. One by one, the other ponies followed, slipping unhappily into the torrent, and suddenly it was a mass of splashing, swimming animals surging forward as one. Some tried to break free but Calum kept a firm hold on their minds, guiding them back to the group the way he'd once seen herding dogs do. The men were there with ropes, lassoing the weak and young horses and using all the strength they had to pull them to safety.

The lead mare reached solid ground and heaved herself out, pausing to give a great shake before meeting the women, who'd stayed on the shore with blankets and towels to rub life and warmth back into exhausted limbs.

Calum slumped where he was, tired from the effort, when another strong presence nudged his mind.

Zandru's hells.

In the desperation to save the mares and geldings, they'd forgotten the stallion who now ran frantically back and forth over his quickly-diminishing patch of land. Instinct called to him to follow the herd, to defend his mares, but he was trapped.

Calum sought a grip on the stallion's mind and held tight to it, using more force than he'd needed with the mare. *This way...*

The stallion resisted; dry land was safer, but he was rapidly running out of that.

Through the water. This way.

The stallion balked. He did *not* want to go in the water. The mares were over *there*, and that was the direction he desired. He pranced, flinging up clods of mud with his sharp hooves.

This way. NOW.

He was strong, and so very different from Canissa, full of life and energy and desire. Calum drank it in, intoxicated by the power and masculinity the stallion effortlessly bore. He simply *was*. There was no shame, no doubt, none of the annoying human emotions.

Calum. Bredu. *Bring him, or leave him. Don't become him.* The frantic mind-voice cut through Calum's focus. *Stay you. Stay human.*

But Calum wouldn't let another life extinguish before its time.

He plunged into the water, heedless of the cold and the rising depth. More than once he was swept off his feet and only just managed to grab a branch or find a foothold against a stone beneath the surface to right himself again.

CALUM!

Gethin shouted at him, but Calum had neither the time nor the energy to spare an answer. He crawled onto the stallion's diminishing island, narrowly missing being trampled.

Be still!

The order startled the stallion just long enough for Calum to be able to grab a hank of mane and haul himself up onto the slick, soaked back. The stallion bucked and tried to rise on its hind legs, but Calum kept a firm grip on the animal's mind.

We go. Now. Through that.

The stallion surged forward. Calum pressed his calves into the animal's sides, both to urge him onward and to keep whatever grip he could. Water soaked him to the waist but he clung on, certain that if he let go both he and the stallion would perish.

But strong as the stallion was, the waters proved stronger. The trunk of an uprooted tree swept toward them, and there was no way for the pony to get out of the way. The tree hit them with a sharp *thunk* that drove the air out of his chest and sent the stallion tumbling from his feet.

The next breath he took was nothing but icy, gritty water. There was no way to tell which way was up and which was down. By some miracle, his fingers were still tangled in the stallion's mane, but as the water grew colder and darker around him, he knew that wasn't enough.

We're going to die. That thought didn't frighten him as much as it should have, but another saddened him.

I'll never see Gethin again.

Bredu!

The mind-voice called to him again and again, plaintive and hopeless. Calum heard it as if from a distance, like an echo, but didn't have the heart or strength to respond. He was too cold and tired to move.

The rain still sluiced down his cheeks. Beside him, the stallion stood with his feet planted in the mud, head and tail slack, hindquarters to the wind. All the fight had left him, and he was as chilled and weary as Calum.

Bredu!

Calum knew he should answer, but he held back. He wasn't any good to Gethin, or anyone. He'd nearly gotten the stallion drowned, and the last thing he wanted was to get close to anyone again. If he stayed here, no one would find him, and he could let the cold carry him peacefully away.

The stallion didn't care for that idea, though. He wanted food and warmth and his mares. He raised his head and let out a thread, high-pitched whinny and Calum was sucked into the pony's desperation to rejoin his herd. Ponies and horses, even *chervines,* didn't live alone. They were social creatures, dependent on each other for protection and companionship. The need bit deep, no matter how much Calum resisted.

But he wasn't a horse or pony. He was a man—one who didn't want to spend the rest of his life alone after all.

Only men laugh...

Only men weep...

Only men dance.

And without Gethin, he'd do none of those.

The next time Gethin's plea came, Calum summoned the last of his resources and called out to him not with his mind, but with his heart.

After that, it was only a matter of minutes before Gethin and two men from Aldaran came pelting down the trail.

"*Bredu.*" Gethin dropped beside Calum and wrapped a blanket around his trembling shoulders while the other men saw to the stallion. "I thought I'd lost you."

"No. You found me." Calum leaned into his embrace. He lowered his barriers and sought the intimate, mind-to-mind contact he'd come to crave. "Teach me to dance."

"I think you'd better prove you can walk first." Gethin squeezed his shoulders. "But after that, I promise we will dance. That, and so much more."

THE WIND

by Shariann Lewitt

Shariann Lewitt has published seventeen books and over forty short stories, including "Wedding Embroidery" in *Stars of Darkover* and "Memory" in *Gifts of Darkover*. Her story, "Tainted Meat," provided the owl and swordsman featured on the cover of *Realms of Darkover*. When not writing she teaches at MIT, studies flamenco dance, is accounted reasonably accomplished at embroidery, and has visited Antarctica.

Here she delves into the recurring effects of the Ghost Wind, when unseasonably warm weather unleashes storms of psychedelic-laden *kireseth* pollen on human habitations, even those of "ordinary" folk. Such occurrences transformed the early settlements, but the danger—and the opportunity—remains.

"I never wanted to do a wrong thing," he told the *leronis*. "I only wanted to do right by Romy. I just have a talent to help crops grow. Even Da says that, and there's not much good he says about me."

Tom looked at the Lady before him in the red robes of a Keeper. He'd never met a proper Lady in all his sixteen years, nor had his Da nor his Gran nor anyone from his village. And Keepers were even more rare than proper Ladies. She had brilliant red hair that lay in a mass of curls across her shoulders and bright sky-blue eyes, the coloring he had heard marked the Comyn. Not that he had ever seen one of those ruling aristos, and never thought to see one in his life.

Not that she was prettier than Romy, of course. Romy's brown hair shone with streaks of dark honey when she moved and she had dimples in her cheeks when she smiled. Which she did, often. This Lady looked as if she had never smiled in her life.

And here he was in a Tower, so far from Upper Siddich Falls that he couldn't possibly figure a way to get home. He thought it would be grander, but everything was made of bluish gray stone and shivery cold. Even the fire in this room didn't warm it so well as their little house back home, with earth floor covered with reeds and a thatch roof that let out the smoke and a warm yellow kind of stone that soaked up the heat and kept the space toasty. Not like this tiny fire, fighting against the cold gray.

He had arrived last night, had been given a generous meal and a comfortable bed in a room all to himself. There had been a fussy man who had shown him his room, the clothes they had laid out for him (some shapeless thing he had refused to put on) and had insisted that he take a bath before dinner. Then there had been the man, not terribly older than himself, in a white garment who had made his insides feel all mixed up. The man looked Comyn like the Keeper, only his hair was dark red and curly and his eyes, clear green.

There were guards, of course. Three of them, now that three had returned to Aldaran. Not that he needed any guards. He had no way to get back home, no money to buy food on the way, and he didn't even know the way. Of course, he could just run off and take his chances, but he had a certain amount of sense. Running off without food or any supply, without a chervine to carry him, was just plain stupid so far as he could see. No one, not even Da, had ever accused him of stupidity. So he knew he had to bide his time and make his plans.

The place was called Neskaya, and he knew he didn't belong there. He only wanted to get back to the village, to Gran, and to Romy. He—*liked*—Romy. He didn't want to hurt her, or even worry her. He had just hoped that he could get some idea of what she thought, so that his jaw wouldn't freeze shut and he wouldn't stare at his boots whenever he saw her. So he could say something like, "You look real pretty today, Romy," or "I picked this spiceweed that I grew for you 'cause I know you like spiceweed cookies."

Just cause he liked her and wanted to be able to talk to her, that was all. That had caused all this mess in the first place and everything had gone horribly wrong.

"You know the saying. 'An untrained telepath is a danger to themselves and everyone around them.' I'm afraid you've proved this more than amply."The *leronis* sighed.

A Keeper couldn't be wrong, but she was. He didn't hear any thoughts. He wasn't any kind of telepath. Well, he hadn't done before the night of the Ghost Wind and then he knew he shouldn't be hearing what people thought. *People*, especially meaning Romy, and *thought*, especially meaning that she wondered why he didn't like her because he never talked to her and always seemed to run away. And he'd felt so bad and tried to tell her that she was wrong and he did so like her, just way too much. Only he didn't say it with his mouth, he'd shouted with his mind. And now every single person in Upper Siddich Falls knew.

Maybe he was lucky he couldn't get back home. He didn't see how he could confront anyone there, now that they all knew, and knew that he knew their secrets, too .Like that Da stepped out with Clea over by the spring pasture (disgusting, he could barely think on it) or that Rafe's Da had actually stolen the sheep that started his herd. Though why he thought about that on Midwinter Tom could not begin to guess. But how could he face his best friend now?

He'd told the Lady over and over that he didn't hear thinking, just like he'd told the men who'd taken him to Aldaran, and then to the *leronis* there who'd done some strange thing to him that made his insides feel all mixed up.

No one had asked him what he wanted. No one had even asked his Da, or listened when his Da protested and said the boy was needed on the farm. Tom had never seen anyone before who didn't obey his Da, not the villagers, not Gran, not even crazy, dangerous Old Sig who lost his mind but not his strength and used to be blacksmith. Da was the only one who could calm him down when Sig went on about seeing some great fire Goddess in his mind. Which probably drove him crazy. Sometimes that just took folks, age and the crazy and the wind. Most became just kind of sad or afraid or forgot everything, and were gentle as sheep when you talked soft to them and led them back to their houses and gave them a nice warm cup of *jaco* and a slice of nutbread.

The Keeper's expression did not convey anger, at least not the kind Tom knew. Not the kind when Da slapped him for forgetting to draw the morning water for the sheep before he went to bed. She didn't seem disappointed the way Gran did when he tracked mud all over her newly swept floor or brought a group of friends for dinner without telling her first. The Keeper appeared to study him, as if he were a stalk of bluegrain Da suspected of harboring blight.

"I told you, Lady, I'm not a telepath. I don't hear thinking, I didn't get sick when I turned thirteen, I don't have copper in my hair or any Comyn in my blood. I'm just a farmer like all my people. We grow good food in Upper Siddich Falls. We sell a lot of our bluegrain, and some of our fruit, too. I'm good at that. I have a gift, my Da says, for making things grow. It's just a talent, like those what can gentle a chervine or do their sums fast."

He did not add that he was one of the ones who could do his sums fast, and read easily and young. Old *mestre* Brannon said if they lived in a town he would go to a proper school and study history and geography and science with trained teachers, and even be tested by a *leronis*. Not that his Da would let him stay in school when he could work, since he'd finished everything *mestre* Brannon could teach him by the time he'd turned ten.

Someone, maybe Romy's Auntie Glyn, had said something about him being tested by a *leronis*, but Da had only laughed at that, as any sensible person would. No *leronis* ever had come up to the village of Upper Siddich Falls since Gran's Gran was a girl, if her stories were true. No one ever came to the village of Upper Siddich Falls except for two traders. His Da dealt only with the one man, Stephen from Aldaran. He said that the Renunciate trader, Dorilys n'ha Elonie, wasn't fit for this kind of work, even if her prices were often better. Tom was better at sums than his Da and once figured they'd lost nearly two coppers by trading with Stephen, but his Da said he must have got it wrong.

The Lady still looked at him. "Hold out your hand," she commanded. Her soft voice was nothing like his Da giving order, but Tom had no doubt that her orders could not be disobeyed. Not like the times he disobeyed Da and went off at night to Rafe's house, where Rafe's Da served them beer and taught them to play cards.

She put a blue stone in his palm, a little one but it seemed to have a life of its own. It glowed brightly when he took it, and as the glow appeared to gather itself inside, he could see that it had a pattern inside like a star. It shifted around like it was dancing and made him think about Romy skipping over the rocks up by the Falls. He had never seen a prettier thing in his life and he thought how much he'd like to give it to Romy, how it would look on a ribbon around her neck.

"It is now keyed to you," the Keeper said. "You must keep it with you at all times and no one, let me repeat, no one must touch it except you and your Keeper. You wear it like this." Her hand went to a cord around her neck and she pulled out a little pouch. "I'm sorry, Tomas, but if you did not have *laran*, that stone would not have responded to you as it did."

Tom shook his head. "If you'll excuse me, *vai domna*, t'ain't possible. Hasn't been a Comyn in Upper Siddich Falls since anyone can remember, not a one. And if you'll please, my name is Tom. Tomas is for some red-haired boy with copper in his belt. Not for the likes of me."

"Tom is the intimate, friendly form of Tomas. If you wish me to address you as a friend, I would be pleased to do so. But I would not presume to take that intimacy without your invitation."

Tom shook his head. He simply did not understand. His name had always been just plain Tom. If he had ever been called Tomas, he would have been accused of putting on airs. Which people in Upper Siddich Falls didn't take kindly.

"So, *vai domna*, am I going to be held here as punishment?" Tom finally found the courage to ask the only question he truly cared about.

"Please, call me Rafaella, Tom. Yes, you must stay here for a while, but you are not being punished. You are here to learn. An untrained telepath is a danger to himself and to all around him."

There they were, back at the beginning again.

"Mikhail will come and teach you to fully tune your starstone, to feel it and work with it. He'll be your tutor as you learn to use your *laran*. You can read and write?" She waved her hand, and in a few moments the young Comyn arrived. He smiled so warmly at Tom that the farm boy found it hard to resist. Not that he could, anyway.

Seemed like a good idea at the start. He'd been sitting with Rafe on the sheep corral. They'd just finished repairing the fence before the autumn snows began in earnest, shoring up a barren spot. Not that the sheep tested the enclosure so much as they liked to rub their itchy noses and flanks against the rough raw wood when insects assaulted them. They pushed and scratched, so posts as well as bars came down. But now the herd was safe and only a soft flurry of snow wafted through the air. The two young men, pleased with their accomplishment, sat on a large rock where they could watch the timid animals reclaim the field.

"What do you think of Romy?" Tom asked.

"She's okay," Rafe answered. "But I like Mika better. Now there's a girl, so tall with that fluffy, soft hair."

"How do you know it's soft?" Tom wanted to know if Rafe had actually gotten to touch her. He'd barely even been able to speak to Romy since he'd left school.

Rafe colored slightly. "Looks soft, doesn't it? I bet it's like touching a cloud. And when she walks she looks like water coming down the stream. Yeah, Mika."

"You're such a goof," Tom punched Rafe in the arm. "How do you know what a cloud feels like, anyway? You're just making that all up. But good, you like Mika. I like Romy. That's good; we don't both like the same girl."

"But Romy's so short!" Rafe protested.

Tom snorted. "She's not that short. Mika's so tall, she's as big as you are. And she can put up a fence post as well as we can. Besides, Romy always looks like a bird that's about to fly. And she laughs and smiles all the time."

Rafe shrugged. "When the time comes, I'll want a wife who can work the farm with me. I don't have your special talents with plants."

"I put 'em in the ground and water 'em, same as you."

Rafe rolled his eyes. When Tom's Ma died in childbirth, Tom took over the entire garden. He'd been only twelve at the time, and yet the garden, which his Ma had tended so carefully, had suddenly doubled its yield. Then his Da had given him the orchards and the nut trees, and finally the bluegrain acres. His Da bred the sheep, made the cheeses, and sheared the fleeces, as well as butchering the meat. They had the best farm in the valley, so people said.

"You gonna ask her to dance at Midwinter?" Rafe asked.

"You gonna ask Mika?"

Rafe smiled. "I am. I've got it all planned out. I'm going to leave snowflowers at her door. And then when she starts work I'll be at the window near the oven when she starts the bread, and I'll let her know I left those flowers for her."

"Yeah, and where are you going to get snowflowers at Midwinter?"

"From you," Rafe replied. "I know you have that little glass house where you set plants over winter and make flowers and some fruit bloom out of season. See, that's what you should do for Romy. Give her some of that fruit. Who can resist fresh fruit in Midwinter when the apples are starting to get dry and wrinkled? You give her some nice, juicy ones, or berries, and she'll be so impressed she won't help but want to dance with you. You see? Easy."

"Sounds good," Tom replied without conviction.

A ewe bleated gently and the herd took up the call. Time to return to the barn for hay. Tom and Rafe got up and entered the barn through the side doors and started to pitch down feed from the hayloft for the animals waiting patiently outside. Then Tom filled the water trough and they unbarred the large doors from the inside. The animals plodded in placidly following the lead ram.

"You know, it might help a bit if you had some, umm, medicinal aid," Rafe suggested once the herd had found their spots around the feed racks. "Like beer, but maybe stronger."

"I don't want her thinking I'm a drunk," Tom was clearly insulted.

"Not like that. Everyone has a drink at Midwinter. But maybe a little beforehand, you know, to steady your nerves. And relax you. You're tied tighter than a catman brought as captive, Tom. You got to let go a bit."

Tom thought on what Rafe said, and his friend had been right. The only time he felt good, felt safe, was when he was out by himself in the fields. He liked to walk the neatly turned rows, most of which had already yielded their crops, the surplus sold to Stephen barely four tendays before. Coins, silver and iron and some precious copper, hidden safely behind the loose brick in the chimney, meat in the smokehouse and the icehouse, roots in the cellar, and strings of vegetables dried in bunches over Gran's old table where her honey pots sat full. They'd traded some of the honey, Gran's fine beeswax candles, raw bluegrain, and six thick fleeces for two full barrels of flour, two good bolts of heavy wool and one of fine spun linen, and a full supply of embroidery silks in rich colors. Gran had already begun making Tom and his Da complete new outfits for Midwinter, rich with embroidery around the collars and cuffs. Tom loved watching his grow, thinking how he'd make a good figure at the party and how Romy might find him fine to see.

So maybe some beer could help him. Maybe two or more would loosen his tongue and get him to talk to the girl.

Then the first real storms of winter pounded down from the heights and locked them in. Plenty of food for the herd, though chipping the ice between the house and the barn took Tom and his Da almost a full morning. Then it took another hour to melt the ice so the sheep could drink. Tom packed the hay around the basins to insulate them from the cold and made sure they were heaped with snow. The large, shaggy animals huddled up around their food and pressed into each other for warmth, and their combined heat kept the water melted.

Back in the house, Gran had a pot over the fire filling the whole house with the smell of mutton stew rich with chopped roots, onions, and dried berries. On the table she had two loaves rising under a damp cloth and had rolled out thin dough to cut into noodles to add to the stew at the end, the very thought of which made Tom's mouth water.

Outside the two tightly shuttered windows the storm howled.

"This reminds me of the story my Gran's Ma told her, about a Midwinter when she was a young maid, pretty and free." Gran began. Tom knew the story, could probably tell it himself, but he settled back to listen. Gran told a good story, and there was little else they could do. He liked to read, but they couldn't waste the candles or the fat for the lamp, not when the storm could keep them for days and they still would have to dig out to the barn before dinner.

"She was the village beauty and everyone loved her. She had hair like the Falls, rippling down her back so long she could sit on it, the color of bark touched by snow and rich meadows. And her skin was just like honey, smooth and warm as summer and golden sweet Or so my Gran said. All the boys were crazy for her, but her heart was free as the wind, as the snow that danced in the autumn. That Midwinter the boys had decorated the grange with evergreen boughs and white ribbons. And Linell, for that was her name, Linell had a new gown of palest green all embroidered from her cuffs to her elbows, from her neck to her breast, and a from her knees to the floor. She had two silver clasps for her hair joined by a little chain. I have seen this dress and your Ma, Tom, she had those hair clasps. They will go to your wife and your baby girl some day.I have them safe for you." She smiled at him and winked.

Tom wondered how they would look in Romy's fine silken locks and blushed.

"No one had seen such a dress or such jewelry in this village before or since, I can tell you," Gran resumed telling the story. "So the grange was all decorated and the boys finished clearing the paths in the center of town so that everyone could make it to the dance. But the weather warmed considerably and most of the paths melted clear, if you can imagine. Such a Midwinter melt as we have never seen! The center of town was full of water from where the ice had drifted. So the women had to think about how to guard their fine skirts from the mud. The way I heard it, the women and girls of the town just kilted up their embroidered skirts and wore their boots over, and then changed over to their dancing slippers and untucked their skirts when they arrived.

"It was so warm that Midwinter that almost no one wore a fur. Most wore light autumn cloaks, but it was so warm and rare and fine a night that everyone wanted to enjoy the pleasant breeze and even the slight hint of sweet spring on the air. A gift of the Gods, though for what no one could say.

"Some said it was my Gran's Ma, that she looked so like Evarra herself that the goddess had descended on her. But that's all nonsense. Such things might happen with Comyn and with the *leroni*, but we're not grand enough for the gods to notice us. Not even for a girl as beautiful as she was that night. So don't go believing any of that storytelling.

"Musicians had come all the way from Honey Ford to play that night, and they were likely the only strangers in the place. But the folks from Honey Ford are no better than we, even if they have some fine musicians down that way.

"Still, others have told that there were three strangers, not from Honey Ford, two men and a woman with finer clothes than anyone has ever seen. And all of them with a glint of copper in their hair. Now, we know that no Comyn has ever come up this far into the county and I think that people are all for tall tales of Midwinter in any case. Besides, how could they have come without us knowing? And how could they have gone afterward? No, I think maybe some of the friends of the musicians had decided to come along to our party instead of staying for their own, and foolish folk have embroidered to make a better tale. Some even say there was a *chieri* there, so we know this is all as silly as can be. No, there was no one but us plain folks, though there was that band from Honey Ford and maybe a few of their friends, don't you believe anything anyone says different."

In fact, Tom had heard all different versions of who had shown up like magic that night, *chieri* and *Comyn* and *leroni* and even *Terranan*. Rafe's Da said that people got so crazy out of their heads that no one could tell up from down, so how would anyone know a thing that happened anyway?

"Strange things happened during Ghost Winds, everyone knows that. The *kireseth* field high above the summer pastures makes sure that the valley has Ghost Winds, but not as often as a lot of people feared. Sheep love to eat *kireseth* in the summer, and they'd chew it right down to the ground if they could. They keep the great fields in check, and the flowers keep our herds happy and fat, and our cheese among the best on all Darkover. Sometimes if the fields become too full, we'll wear masks and harvest it, then bundle it up and let it mature where it can do us no harm. Then we can sell it to the traders, who take it to the cities and Towers to be made into medicines," his Gran continued.

Tom had harvested it many times, and it had never turned him into a telepath. He could feel it grow, just as he could feel any planted thing. Sometimes he could feel the full crop on the side of the mountain, could feel when the flowers bloomed and when they were ready to spread their golden pollen. He knew when it would be safe to harvest and bag, and how long it had to wait before it could be sold for good profit. But that was no more than he knew of any plant, and he thought about the *kireseth* rarely. The more responsibility he had for his own fields and orchards, the less attention he could pay to some wild thing that the villagers did not truly own.

Inside of Gran's story, he reached out and felt the *kireseth* on the mountainside, a great crop this year. None of the valley villages had harvested in several years; they had had good weather and full larders and plenty to sell to the traders. They had little reason to go so far above the summer fields and wear uncomfortable protective clothes when there was so much plenty at home. The *kireseth* had multiplied again and again over the years it had not been cut, and he could feel the great massive weight of it, all starting to sleep under the deep blanket of ice.

Starting to sleep, but not entirely gone for the season. Not like the onions and bluegrains that had already been turned in their rows. No, the *kireseth* were native plants and they did not enter their deepest sleep until after Midwinter.

And here a thought began, just a small touch in the back of his mind that he pushed aside. He ignored it to listen to what Gran said in the shadows, for if he let his mind stray too far he would start smelling the stew and he wouldn't be able to ignore the hunger that threatened to drive him to empty the pot before she had even added the noodles.

"So the music was playing and Linell danced with all the boys, but as I said, none of them took her eye. I heard someone say that a fight broke out early in the evening, over drinking or some slight someone remembered. Some said it was over Linell, over which boy could dance with her twice and that it turned into a brawl. I expect the youngsters threw a few punches and were promptly thrown outside.

"And then the wind stirred. As I said, it had been unnatural warm all of the day. Now, without getting cooler, the warm wind started to blow down from the high peaks From where the summer pastures are. From where the golden flowers grow.

"It was the greatest Ghost Wind that the valley had ever seen. The next day everything was pale gold from the pollen. Even the newly scrubbed grange, the temple steps, everybody's white shirts and sheets and tablecloths were coated in gold. The stuff lay on everything, in every crack in every table, on every plate, in every bowl, floated on top of everybody's wash water. So the next day everyone knew what had happened and why, though what they experienced when it happened was for anyone to say.

"Linell woke alone. In due course she gave birth to a daughter, my Gran. She told her daughter, my Gran, who told me, that that night she had lost her mind. She had seen things she could not see and heard things she could not hear. She knew what everyone in the whole village thought. Those boys who wanted to court her, every single one thought that she was only a thing to look at and not a real person at all. Or they didn't really like her but it was all a competition and she refused to talk to a one of them.

"Linell said that when the golden powder sparkled throughout the room, everyone in the grange started to take off their clothes and it was one great carouse. Across generations, even, young and old, doing everything you could imagine and some you possibly can't. But she said she could hear everything they thought and felt what they felt and it just made her sad and she wandered away into that warm, warm wind away from the grange. She put on her boots, walked up the High Street and across the fields and through what's now Mhari's spread, up toward the summer pastures. And even though it had got warm, there was still snow and ice up to her waist at least and maybe higher, and mud past her ankles at least.

"I don't know who it was she found, or where, or where they went. She never said. She said only that his head was quiet. Not silent, mind you, but quiet and calm and not crazy like everyone at the grange. And she thought him fine to look upon, with clean hands and no dirt under his nails. Not a farmer. Not from the valley. But like I said, I think she was also too gone with the *kireseth* to know. Just that he was my Gran's Da, and he disappeared and no one ever saw him. Only Linell.

"And Linell herself, she waited around until her daughter was seventeen and decided on a freemate of her own. And then Linell just disappeared herself, just like that. She left her farm, this farm, to that girl, my Gran, and it's been in the family ever since. No tracks led away from the house, my Gran said. They searched for her all over the valley but no one ever found any trace of her. And that's the end of it."

With that, Gran scooped up the long, thin noodles she'd sliced and threw them into the pot. "Now when you get back from taking care of the sheep, your dinner will be ready."

That wasn't the first time he'd heard the story, nor the twentieth time, either. He could recite it himself in his sleep. He'd just never thought that he could *do* anything.

But *kireseth* were plants like any other, and he could coax plants to grow and bloom and he could sense when they needed rain or some extra warmth and—well, he never thought he'd done anything special. Sometimes he prayed to Aldones the Son of Light for those things and sometimes he just sent out a wish to the world, a wordless desire for the plants themselves.

The conditions he asked for didn't always come. Sometimes there was drought when the crops needed rain and sometimes the rain came, but far too much of it and it drowned the fields. Once the Siddich, which was more a creek than a river except at the Falls, except during the spring thaws, flooded its banks and half the population of Honey Ford had lost their homes. Tom knew that had nothing to do with him. He only tended the land and what grew on it.

Once long ago, this land was considered played out, good for nothing but sheep and goats. But the Siddich had flooded many times and brought rich run-off, and gradually the grasses and wildflowers renewed the soil. With only four small villages, most of which nurtured the herds, spun and wove woolens or knit fine garments, only a few fields now showed that the land had become fruitful again. Tom knew the best spots. He could put his hand into the loam and tell the tenants whether to plant the plot in wind berries or bluegrain.

But he had never thought he did any more than observe and make careful choices.

Now, though, well—he still did not believe he could truly

influence events of sun and wind and snow. But he could send extra energy out to the *kireseth* on the mountainside and pray for what the flowers most desired. Treat them as his own, as it were. And hope. If he were wrong, well then, no harm done. He would be no better or worse off. Best, he need not tell anyone of his plan. Everyone knew what had happened in the past. Everyone would believe it was only the will of the gods, and who was he to say or even think anything different.

And so as the sheep sheltered in winter quarters, Tom took to wandering high in the hills, his boots crushing through the sparkling snow crust as he reached deep below to the *kireseth* lying quiet beneath the white blanket.

"You really did all of that without a starstone?" Mikhail asked.

"I didn't really do anything," Tom protested. "I thought that was clear."

They had worked together for four days now, and Tom could already shield his thoughts from the monitor and could keep himself from listening in when he wasn't invited. Not too bad for only four days, Mikhail had told him without words. But he caught the inflection of emotion under that and knew that Mikhail had been impressed.

"You've got to stop studying me like I'm some sort of bug," Tom protested. He was careful to shield the rest of his feelings, that he felt out of place with these people who came from noble families and had been trained to *laran* for generations. But who also never worked with their hands as he had, who had servants to make their food and wash their linens and sweep their floors. No one he had met so far had any idea how to make cheese or milk a sheep or a goat, or how to weave.

And still, as much as he desired to leave, he found every day revealed some new wonder in his own abilities. This *laran* that they claimed he needed to train kept unfolding and showing him possibilities he had never imagined.

"So why was I never sick, like you were?" Tom asked. He felt it only fair that Mikhail have to tell as much as he learned from Tom.

Mikhail shook his head. "We aren't entirely certain. I think you must have had a reasonable share of *laran* before the Ghost Wind, but that was the catalyst. It appears a number of people in your valley have shown abilities no one ever suspected."

"Never been no Comyn in our valley," Tom said. "Tax collector comes once a year and we pay up. The children like to see his horse, only real horse anyone in our parts has ever seen. So it's like a big party when he comes in to collect our taxes and rents with his pony trap. We're usually third, so the cart is pretty full with the ewers of honey and knitwear and woolens from Lower Siddich and Honey Ford. Tax collector may have some Comyn blood, may be a distant cousin of some noble family. He dresses better than the rest of us, that's sure. But otherwise?" Tom shrugged.

"That doesn't necessarily mean that you have no Comyn blood at all," Mikhail responded. "Sometime in the past, some Comyn might have taken shelter in one of your villages. During the Ages of Chaos and the time of the Hundred Kingdoms, many nobles had reasons to disappear."

Tom shook his head. "You think we're just country bumpkins and don't know our own past. We do and we remember, and we've never had anyone noble or any *laran* among us. We're proud of who we are and what we do. We'd know."

Mikhail shook his head. "You don't understand. We need you, Tom. You and your village and all your people who seem to have suddenly gotten *laran*. We need to find out what happened and if we can duplicate it."

Tom made a face. "Isn't that why you're the nobility and get to live in fine castles with the likes of us to do your chores? You have the magic and you can take care of things we can't."

Mikhail sighed. "Used to be that way, but now there aren't enough of us. Not just Comyn, but *laran* Gifted. We need every telepath. Look at this Tower, Tom. Think about it. Doesn't it seem awfully big for the twenty-two people living here?"

Tom had to agree to that. Fifty people could fit in the Tower dining room easy, and he'd never seen more than twelve at a go.

"Back in the day, there were three full working circles here at Neskaya. Now we're at barely two. All of the Towers are like that these days, and several of the Towers have closed. We can't do many of the tasks we used to, we've lost the knowledge. But even things we do know how to do, that we need to do, we don't have the strength to keep up with the need. We can't even make all the firefighting chemicals we need, let alone deliver them quickly where they're needed. We used to test every single child for *laran*. Now we can't. We don't have enough *leroni* who can test them, and we lose those we have from their work at the Towers. All of Darkover is in danger. And your village, Tom, may be the key to bringing back our strength."

"It were just a Ghost Wind. That happens in the mountains," Tom protested.

"But you made it happen. And now nearly a third of your villagers are showing signs of strong *laran*. So we need to learn what you did. And where the latent ability came from in the first place. If we can replicate it..."

It was no use to protest. Mikhail didn't believe him, and the more he showed the young monitor, the more the Comyn refused to believe the truth. There was nothing to do but show the rest. Then, maybe Mikhail would answer his questions as to what became of Romy, or Rafe, or his family. Above all, Tom worried that Romy had been hurt. He hadn't seen her or felt her after and no one told him anything, not about anyone except his Da and his Gran. And all he knew about them was that they were unharmed.

So Tom lay down again on the neatly made up cot in the monitor's examination room. He pulled his starstone out of its small silk pouch and let himself fall into the patterns in its depths. *Focus*, he told himself, as he concentrated on the coming of the winter snows.

They slept lightly, slightly aware when the chilling winds of the Hellers died down and the storms abated for a day or two. Just a tenday before Midwinter, he felt them sleeping like a good dog partly on watch, ready to be roused. He felt the warmth, the desire, their readiness, their pollen full to burst golden over the pristine snow. He could not quite understand how he drew the light, to that particular mountainside and field. Only that he begged with all his being for the warmth to arrive. He needed a slight thaw, not too much. The flowers were not greedy; they were not ready for summer, and true heat would only confuse them. But a little bit of thaw, the sun kissing the ground, the snow gently melting into the soil, the flowers awakening ... he called to them, to the sun, to the air itself every day.

Every day, all day, he thought of the freedom to finally face Romy and tell her—well, maybe ask her if she might dance with him? That would be a good start, better than he had managed so far. That was all he hoped. Truly.

He felt the sun grow warmer and saw the dirty puddles slosh up on the low parts of the paths. Gran complained about everyone tracking mud into her nice clean house, so Tom and his Da had to take off their heavy boots just outside the door.

This year it was the girls' turn to decorate the grange, so Tom and Rafe had no idea what it would look like. The girls decorated and chattered all day while the boys took baths and put on their new clothes. Gran had added a decorative band to the bottom of Tom's trousers, as he had grown a good two inches since she had finished them off when the sheep had come down from the high pasture. He marveled at the fine wool of his vest, dyed a rich russet to match the pants. The creamy shirt of linen finer than any he had ever owned before, and around it his father had given him a worked lambskin belt dyed warm nut brown with a heavy brass buckle.

"Wore it when I married your Ma," he said as he fastened it around Tom's narrow waist. "You'll do the same, I expect."

Marriage? Tom couldn't even talk to Romy. He couldn't think the word *marriage*, and already his father was talking about it and his Gran was beaming. He felt like a complete dolt, and he wanted nothing more than to run up the mountainside and lay down in the flowers.

The warming flowers that lifted their star-like heads to the sun that had set hours ago, that felt the weight of their pods straining against the delicate membranes as traces of the day lingered even as the evening chill set in. He felt almost split in two, one of him saying goodnight to Da and Gran as Rafe pounded on the door, the other of him deep inside the pollen pods, knowing that in minutes the fragile sheaths would spill their golden powder over the snow and down the mountain. And the wind...

He called the wind, feeling the slight rustling of a breeze high in the crags, picking up speed as it funneled through the narrow Falls onto the *kireseth* meadow. Rafe dragged him by the elbow, talking incessantly of Mika and how he thought she would look, but Tom could barely see Rafe's finery. Green, maybe? He could pay attention only to the wind and the golden pollen...

The girls had hung the grange with the traditional evergreen boughs and flowers made of ribbons and scraps of fabric left over from making all the new Festival clothes.

"They must have been working on this for months," Tom said, staring in wonder at the opulent bower that had transformed the workaday grange.

Not in the history of Upper Siddich Falls had the grange ever looked so sumptuous. The young men, the elders, all gazed around in complete amazement as the girls laughed with delight, colorful in their new dresses as the flowers themselves. The elders, as always, had taken care of the food tables, and as this had been a prosperous year, the great trestles groaned under the weight of cheeses and honey cakes and roasted nuts coated in spiceweed and tossed with dried summer fruits. Three kinds of cider scented the hall next to many beers, including Rafe's father's very best.

There, across the grange, stood Romy in a dress the color of the winter sky, all embroidered in shimmering white and pinks and yellows. Tiny blue ribbons held her hair so that it moved and reflected the lanterns set around the room. Tom gazed at her, drinking in her presence, her lively smile, the toss of her head, the flash of confidence in her eyes.

And then, before the beer hit him, while he could feel the *kireseth* pollen riding the wind down the mountain, she walked over to him and looked him in the eye. "And you, Tom, why do you look at me that way? You never speak to me and every time I see you, you run away. Do you dislike me so?"

Horror. How could she think he disliked her when—no, he liked her far too well. Tom dropped his eyes and his tongue stuck to the top of his mouth. "I... I... Romy..." Words fled.

And then the wind hit the grange. The doors and windows rattled, and yellow pollen filtered through every crack in the old wood, between the old stones, everyplace the thatch had thinned, every gap between the doors and windows where the years had settled the perfect angles out of true. The pollen overcame him, all of them, engulfed his brain, and he suddenly saw Romy in a new way. She shone like a star, like his favorite moon, beautiful and lavender high in the sky flying high above the peaks.

Then he saw into her mind and knew she could see into his and he no longer needed words. Silly things when she could taste how he felt, touch how he saw her, know that he barely thought of sheep or orchards or bluegrain without thinking something of her. And she could see how he was embarrassed that she knew that now, knew all his secrets—but he knew hers as well.

And—she liked him back! She had been watching him as he had watched her. She had giggled with her friends because that was just what girls did when they liked a boy. That seemed so strange, and yet in Romy's mind it made so much sense. She had wanted to talk to him a hundred times, but he had always run away. She had remained with her friends, hurt and confused, and now he reached out to soothe that hurt and confusion away. He had to let her know, and she knew, and then she was touching him and her skin burned his and he had never imagined anything could feel so delicious, so delightful, as her fingers on his hand. So he petted her at first, her face, and then ran his palms over her hair, which was sweet and softer than he had ever conceived hair could be.

He kissed her, or maybe she kissed him, and they were both inside each other and he could feel everything she felt and everything he felt and every other thing as well. For a moment he had a taste of horror, his Da with Tessa who strung looms. He flinched away from the knowledge, from his Da's mind entirely and returned complete to the moment, to Romy and the taste of her skin, to the little shivers when she responded to his touch. Her clothes came off one layer at a time and somehow his seemed to dissolve, and throughout the grange the scene repeated over and over. Piles of clothes became bedding as couples experienced each other, as Romy and Tom found new uses for their new Festival garments, and new uses for their bodies as well.

The next morning he rose next to her, stiff and sore from having slept on the cold grange floor. Her eyes fluttered as she woke, and Tom could feel her thoughts as she rose, but still could not help but apologize. "Romy, I am so sorry, I never meant..."

"Oh, hush, you silly boy." And then she said no more, but the wonderment of the night before, the ability to see into her mind, had not disappeared. Tom could still feel her content along with her cold, and the pleasure they had shared lingering over the knowledge that this dawn brought a new way of the world. She reached out to his mind, and he invited her in, tentative and afraid, and she entered into his own delight and hopes and thoughts of their future together on the farm. He experienced her satisfaction at the thought.

"Do you think this will end?" he asked, meaning the telepathy, though he could not form the word. Telepathy was for Comyn, not for the likes of them.

She did not answer with words but he felt her mental shrug, and he knew she didn't truly care, that sharing this one night and moment was enough.

Late that evening the Guards had come and taken him to Neskaya.

"Where is she?" Tom asked Mikhail. "How is she?"

Mikhail smiled. "You can reach out to her, you know. Use your starstone. Think of her, of the feeling in her mind, of the closeness you shared. That will bring you to her."

Tom refused to point out that he had no idea of where Romy was and that it was Mikhail himself who had taught that entering another's thoughts was the deepest violation of a telepath's oath and honor.

"You are not entering her mind. You are only reaching out to touch her, as if you would tap her on the shoulder to get her attention," Mikhail said. "And you were projecting your thoughts. You need to shield naturally, without thinking of it."

Tom sighed. So very many things to do. Well, he could try to tap Romy on the shoulder and see if he could reach her, see if she was well. See where she was.

He gazed deeply into his starstone and watched while the patterns shifted and drew him in. He remembered Romy in her Festival dress; he imagined Romy's mind, her laughter, her confusion, and her contentment. Most of all, he reached out for the essence of who she was, of the center of the being he had touched for those few hours when they had been united.

And there she was. He could see her in a stone Tower room much like the one he occupied. He gently touched the image to let her know he was there and felt himself drawn into her mind, her experience, which had been much like his own. So very much they shared, the wonder, the strangeness, and the homesickness as well. So cold here in a Tower, and so lonely with the few Comyn with whom they trained and with whom they had to be so proper and formal. No one else like themselves.

"Where are you?" Tom finally formed words inside their shared experience. "What Tower? How far away?"

And he heard Romy laugh once again. "Silly boy. I'm in Neskaya, two floors up from you in the Virgin's Hall. Now that we know; we should be permitted to meet for dinner."

"Why didn't you tell me?" Tom demanded of Mikhail when he finally regained his body. "She is right here. And except for the Keeper, I've seen no women at all."

Mikhail smiled. "So you have passed the test. You are both *leroni*. What you care to do about that, after you are trained, will be something for you to decide. But we would very much like to have you stay and work here in the Tower, at least for a time. We need strong *leroni*, as I have said. And we need to understand what changed in you, in both of you, for the good of all of us."

"But a *leronis* cannot marry!" Tom protested. "And besides, you know that Romy is no virgin."

"Only a Keeper must remain virgin," Mikhail corrected him. "There is so much for you to learn, and to do. More than making a Ghost Wind."

DARK COMFORT

by Ty Nolan

In the Introduction, I mentioned the "variations on a theme," unusual forms or applications of *laran*. Not to be confined to one exception form of psychic talent, Ty Nolan invites use into the pavane, a stately dance, between two mental Gifts, one a uniquely Darkovan form, the other possessed by a star-faring race.

Trained as a traditional Native American Storyteller, Ty Nolan had his first short story published by Marion Zimmer Bradley in *Sword of Chaos*. His book, *Coyote Still Going: Native American Legends and Contemporary Stories*, received the 2014 BP Readers Choice Award for Short Story Collections and Anthologies. He is a *New York Times* and *USA Today* Best Selling Author. He currently splits his time between Arizona and Washington State.

"Gods," he slurred. "You're so ugly that when you were born the midwife said if you didn't cry right away then you were a tumor." The drunk in front of him tried to finish what was in his goblet and missed his mouth.

Balik sighed and wondered if there was any point in responding. He walked away and heard the speaker falling over while calling out *"nedestro!"* and the stool soon followed with a satisfying crash. He went to the bar for a refill. He couldn't seem to get warm. Cottman IV was a miserable planet with a feeble red sun. The local version of alcohol helped. He looked out the window and tried not to shiver at the thought of having to walk back to the Space Port. The odd lighting depressed him. It felt as if he were too often a few steps away from darkness and then another moon would crowd into the sky.

"Not from around these parts," the bartender said as he pushed the heavy stoneware cup back to Balik. The older man's accent was almost as thick as the liquid in front of him. It tasted like half-distilled piss, but after a couple of sips his tongue would be numb and he'd feel slightly warmer. Balik prided himself for how quickly he could pick up languages. Walk far enough from the Space Port and he had a problem even understanding the Terran Standard being used. The Dry Towns trading jargon was simple enough and about as expressive as the cup he was holding. He actually had enjoyed the musical tones of the Darkover aristocracy when they'd walk by speaking *casta*. He looked at his empty cup and decided against another. This wasn't the best of times to be drunk. It had been a stressful past few days for him and he had just wanted to put some distance between his life and his work. He had tried to rent a flitter to go back to a mountain top with a spectacular view but everything was already reserved. Between Terran and Darkover there far too many holidays he had never heard of.

He took a deep breath. The scents and stinks formed colors in his head. All of his kind had a radical form of synesthesia and a sense of smell far beyond any human or most of the other sentient species he had so far encountered. The colors were dim and as inviting as what the locals called the bloody sun. If he delayed any longer, he would order another drink. He pulled his coat more tightly around him. He had paid extra for it when he knew he would be doing contract work here. The salesperson had promised him it would be superior to anything he would find when he made landfall. The sales pitch had smelled honest enough but he had come to realize the vendor was simply ignorant and not truly telling a falsehood. A gust of icy wind blew a brief flurry of snow into his face and he sneezed. He considered going back in for one last drink. He trudged glumly back towards the Space Port. The ground had refrozen while he was inside and it was dangerously slippery. He was frustrated that he could be so easily sent across the galaxy but still not be able to find an adequate pair of boots—let alone a decent coat.

He sneezed again. Even numbed with the cold, he could still smell the coppery scent of blood. A flood of vivid colors alerted him. Blood always seemed to smell the same to him regardless of worlds or species, and formed a similar pattern of hues within his mind. He followed the scent, conveniently located before him. Balik considered pretending his awareness was no greater than the humans around him. He had a difficult time telling himself lies. They always smelled bad and his heart constantly pointed due truth. He saw a slight figure crumpled in the faint shadows caused by the little moon overhead.

He leaned over. The scent was female with a mixture of an odd combination of colors he had not experienced before. A bad cut above one eyebrow had cost her enough blood to soak her cloak. Her hair was cut unusually short for a local woman. Blood had caked in her reddish hair where she had been unconscious on her side. It looked black under the moon's light, but the colors he smelled intrigued him. He noticed a sliced through leather pouch tied to her simple belt. The inhabitants of Cottsman IV seemed about as noble and honest as those of the other human worlds he had visited. Balik's kind could always smell a true lie. It forced a strict and instantly direct honesty among his own. He knelt down and gently felt for her pulse. Her smell had told him she was not severely hurt, but he had long ago learned to use more human standards when something might involve the law of whatever world he stood upon.

Her eyes jerked open. His first impression was that he was unclear if they were gray, green, or pale blue. He wondered if it were a trick of the alien moonlight. "*Latti!*" she screamed at him. *Leave*, he recognized both the phrase and its tone. She smelled of fear and anger and this caused a fascinating mixture of colors in his head.

"*Permanedál*," Balik said firmly.

She laughed as she tried to sit up. "You are obviously from the Space Port but you quote me the Hastur's family motto. *I shall remain*. Know that I need no man's assistance." She looked at him intently. "Different." She touched her forehead and stared at the blood on her fingertips. The scent of her blood and the colors it engendered for him focused his vision. He noticed her thin hand had six fingers. "But who am I who has been judged so much to judge?" she said, almost to herself. "Outlander. Off-worlder, yes? Since you know enough of our language to be more than a mocking bird, do you know what *Comhi-Letzii* means?" The words felt odd to him. It had something to do with a community or society, but he was unsure. He shook his head slightly.

"We are sometimes called Free Amazons. Renunciates. Sworn to belong to no man and to be independent." Her small hand felt at her ruined purse. "And I shame myself by proving so poor at my independence."

"I offer you the concern and aid I would to any man, woman, or other gendered individual. It's part of simply being civilized." Now it was his turn to look awkward. "Or as civilized as I can claim to be." He stood up and offered her his hand to help her to her feet. *"Never look down at anyone unless it is to help them up,"* he remembered his grandmother telling him when he was a child. He was lost in a swirl of colors and scents remembering her. *"They are not dead who live in the hearts they leave behind,"* she had told him when his grandfather *died. Now he comforted himself once again with her words.*

Then another blast of wind hit him in the face and he was once again standing on a miserable little planet touching the warm hand of a stranger. "You're not badly hurt, but you'll scar if the cut above your eye is not treated. Come with me. It's not far and there's an auto-clinic that I can access for you." She started to object and he smelled her fear and frustration. Colors glittered within his mind. "You've been robbed. I suspect you have no resources and you seem to be alone." The only touch of recent others he could sense on her was the man who had robbed her. He could smell the male scent and bitter metal of the knife that had been used to knock her senseless and cut through her purse. "My contract provides me emergency healthcare, so it will cost me nothing. My ID will clear you through the gates as long as we stay close." The wind was picking up. He felt miserable but realized she felt worse.

He watched her, tracing her thoughts and smells as she considered his words. He was aware she had a level of arousal that frightened her. The scent of arousal started at a hot pink and extended into crimson. "And I offer you what I would any man or woman or other gendered individual. I do this not for sex or any sense of ownership. I was raised by my grandmother to help another in need in the hopes that when I am in need I will be treated the same." The color of an iridescent pearl eased around her, indicating a scent of relief.

"My name is Esme," she said quietly. As they moved forward he was noticing other emotions. Her energy level was low. She smelled of hunger, more of a physical need than of eroticism. Her scent had a tinge of near exhaustion. His heart went out to her.

"Balik," he said simply. "When was the last time you had something to eat?" The murky color of a lie emanated from her, but then cleared. A lie, but not spoken. She had decided to opt for honesty. That made him feel better. Lies had a stench that tended to linger.

"Two days?" she said quietly. "Some details are clearer than others. Our Guildhouse was destroyed in a fire set by a cult group that hates Renunciates." Her voice caught and an overwhelming scent of sorrow swirled with loss nearly overcame him. "So many of our *bredini*—our sisters—were elderly. The only threat they offered was their independence. They were simply living out quiet lives. I was away from the Guildhouse trying to gather some medicinal ice field herbs with Cassie." She lapsed into silence. His mind attempted to sort out the complexity of colors and smells as she tried to make sense of her experience.

When she had survived her threshold sickness, she was shunned—feared and hated in a way she didn't fully understand at the time. By her fourteenth birthday she had realized she had no future among the Comyn and even her own family. She considered killing herself. She wondered if she could survive a lifetime of being alone. She had grown up hearing of the Renunciates—a pitiful group of losers who couldn't find husbands. Abominations. Women who couldn't be with a man. Female *ombredin*. It took her another year to accept joining a Guildhouse would be at least a little better than being an abomination in her own home. Her family was only too happy to let her go. She glanced around at the cropped hair of the women everywhere she looked. She cried when they cut her hair. She had considered it her best feature. When she told the Mother of the House what she was, she was met by silence.

"Never touch our healer," the House Mother said, and never discussed the matter again.

"You have great anger," the healer said. "You must learn to understand the anger behind the anger. Otherwise you will make many mistakes." She sipped the mint scented tea in front of her. "You will think you are angry at me when you are angry at yourself. When you are angry at your family."

She hated the rough feeling of the drab clothing she was given after a lifetime of wearing the highland silk and the clean smelling linen she loved. She hated their rough manners and even the raw sounds of the *cahuenga* language they used. She kept to herself and realized there was very little difference of being at the Guildhouse and being in her home when it came to her pain. Eventually, like an injured animal, she accepted the friendship of the other Renunciates. She grew closest to Cassie, a kind and round-faced older woman who reminded her of her aunt. Esme learned about the gathering of herbs and how to dry them so they could be used later on. She thought of herself as little more than a servant and decided it didn't matter if she was a slave in her own home or in the low caste reality of the Guildhouse. She sat through endless discussions of how superior the Free Amazons were to the Comyn while all she could think about was how much she missed being the Comyn she was born to be.

When the House Mother talked about their meaningless future, Esme dreamed of a formal *di catenas* marriage and all the glory it would entail—claiming the status she deserved. She pushed at the tasteless food in front of her. She missed the bards and musicians of her rightful place and listened to the off-key entertainment her Guildhouse offered.

"We watched the House burn from where we were. We listened to the screams. We heard the triumph of the *gre'zuin* as they celebrated their victory over frail old women." It was times like this Balik wished he was nose and mind blind. It was why he sometimes drank too much. "Cassie ordered me to follow her away from the burning house, to report what had happened and to petition to join another Guildhouse. That was nearly ten days ago. I didn't know the area once we had gone more than a couple of days away." He could see the Space Port gates. "Cassie stumbled and fell as we were descending a ravine. She was already dead by the time I found her. I didn't even get to say goodbye." She turned and looked at Balik and the pain in her eyes was so great he tried to blot out the scents that flowed from her, blinding him with the intensity of their colors.

He held up his left hand. His implanted ID triggered the opening of the employee gate and he touched her shoulder gently as they walked through. He knew it was just his emotional response—the alien planetary smells were still strong on this side, but there was a scent of relief and anticipation of finally being warm again and in a civilized environment. Alien worlds were exciting, but he didn't need to regularly encounter bloody victims at his workplace. "I buried her. I said the prayers. I kept walking. I tried to make the little travel food I had last as long as I could. I wasn't able to find food under the heavy snow. I saw the towers of the Space Port and headed here, figuring I could get my bearings and ask directions."

He led her to the auto-clinic and touched a pad to ID himself and initiate a scan. He had her sit within the dimly lit circle and a holographic image of her formed with resulting readouts of her body. In the bright light of the infirmary she looked like a starved child. The initial scans confirmed what he had scented. Her overall health was excellent. A few meals and a simple treatment of her wound would be easy enough to prescribe. He had nothing he could offer her for heart and its grief.

"Keep talking," he said softly as he keyed in the prep. "It will distract you. This may sting a little." He silently chided himself and smelled his own embarrassment. The woman had just endured a massacre, starvation and being beaten in a robbery. The application of the cleansing antiseptic would be like a paper cut after having her arm amputated without anesthesia. He thought for a moment and keyed in a basic array of vaccines. The last thing he wanted was for her to die from the exposure to some alien entity in transit after she had entered the Space Port for a simple medical treatment.

"I only had a few coins with me. They were just tokens of memory. We're supposed to give up our old lives, but they were gifted to me by my mother when I was barely five years old. They were to teach me to save and be patient. I had wanted a special sweet and she gave them to me, telling me that when I had collected enough I could buy my own sweets." Esme's voice was distant. "She was trying to teach me to be independent even then. Who knew she shared something with the Free Amzaons?" She touched her ruined pouch. "Whoever stole them ran off with coins less valuable than the leather that contained them. Their only value was sentimental."

The machinery smelled of sterility and raw metals that provided disconnected colors. Sentient beings gave off colors that ended up mixed and blended. Only infants had singular smells and colors. Equipment like this were like being shown a color chart. Each one distinct. Clean. It was comforting to him in a way. It was why he did the work he did. He watched patiently as the final salve smoothed over her injury. It almost smelled of a combination of basil and the Kynick flowers that bloomed outside of his home back under a proper sky with a single moon and a sun young enough to keep him warm. The colors of the smell were light blue swirled with purple. If he wore cologne, he would like to wear something like this. The last vaccine showed that her body was responding normally so there was no danger of a later allergenic reaction. The holographic display switched off and the pad signaled him to confirm the transaction.

"First," he said softly, worried what the experience of walking into true civilization after a lifetime on a Class Six planet stuck at a pre-industrial stage might have on her, "let's get something to eat. I'm a terrible cook and I don't think I have anything other than a couple of cheap bottles of wine in my quarters. I'm hungry too. There's a place nearby that serves simple food that I enjoy." He monitored her. She smelled of curiosity rather than fear and confusion. Curiosity was mostly orange with flashes of hot yellow.

He ordered for them both after asking if she preferred vegetarian. He wasn't surprised she was an omnivore. Most inhabitants of Class Six societies were. He noticed that she was fading, giving off a calming scent of approaching sleep. He charged the meal and guided her to his quarters. He explained the recliner in the media room converted into a bed where he would sleep, and then opened the door to the bedroom and showed her how to engage the bathroom options and then turned down the bed and left her alone, telling her he would see her in the morning.

He pulled up his work schedule and cleared the next two days to be available for her. He didn't understand why he felt so drawn to her. He had bedded a number of human women and a few others of compatible species, but they had meant little other than physical pleasure.

He spent some time looking through any information he could find on the *Combi-Letzii*. The Renunciates had a fascinating history. An understandable survival response in a world of utter male domination, but one that took a level of courage that he admired. He got up and poured himself some wine and sat back down. He decided that Esme would best respond to a transactional exchange. He'd ask for her help with language and culture. That would support her underlying need to be independent from men. He set up a program of basic questions for her to answer that he had used many times from his introductory course in xeno-anthropology.

He yawned and gave a verbal command for the bed-mode and was asleep while trying to imagine the life of a Free Amazon in a world of swords and women who too often died in child birth.

He woke up a few hours later. He needed less sleep than humans. He pulled up the holographic scan from the night before and used it to determine her clothing size. It wasn't necessary. She would obviously wear extra-petite. He brushed the screen to have some basic items delivered. He thought about ordering them in bright colors but realized that would be what he would wear and she might perceive it as him dressing her like a doll. It was the last thing she needed. He chose simple organic colors similar to what she had been wearing. Her emotional colors would provide him enough stimulation. He smiled. He took her bloodied cloak and placed it by the door to be sent out for cleaning.

The clothing and breakfast arrived at the same time and he exchanged the packages for the cloak. He heard her moving around and let her know food was ready when she was and that he would leave a change of clothing outside the door. He returned to the media room and saw her small six-fingered hand pull the clothing in and then shut the door. He sipped his hot tea and looked over his communications hub. He finished up his most recent assignment, making him feel better about taking some time off. He had earned it. He poured some more tea. He enjoyed it for the colors of its fragrance rather than for its taste.

She smiled shyly when she left the bedroom. Her short cap of auburn hair was still damp from her bath. The clean clothing seemed to suit her. "I've made an appointment later on today at the Darkover Embassy in the Space Port. You can report on the atrocity that was committed and find out where the closest of the Renunciate Guildhouses might be. I tried to find out but the Port's database is only showing fragments of information you might find useful and some of your history. If you would like to barter for what I can offer you, it would be a great help to start filling in the gaps of our knowledge. Perhaps in the future such information may help another Renunciate in need. I would also appreciate learning more of your language. Linguistics is a passion of mine." He scented her relief. The colors made him feel more relaxed. "It would be best if you were here for the next couple of days to recover and to make certain you don't require any further treatment for your injury. Then I'll help you to get to your new Guildhouse."

"*Su serva* ... Balik." She hesitated. Her smell of relief grew stronger and was touched with the orange of curiosity. Her eyes confused him as much as they had when she first opened them. As someone whose life constantly overflowed with colors, they seemed to shift as much as her emotions. He had never seen eyes like hers before. At times they almost seemed silver.

He rose and set out the breakfast items and poured more tea. She seemed to whisper a prayer before she ate. At the first taste the curiosity ramped up and he enjoyed the flashes of yellow within the orange. He then realized the silent questioning was being directed at him, rather than at the novel food.

"Do you have *laran*?"

Now it was his turn to be curious. "I only know that word to mean some sort of gift, but I could not tell from what's in our database if the word means something spiritual or something more literal." He cut himself off before he added what he had read so far seemed more like the simple superstition he would expect to find in a Class Six society.

"It just seems as if you have been reading my mind since you first met me. You keep watching me as if you are anticipating my response before you even speak." She had a little more tea. "My uncle and his children have that sort of *laran*." She laughed. It smelled of lavender and silver. "I always felt left out. They'd look at me the way you do. Then they would look at each other."

"Telepathy is considered extremely rare among humans," he said hesitantly. "Perhaps they were just excellent at reading body language."

She laughed again and he sat back, admiring the colors. "Oh, no," she said. "Not so rare among the Comyn." She smelled of the dark blue characteristic of complete belief. So it was true for her.

"Do you have *laran?*" He automatically tried to distract her from asking more about his own ways of knowing. His kind kept that as much of a blank space in the databases as possible. It was why so many of his relatives were diplomats, negotiators and security heads. Their senses gave them a distinct advantage that could be lost with a strong disinfectant or something that could more seriously rob them of their sense of smell. Better that their employers didn't know why they were so remarkably good at their jobs.

The laughter suddenly stopped. The lavender and silver were replaced with a pained gray. "I had threshold sickness. I was comforted by being told I would soon be like my cousins and my older brothers." Her scent became drier and the gray became more solid. "But I ended up with one of the rarest types of *laran*. I'm a *nula.*" The gray began to shade into a thick black. Then he made the connection of the word and her emotion.

"A null? You cancel things out?" He knew he was seeing the colors correctly, but his logical mind couldn't twist them into anything that made sense.

"It is a sad joke," she sighed, pushing the tea away. "My cousins say that I move at the speed of dark. Minds are walled off to me, and no one can easily read mine. I don't see the future," she laughed bitterly but it wasn't lavender or silver. "If I had, perhaps my sisters would still be alive and no thief would have surprised me. But if anyone with *laran* touches me, their own abilities are, as you say, canceled out. Who of the Comyn would want to touch someone in intimacy and lose their Gifts?" Her scent made him hurt. He automatically reached out in sympathy and took her thin hand in his. The mental colors that always surrounded him were being smothered by the blackness she was giving off. It was as if— as if true night had fallen and that was all that he could see. It was overwhelming—and intoxicating. "When they had me touch a starstone, I killed it."

She looked at him, and her eyes were a true silver. He could smell only the icy air of the mountain top he had visited his first month on Darkover. He suddenly realized he was crying for her because she could not shed tears for herself. He unconsciously wiped at the wetness on his cheeks.

"They brought out another two stones and when I touched them their bright blue fire was extinguished. I could feel their life go out." She sat back. Balik pushed at the darkness around him, fascinated. "Then no one would come too close to me. I lived as a pariah, only permitted to be around servants and others who lacked *laran*. After two years of that I left to join the Guildhouse, knowing *laran* is not commonplace among the Free Amazons, since most were not from the Comyn. I let the Mother of the House know what I was. The only one of my sisters there who had *laran* was our healer and we carefully kept our distance." She lifted her head. "But at least I felt useful. They didn't look upon me with contempt or pity." There was a sudden sharp smell of cinnamon and the blackness started to fade. His sense of smell began to return and her colors increased in their complexity. He had never heard of any of his kind who had experienced anything like this other than those with traumatic brain injuries. They didn't recover and soon died.

He watched her carefully, as much interested in his own reactions returning to a familiar comforting level as he was at how her scent and emotions kept shifting. She was beautiful. He was puzzled that he hadn't really noticed that before. Her eyes now appeared a pale green rather than the silver he thought he had seen before. She seemed so small. He knew from the scan at the auto-clinic she was barely twenty. She seemed younger. She smelled of vulnerability and it matched the barely there greenness he saw in her eyes. Then her inherent strength—that of someone who buried her dead and endured the primitive wilderness of Cottman IV emerged with the smell of bronze and flashing flecks of gold.

"And you?" she asked. She picked up her tea and looked at him over it, examining him with the attention he paid to her. She smelled yet again of orange and hot yellow. He knew she saw him as an unusual looking human. He considered his answer. She had not yet lied to him. He didn't want to now do so with her. All who left his world took an oath of silence about what they experienced with others. He wondered what his grandmother would think of him at this moment. *"Always follow your heart, even if you don't always follow the rules,'* she had told him one day when they were alone and she was fixing dinner.

"From far and far away. A world you've never heard of called Kaliph. As far away from Darkover as Terra is, but on the opposite side." The orange intensified. He automatically moved her attention away from him by telling her more about where he was from. 'The sun is younger and burns a bright yellow. We have a single moon. Like Terra, our world is more water than land. You'd probably find it too warm, just as many of those from off-world find Darkover too cold." He told her of the Lorket he had as a child and how its song sounded like tiny bells. He told her of his curiosity to see the worlds he had only known as stories. He heard a chime from the media room that reminded him of the Lorket. "We need to leave soon for the appointment at the Embassy."

He put on a formal tunic for the meeting and held open the door for her to let her enter the corridor. They would need to take a change of tubes to get to the Ambassador's office. "It isn't far," he told her. "When we came in last night, I brought you in the fastest way I could to treat you and then to have dinner. We'll need to pass through a much larger and busier area. If you have any questions, feel free to ask them. I suspect it might be confusing. We'll have to enter a transportation center that will be faster than any horse, but will a far gentler ride than anything with hooves. We'll be moving out of the Terran specific spaces to ones that are shared by other species."

She nodded and followed him closely. Esme was alert and gawking at what she saw around her. They had left early, so he felt no pressure at letting her take her time, sometimes stopping to look at something that he hadn't even noticed. A young Tromley half her height rolled by in its liquid filled sphere and she followed it with her eyes, her mouth as round as its transport globe.

"Many wonders," he whispered. None of the Kaliph would contract with the Tromley Empire. They had no scent. For his kind is was like being with someone who had no soul.

"We're being seen by an Aidan Ridenow," Balik said as they

continued on. "I told him you were a Renunciate whose Guildhouse was attacked and burned down and that on your way to the Space Port you were rendered unconscious in a robbery. That was enough to secure the interview and I thought it best for you to give him more details directly." He slowed his pace. "I hadn't thought of it, but will there be a problem? As I said, our database has many gaps but I got the sense anyone high-ranking enough to hold the title of Ambassador from a society that doesn't see women as equals, may not be very supportive to someone like you." She smelled of confidence, but mostly nervousness. It was like watching bubbles of a dark emerald popping into browns.

"He should be civil, particularly in front of someone representing the Space Port." She looked at him. "Perhaps if he believes you to be Terran, it would be for the best. Growing up, many of the Comyn men I've been around have enough difficulty accepting Terrans without having to stretch their minds even more by acknowledging Darkover is only one small world among many so much larger and more powerful."

They were shown in after a wait of a few minutes. The desk the Ambassador sat behind was impressively intimidating. He smelled slightly of contempt which Balik read as a feathery tan. Balik found it unpleasant and realized it was directed as much towards him as it was to the woman with an oath freeing her from servitude to a man. About halfway into the interview, Ridenow stopped and said something in *casta* Balik couldn't follow. The Ambassador smelled of anger mixed with curiosity.

Then he realized the man was asking why he could not read the minds of either one of them. It surprised Balik. As he had shared, telepathy was virtually unknown among the Confederation of Empires. He had no way of knowing a Kaliph mind would be as inaccessible as that of Esme. He kept his face blank. The Ambassador frowned and Balik felt a sort of tickling inside of his head. He sat quietly and let the feeling fade. Ridenow's scent increased in anger and Esme simply seemed frustrated but calm. Perhaps she was used to being beyond the reach of what she called *laran*.

"*Nula*," she said simply. "It is what I am."

That triggered more rapid *casta* from Ridenow and although

Esme looked subservient, she smelled of anger and quiet control. "As long as we do not have physical contact," she said softly, "you are in no danger." She took a deep breath and let it out. "It's why I left my domain and joined the Guildhouse, where touching me would not matter." She raised her head for the first time since they had been seated. "Did you think I cut my hair and took the Oath willingly? Do you think I renounced my birthright to humble myself as a Free Amazon?"

Ridenow cut her off. "I know you, do I not? You were just a child. Esmerelda Aillard. You were supposed to be promised to a Hastur but there was some scandal that I..." he looked at her and then at Balik. "Oh, I guess that explains it."

Balik watched Ridenow closely. His scent faded into something he recognized as the tinny smell of calculation. His older brother had taught him a term long ago—*weaponizing*. He looked back and forth between the two. He could tell Ridenow was no longer paying attention to her. He smelled of smugness, which almost stank as much as a lie. If Esme was correct about the role of *laran* among the Comyn, a *nula* would be a potential gun to hold to the head of a rival. One touch and the advantages that apparently gave the Comyn men their rule could be forever extinguished. An eternal mental darkness.

He began to more fully understand why her people could fear her and why she might seek refuge among the Free Amazons. His mind was racing. One of the reasons his kind were frequently hired to head security teams was their ability to detect an assassin. Esme was a perfect weapon. Beneath notice in a society that saw women as little more than servants. The arrogant paid no attention to servants except to order them around. Esme was high-born and cultivated to fit into their aristocracy. No need for a knife or poison that could be found if she were searched or scanned. He recoiled from his own scent of fear.

"*Evil enters the world when people are treated as things,*" his grandmother had told him as he prepared to leave for his formal training. "*Watch out for those who do so. Never do so yourself.*" He was too young to fully understand what she had meant. Now he was too old to deny her truth.

The Ambassador told them he would look into both the

destruction of the Guildhouse and direct the local authorities to begin a search for the thief. He stank so much of lies Balik almost curled his lip. They walked out. He could smell the frustration on her. It held dimness and the sourness of unwashed laundry. When they were a few minutes away from the Embassy, she said, "I don't need the *laran* of a telepath to know he won't follow through."

"In a Class Six society," Balik began and then stopped. "In your world, power is held by those locked into hereditary positions. In my experience, that encourages intrigue and power grabs."

Esme looked at him. Her eyes seemed the palest blue he had ever seen. "Is all that in your database?"

"Let's just say I come from a family that is all too familiar with how power functions. If the gift of *laran* supports your males who control the domination of your people, what happens if a *nula* reaches out and—to use your words—*their fire was extinguished?*"

Her eyes widened. "It would be like cutting off their balls," she whispered. "I've spent so much time in self-pity of my own rejection I hadn't thought beyond it to consider the underlying reason as to why everyone around me stepped away." He was fascinated by the quick changes in her scents and the accompanying colors. Her eyes seemed more of a soft gray. "You think he wants to use me?"

"I think he wants to own you. I think he wants to decide when and where to deploy you." She stopped walking. "I think you are a weapon that can only be used a limited number of times. I think..." He pulled her into an empty corridor, "...if he uses you to advance himself, he will need to rid himself of you and distance himself from potential responsibility and blame."

"Then I would endanger any Guildhouse I entered. Ridenow would just consider it a place to store me until he wanted to use me."

"If another Guildhouse were to burn, it would just be seen as the act of the fanatics who destroyed your last one." He closed his eyes, smelling the fear rising in both of them. "My aunt told me of a murder case she had investigated. It was initially judged as a random mass murder. But it was an arranged murder hidden among all the innocent bodies. A second Guildhouse in ashes would mean no trace or records of you having been there and why."

"What is it like to live in your mind?"

"Let's just say it's a very colorful place. I would like to comfort you by saying I'm overly paranoid but I don't think this is the time to start handing you lies."

She nodded. "I don't think it's ever the time to lie to me." They walked back to his quarters in silence. He poured them some wine and heard his communications hub chime. "It's from Ridenow," Balik said. "It's an invitation to a reception he's holding in honor of someone named Rafael Serrais." Balik's fingers flew over the screen. "Rafael Serrais..."

"Is next in line of succession for his domain," she said putting her wine glass down. "The Ridenow and the Serrais bloodlines are woven together. I suspect the Ambassador has chosen his target."

Balik nodded. "The rest of the message is to let you know that after the reception he will provide you an escort to your new Guildhouse." She came over and looked at the communiqué.

"I've heard of this one. It's even smaller than my own. More than two weeks away by horse. There are others closer. If I were going to dispose of a Guildhouse and hide it among innocent victims like my poor sisters, I would choose one like this. Unimportant. Too inconvenient a location for detailed investigation if it were destroyed. It's the one I would choose if I were a *kyorebni*, used to feasting on carrion." She smelled of anger and disgust. "May he rot in Zandru's darkest hells!"

Balik spent more time busy at his screen. "Forgive me," he said, "This is something important I need to do. I'll explain it when I've finished." She fumed, finishing off her glass of wine and poured herself another. "And what about you," she asked. "Aren't you another loose end?"

"There are advantages to having people here assume I am a Terran. Regardless of how your Comyn may think of themselves, the Terran Empire considers this place to be a colony. My world is not part of the Terran Empire. I come with a different set of rules to be followed."

"So you are protected from Ridenow's machinations?"

"Not at all. I'm merely more difficult to extradite once I'm off-world."

"And when will you be off-world?"

"There's a shuttle leaving less than two hours after the reception begins. It will connect with a pleasure cruise a few days later that will be headed to a different quadrant." He smelled her frustration. "That just means it will be very far away. It has a final destination that will be close to my own planet. I'm used to traveling a lot with my work."

"And I'll be on my way to a Guildhouse destined to burn…"

"Or you will be sitting next to me on the shuttle. If I register you as my Domestic Partner, then you will hold the same non-Terran rights I enjoy." He turned in his chair to watch her. She smelled of confusion, excitement and arousal. It was a very heady combination and the colors were making his head explode. "I have no *laran* to lose by touching you. We have much to talk about but with what I do possess, your touch can be more intoxicating than any wine. I suspect being married isn't the worst of fates for you, although I know you would prefer to experience it on Darkover. The Domestic Partnership I offer will give you protection if you decide you don't want to remain with me any longer than to go off-world and away from Ridenow. But if we stay away for a few years, we might be able to return with Ridenow no longer in the position he is in now. Caught in a bungled coup, Ridenow would not be in a place to confess details to implicate us, and I'm certain he is a man with many enemies of his own."

"You would do this for me?"

"I would do this for *us*. It's a dangerous plan because we face a dangerous man. We have a saying back home: *If you are going to die, then you will die in the dark even if your family makes candles.*" He smiled at her. "We will have to do it together, though. A single finger cannot lift a pebble."

She touched his face gently. She smelled of wonder and excitement. Her arousal was spiking.

"What is a Domestic Partner? Is it like what we call a freemate?"

"Among the Confederation of Empires it is considered to be equivalent to a marriage. But it is a specific legal and binding contract that would provide you with all the rights of a true marriage to me. It would be like a merger of companies."

"How romantic," she whispered and she smelled of regret.

"It would be less romantic if I assumed you would be willing to marry me simply because you wish to save your life." He took a deep breath and let it out. "Wouldn't that be what you were taught in the Guildhouse you should never do? Depend on a man? Even one who isn't human? No. I would not want to hurt you by forcing a marriage upon you. That is why I suggested a legal contract instead."

She looked at him, her eyes almost silver again. "Perhaps you don't fully understand what *di catenas* means to those of us of Darkover."

He frowned. "The term means to be chained, right?"

She laughed, but rather than lavender and silver it was topped with a bitterness of burnt almonds. "Yes, that is its literal meaning—but it means an unbroken connection. An eternal joining. If it's a type of slavery, it is one every woman—indeed—every man, is born to desire. It's a sense of completion." She turned her back to him. "It's something I have dreamed of—and once I learned I was a *nula*—knew I could never have."

He sat silently, watching her swirl of confused colors. "We have true marriage on Kaliph. Perhaps it is not as elaborate as what you know. You asked if I have *laran*. Not as you know it, but I am not human. I think I have a gift that is similar. I know that you respond to me—that among your many emotions there is desire." He watched her turn to face him. "Know then that I also desire you. I hadn't originally thought of true marriage. We are a long-lived people. I would not have considered true marriage for a number of years. We travel. We learn about others. We say in our language, *Nottda longa*—we gather stories. That is then what we offer to a potential spouse. It is what we value. I didn't think I would have enough to offer you." He smiled. "But I think it is what you offer to me. Would you be willing to have more than a Domestic Partnership? Would you be willing to be chained to me?"

She laughed. "It sounds so formal when you say it in Terran Standard. *Di Catenas*? Oh, yes, it is what I have always wanted for myself. And you are kind. And wise. You reached out to a stranger and found a heart that is not that of a stranger after all." She leaned over and touched him. "And if you really do have such an alien form of *laran*, then you know I want to know you as more than an outlander. I want to know you as a man." She laughed again. "I want to know you as my chain." Then she stood tall. "No—I want to know you as the chain I hold. I hated my time as a Free Amazon. But I learned to value what it means to be independent. If a Domestic Partnership means we would be equal, then I want that—to be equals."

He looked at her, her eyes a pale blue. "I was taught that in a true marriage, we would be equals. I'm not a man of Darkover. I'm from a bigger universe. I would be honored to enter into true marriage as equals. Let us leave this place of small hearts and minds that only sees women so less than males you needed to live alone, protected by an Oath. Come with me and see what a Confederation of Empires can offer." He held on to her hand. "What I can offer." As he looked into her eyes, he realized her simple touch didn't trigger the darkness. It apparently needed her emotional connection as well. That was useful to know.

"Do you wonder what my work is?" She shook her head. She did so carefully, as if it were very full. She continued to smell of arousal. Her scent told him she was still a virgin and that it was not her time of fertility. He wondered what it was like for her to always have to monitor her touch, to wonder if she might ever be able to be intimate with someone she cared for. "I'm a xeno-physician. I can pick up a contract almost anywhere. I've just terminated my contract here. That was one of the things I was doing on the screen a few moments ago. I was nearly done with it anyway. And I was booking passage for the two of us in case you agreed to go with me." He rose and took her glass of wine and drank from it. "Let's talk." Esme took the glass from him and placed it on the table. Then she kissed him.

In another hour she lay against him, her head on his chest while he sank into the temporary comfort of darkness she could offer. "I don't know if I can give you children," he said. "I'd have to do some tests for compatibility." He turned to look at her. "I assumed you want children. I would like to be a parent one day. I hope that I might be at least half as good a grandparent as mine were to me." He held her hand. "We would have more choices off-world. We can adopt of course, but there are options of surrogates and genetic engineering."

"I know you think Darkover is just a primitive world. But you don't know of our grim history. The star stones can be used to do what you are calling genetic engineering. It was terribly misused and is one of the major ways that women lost our power and the men took it all. Yes—I also want children, but forgive me if I hesitate to do so in a way that echoes what was done so many years ago. That resulted in breeding us for *laran*. Those of us who look like me—the six-fingered—we are descended from the children of the yellow forest. The *chieri* are the indigenous race of Darkover— the source of *laran*. But for those of us who—look more like me than humans—we are often infertile. More so for males, but there was always a question if I could be able to have children of my own." She shut her eyes. "But if we cannot have children together, there is no shame in adopting. But using the star matrix to work its magic within my most private self—it scares me because of the stories I was told."

He sat up, painfully aware of what those stories meant to her. The strong blue of her emotion meant she fully believed in them. After learning that laran wasn't just a superstition, he now hesitated to simply dismiss the idea Darkover might have once been able to do far more than it could now. He was aware of a relatively high infertility rate for the local inhabitants and had wondered why none of them had sought any treatment since he had begun his contract work. "Then let us see what happens." He held her tightly.

Then he stood up and gave a verbal command for the bath to fill. "I mentioned my world has more water than land. My kind feel more comfortable immersed in water. Do you know how to swim?"

"It's too cold for swimming where I grew up," she said. "There are seasons where it is so cold if you fall out of a boat you will die of hypothermia before you can drown. But I have always loved to soak in warm water. It's simply such a chore to fill a tub and keep it warm."

He picked her up as if she were a child. "Here you only need tell the bath controls what it is you want. It will adjust the temperature. It will fill in a few seconds. You can order scented oils but I ask that you do not. My sense of smell can be overwhelmed sometimes if there are too many artificial fragrances." He nuzzled her. "I'd rather smell you." Still holding her, he stepped into the bath and eased into its warmth. "Is the water too hot? Too cool?"

She turned to face him, feeling buoyant in the deep bath. She touched his chest, now slick with the water. "It is perfect."

They made love again, something she had never done in water before. He felt even more connected to her. When they had finished, he used plush towels to dry her, rather than the standard air vents, because it felt more sensual and she then did the same for him. Their scents were starting to merge because of the intimacy. Any sense of lingering doubt over what they were doing was gone for Balik.

After a few minutes of simply sitting together, they dressed and he took her to one of the many shopping centers within the Space Port. This time she smiled and beat him to summoning the tube that gave them passage to the area beyond the Terran community spaces.

"On my world, in true marriage we seal our bond with matching necklaces the way many Terrans do with rings. The symbols are the same—unbroken circles. Joined together. When you said yes to my proposal I provided the data for the jewelry store to create for us what I would have provided for you under a yellow sun and a single moon. Not a Domestic Partnership, but a true marriage—a *di catenas* one. The center stone is one we call in our language *Monthalla*. It is sometimes called the rainbow gem. Its fire is one that you will not be able to ever extinguish with your touch."

"Do you fully understand to us a *di catenas* can never be broken—can never be ended? If you have any doubts, then it would be best to sign the contract for the Domestic Partnership you first offered." She looked at him with silver eyes, not daring to blink.

"I think I have already given you my answer. I realized in the bath that any doubts I might have had were washed away." He took her small hand and walked with her to the front of the store.

He charged the necklaces to his account and took her to an interdenominational chapel where they placed the necklaces on each other and pledged themselves as a married couple. He then surprised her with a ring that had a matching *Monthalla*. Esme smelled of joy and satisfaction. It was almost as enjoyable as the quieting darkness she could also provide. "Let us do this now. Let us do it again later on when I can welcome you to Kaliph." He kissed her. "Then in time we will return to Darkover and you can have as formal a wedding as you desire."

"Do all those of Kaliph move through courtship so quickly?"

"Not always, but because we smell emotions, we are able to skip a lot of the miscommunications I watch among the Terrans. We know when another desires us or isn't interested. It saves a lot of time."

Balik showed her how to use an easy program to design what they both would wear for the Ambassador's reception and the clothing she would take with them on their honeymoon. Everything was delivered to their quarters the following day. She wore a richly embroidered gown that shimmered silver and matched her eyes. He no longer saw her as a non-Kaliph. She was too beautiful to him— she was simply Esme. She was simply the one that made him feel whole. They went over their plans several times more to make certain nothing would go wrong. He returned from the auto-clinic and dressed in the grandest of Comyn fashion.

Clasping hands, they were ushered into the reception. At his suggestion, she wore gloves of the finest silver mesh. It would allow her to touch those with *laran* without consequence. But they were easily removed. "That is Lord Serrais," Esme told him. "He looks like his father. I met the elder Serrais the year before I had threshold sickness. He told me it was a great honor for me." A servant offered them wine in tooled silver goblets that looked as if they were designed for her to hold.

Ridenow looked across the room at Esme's gloves and frowned. He left and in a few moments a different servant told them the Ambassador had requested they meet with him privately. They nodded and she slipped off the gloves as the servant opened a door to a private office. "*S'dei par servu,*" he said as he stepped away. To Balik he smelled of ignorance. It was a welcome scent. As soon as the door shut, Esme stood in front of Ridenow, holding up her six-fingered hands. The light hit her necklace and a rainbow glinted off of the matching ring she wore.

"What is the meaning of this?" Ridenow demanded, smelling of arrogance. Balik moved behind him and slapped a medicated strip on his neck. No one had noticed he had also been wearing gloves, but they were the surgical type that were barely visible. Ridenow glanced at Balik and then fell backwards in his seat with unblinking eyes. Balik counted silently, making certain Ridenow had had enough exposure to the drug. He then reached down and peeled off the strip. He quickly removed his left glove and stuffed the strip inside of it and then took off the other glove and placed them within a hidden pocket. Esme smiled.

She walked slowly towards Ridenow. "You remembered me when I was a child. Do you know how I remember you?" She took another step towards him, watching the fear rise in his eyes. "In the Guildhouse the sisters talked about how important it was to be independent. To be strong. Do you wonder why? Because men like you taught us to believe we only had worth if we served a Comyn man. To believe we were only complete if we were," and then she smiled again, "...chained to someone like you." She held up her right hand. "That was what my mother and her mother believed. I even believed it myself." She pointed her finger at his forehead, a mere hand span away. "And do you know what happens when a *nula* touches you? Well, of course you do. It's what you wanted me to do tonight but to someone else. One gentle touch and you become the same in many ways a *nulo* yourself. Mind blind. As *laran*-less as any of those not noble born. Do you know what I learned from my time among the Free Amazons? Those who are not noble born have just as much value. It isn't about how you're born. It's about how you value others. How long do you think you can hold your office when you can't know what others are thinking? What others are plotting? How much worth will you have then?"

She reached down and held his face in her six-fingered hands. She kissed him in the center of his forehead. "But I know my own worth. I know my own value. I don't need you, Ambassador Ridenow. I don't need a man. But I have the power to choose to be with one. I have the power to choose the man I love. And who loves me." She pulled away and he watched her, unable to move. "I hope you begin to wonder if anyone would ever choose to love you." She watched him, her face hard and her eyes a burning silver. "Or if your wife only agreed to marry you for your position? I wonder how she will feel to be forever chained to a man of no value?" Esme smiled wickedly and watched him shut his eyes as he passed out.

She nodded to Balik. "We're done here." Balik opened the door and shouted for help.

"He was passed out when we entered," Balik told a frantic group of servants in *casta*. "At first I thought he had too much to drink but I worry it might be more serious! Do you have a healer on staff?" When one wide-eyed man nodded, Balik yelled at him to summon him. There were advantages to authoritarian societies when it came to being obeyed without question by servants if you were dressed as nobility. They left quietly among the commotion and went directly to the shuttle where Balik had sent their things before they had left for the reception. In a little more than an hour they were just a happy couple off on their honeymoon. Ridenow would awaken in another three days when they would be away on the pleasure cruiser and he would be *laran*-less and powerless to call them back. Balik wondered how long it would take for the Ambassador's rivals to discover he had no more ability than the humblest of his servants. "I thought it was a nice touch the way you held his face with your hands and then kissed him on his forehead. I wish I could share with you what triumph looks and smells like."

She silenced him with a kiss.

SIGHT UNSEEN

by Steven Harper

Steven Harper Piziks was born with a name that no one can reliably spell or pronounce, so he often writes under the pen name Steven Harper. He lives in Michigan with his husband and sons. When not at the keyboard, he plays the folk harp, fiddles with video games, and pretends he doesn't talk to the household cats. In the past, he's held jobs as a reporter, theater producer, secretary, and substitute teacher. He maintains that the most interesting thing about him is that he writes books. Most recently, he wrote the *Books of Blood and Iron,* a fantasy trilogy, for Roc Books.

"An untrained telepath is a danger to himself and everyone around him," runs the old adage, proven true time and again. Sometimes even a *trained* telepath can wreak devastation with a careless thought, an angry mood. And—echoing Shariann Lewitt's hero in "The Wind"—even a forgotten, "throwaway" orphan can rescue a prince.

The day I turned fifteen, Brother Hiram kicked me out of the orphanage. I mean that literally. Brother Hiram planted his foot on my ass, and I almost went to my knees on the cobblestones outside the front door.

"We're done with you!" Brother Hiram announced unnecessarily. "Beg Zandru for help if you need it."

And he slammed the door.

It was quiet outside. The main street of Haydentown, halfway between Neskaya and Armida, wandered around the city like a stone squiggle. Thank Sharra it wasn't raining. Or snowing. Or hailing. To the west, the city climbed the hills toward Castle Hayden. Behind it, the sun, low and bloody, was touching down on the Kilghard Hills. It was a clear summer evening, the perfect day to be kicked out of the only home you'd ever known.

I staggered upright and turned around. The orphanage seemed to stare down at me with empty, dead eyes that saw nothing. They sure didn't see me. The orphanage was one among a dozen row houses, all huddled close together in the smelly part of town. The shutters were closed tight so that not one scrap of light might escape for anyone on the street to use. Inside, Jerrell and Larion and Giley and the others would be hanging up their socks in front of the fire to dry about now. Orphans didn't stay up late, and they didn't sleep after sunrise. I always wondered about that. What in all nine hells did it matter if we stayed up late and slept in the next morning? We were *orphans*. But Brother Hiram said suffering made us better people, and that included going to bed early and rising before dawn, and using stinging willow switches on my bare legs for looking him in the eye, and locking me in the basement for asking questions during reading time, and beating me with an axe handle on the day my voice broke.

"That's to remind you never to touch yourself for evil," he had snarled. "And that and that and that."

I looked at the white scar on my palm and remembered the hot iron. *That* had been for something else entirely. Huh. I spat at the door.

It opened. My heart jerked. Brother Hiram was coming at me for my disrespect. But it was only Jerrell, in rags tattered as my own. I let out a breath as he slipped outside.

"Kieron," he said in his quiet, familiar voice. "He can't kick you out like that."

"I'm fifteen today," I said, and my voice choked anyway. "So I guess he can."

He reached out to touch my arm, but I flinched, and he pulled back. "Next month it'll be me," he said.

There wasn't anything I could say to that, and a lifetime of Brother Hiram's willow switches and dark basements stole away most of my words, so I kept silent.

"Where will you go, Kieron?" he asked. "Do you have a plan?"

I glanced up the long, winding street, past the shops and inns and houses, to Hayden Castle at the top of the hill. Not for the first time, I wondered if my parents had lived there. Lots of the boys told wild stories about their fathers being generals or Comyn lords, or of their mothers being Free Amazons. Jerrell even had a locket shaped like a star that had been around his neck when he had come to the orphanage. He swore it was actually a matrix, and he only needed someone to awaken his *laran* to make him Comyn. We all scoffed and said he was an idiot, but all of us secretly wished we had a locket, too. I didn't have a thing from my parents. Not even a memory.

We all made up stories about our futures, too. Most of them involved the castle that stared down the high street at us. One day we would be stable workers at that castle. No, we would be page boys. No, we would be knights! And then we would learn that *Dom* Robard Hayden was actually our father, and he would make us—he would make *me*—into a prince. And I would no longer be invisible.

None of the futures involved begging on the street for crumbs, *reis*, or a kick in the face. Which was what I faced now if I started at the bottom.

"I'm going to find work," I said, "at the castle."

"Hello? I'm looking for work. I'll sweep ashes. I'll shovel manure. I'll scrub chamber pots. Hello?"

The people bustling about the castle courtyard ignored me, looked through me, walked past me. One or two snorted and pushed me aside, wiping their hands after they touched my threadbare cloak and patched tunic. One man gave me a cuff on the ear and told me to get on my way before the gates shut. Other than that, I was invisible.

"Hello?" I tried one more time. No one paid me the slightest attention.

I slouched across the darkening courtyard, already mostly abandoned for the night. A few people still bustled about, attending to last-minute chores or errands. It was a trick not to stare at the high stone walls and the actual glass windows and the horses and well-dressed, confident servants. I tried to imitate them, but I was a fraud, a boy with no family, no friends, no—

The air rushed out of me as I collided with something both soft and hard. I went down in a tangle of arms, legs, and suffocating cloth. After some cursing and snarling, I worked myself free and scrambled to my feet. I had run into a woman, middle-aged, running to plump, wound in petticoats and corsets, and carrying a walking stick. Her graying hair—still streaked with red—was pulled back in a butterfly clip. She was splayed in an undignified pose that would have been funny if she weren't dressed like a palace lady.

"Zandru's balls!" she sniped. "Who is that? What's going on?"

Okay, now it was funny. Still, I felt bad for knocking her over. I held out a hand, but she didn't take it. It took a moment for me to notice that her eyes were blank and staring. Blind.

"Sorry, my lady," I said. "I didn't see you. My hand is in front of you, if you want help getting up."

She grabbed my arm and nearly yanked me over again as she pulled herself up like a top coming upright. "Where's my damn stick, boy?"

After I handed it to her, and she whacked my shin with it. I yelped, though after Brother Hiram's beatings, it was barely a tap. "What was that for?"

"Hm," she said. "Interesting answer."

"What do you mean?" I rubbed my leg.

"Most people of your station would beg my forgiveness. You demanded my attention." Her blank eyes met mine. "I can't see you. Why can't I see you, young one?"

"Because you're blind?" I hazarded.

"I'm blind to this world," she said, "but I can see the minds around me. Except yours. Why do you think I ran into your loutish legs? I should have sensed you like I sense everyone else."

I noticed a long silver chain around her neck. It held a locket wrapped in silk. Her matrix. A chill washed over me, and now I did want to beg her forgiveness. My knees wobbled a little. One word—or thought—from her, and I'd be dead. "My lady," I stammered. "Comynara."

"Call me *Domna*, young one. What's your name, since I can't pluck it from your mind?"

I summoned up some courage to answer her. "Kieron. I'm an orphan, and Brother Hiram threw me out today because I turned fifteen, so I'm looking for work here at the castle."

"How nice for you." She reached out to touch my face and, *Domna* or not, I drew away. "I still can't sense your mind. Do you have red hair, Kieron?"

Only the Comyn had red hair. I glanced at the sunset streaks in the lady's hair, and my knees wobbled again.

"You're *Domna* Marya," I quavered. *"Dom* Robard's sister."

"Indeed. And I still expect an answer to my question."

"I don't have red hair," I said. "It's brown, though in some light it's the color of a chestnut."

"Huh." She gestured with her stick. "There's a bench over there. Sit."

Remembering my manners, the ones Brother Hiram had drilled into me, I offered Lady Marya my arm, but she ignored it, and I remembered she couldn't see it anyway. It didn't seem to matter— she found her way to the bench just fine. By now it was nearly dark, and the courtyard was completely empty of people.

"I have a proposition for you." Lady Marya eased herself onto the stone bench with a creaking of joints and corset seams. "You know of my nephew, young Lord Rufus."

"Lord Robard's son." I nodded. "He's younger than I am. And a..." I hesitated.

"Nedestro. Born from that strumpet, Nanna. And the boy is a spendthrift," Marya scoffed. "The child tears through money like a herd of rabbit-horns in a new clover patch. Clothes, gambling, drinking, horses, women. My brother, Robard, indulges him, bastard child or not. But Aric." Her voice softened. "Now there was a Comyn lord! Strong, disciplined, kindhearted. My Aric."

"Aric?" I thought about this and came up empty. "Who's Aric?"

Marya gave a sigh that came all the way down from her shoes and I saw pain crease her face. "Aric was the heir to Hayden. He was *my* son."

She fell silent, and I didn't know what to say. Lady Marya scraped her walking stick on the stones, drawing designs only a blind woman could see.

At last, I said, "What happened to Aric?"

Marya sighed again. "Now there's our problem, my young Kieron." She tapped the stick on the ground. "Last year, Aric and I were down in the hunter's lodge at the bottom of the hill, and we got into an argument. It became more and more heated, in fact, and afterward, Aric was ... gone."

"What do you mean, gone?" Something was tapping at the back of my head, like a faint knock at a distant door, but I couldn't say what it was.

"Gone as in gone, boy. I ... I remember becoming angry, so angry that I couldn't bear another moment of it. It was like thunder built inside me and exploded. I..." She closed her unseeing eyes and touched the silk-wrapped matrix on the silver chain around her neck. "I lashed out at Aric. With my *laran*. And ... well, no one has seen him since." She hurried on. "Now Robard intends to marry Nanna, which will solidify Rufus's claim as the heir, and Sharra help us all when that day comes."

"You killed Aric?" I asked. The tapping at the back of my head was growing stronger. "That's ... that's..." I didn't know how to finish the sentence. She was Comyn and could do as she pleased, right? Even kill her own son? I wondered if my own mother had ever done anything like that.

"I think about it every day," she said softly. "That was the day I went blind, you know. The healers at Neskaya can't do a damned thing except make namby-pamby mouthings about sorrow and things I don't want to see. Balls to them." She turned her blank eyes on me. "What do you know of the ghost in the hunting lodge?"

"The ... ghost," I repeated. "I don't know anything about it."

"Don't you?"

I started to repeat that I didn't. But the tapping at the back of my head burst into the room. It was like remembering a song you hadn't heard in years. "Yeah. I do. Wasn't there some kind of story about the spirit of a prince who haunted the lord's lodge outside of town? And a queen who wept over the loss of her son? And ... gold. Or something."

Lady Marya slapped her knee. "Ha! You remember more than most. Yes. After the ... disagreement, I returned with the servants to the castle, blind and bewildered. I was sure Aric had just gone missing, but no one seemed worried. I ordered search parties to find him. They gave up after only a few hours. No matter how much I railed or shouted, the searchers always came back, with no clue what I had sent them out to find. Even Robard and Rufus didn't seem worried. I set a reward for anyone who could find Aric.

Do you remember that?"

I thought hard, and shook my head. Even the knocking had stopped.

"Within a week, the search parties ended. Within a month, the reward was still unclaimed. Within a year, no one seemed to remember Aric had even existed."

"But not you," I said.

"But not me," she finished. "I did try to find him at the lodge, but the servants I brought kept forgetting where we were going." Her expression softened, like water slipping off stone. "Sometimes I wonder if Aric even existed at all, or if he was just something I dreamed."

I ran my tongue around the inside of my mouth. "You want me to go find him, don't you?"

She drew out a handkerchief and touched it to her nose. "Everyone else thinks he's dead, or a ghost, or that he never existed. But now that we've talked about him, *you* seem able to remember."

"A little," I said.

"It's the *laran*," she said. "Something went wrong with my Gift. I hit him with it, and now ... everyone's forgotten him, and I've been struck blind. A year passed, and I was ready to let Aric go forever. Then you showed up in my courtyard, an orphan boy this blind woman can't see, and who can remember the dead son everyone has forgotten." She leaned toward me, and her voice cracked just a little. "Can you find him? Name your reward."

"Where do I look?" I asked, and noticed that there seemed to be no doubt that I was actually getting involved.

"The hunting lodge," Lady Marya said. "Start at first light."

I spent the night in a warm stable and set out in the morning with more food in a sack than I had ever seen at one time. My stomach was full, I had new clothes on my back, the morning rain was already beginning to lighten, and I was walking toward a Comyn lady's reward. This had to be a good day. Even though I was in a thick forest filled with animals that could tear me in half. And robbers that would take my food and clothes and skewer me with a rusty pike.

These conflicting thoughts stayed with me until the horses came. I heard their hooves pounding toward me through the trees. My heart beat in my throat. The winding road had already taken me outside the city, farther than I had ever been from the orphanage. Hills and forest stretched out in all directions, and I felt alone and nervous, like a mouse skittering across the kitchen floor at noon.

The horses were growing closer. And then something touched me. A cold finger ran up my back. No, that wasn't it. It was more like a rainstorm that showered over me and wandered up the road, except it didn't quite touch me. In my heart, I knew then that someone was looking for me.

I dove into the bushes with my sack and scrambled under some leaves just as half a dozen horses galloped around the bend behind me. At the head of the group was an older guy. He had fading red hair, a silver chain around his neck, and a look of angry concentration on his face, like he was trying to break a mirror by staring into it. My heart beat a quick step. Lord Robard, and he didn't look happy. The pointy swords he and his men carried didn't look happy, either. I held my breath until they passed without seeing me.

A little shaky, I continued on my way, listening hard in case they came back. Lord Robard didn't want me to look for Aric. That was interesting. I thought. Only Lady Marya and I even remembered him. The problem was, Lord Robard had friends with swords.

Why in nine cold hells was I doing this? All I needed to do was turn around and walk away.

Well, the reward, for one. It would set me up for life. To someone with no family, no skills, and no future, that was a roundhouse punch of an inducement. I trotted down the road, more carefully now, and sighed to myself. There was more to it than a reward, wasn't there? I was in my own fairy tale now. I was the orphan boy going off to save the prince—or the Comynara's son, anyway—and people remembered you for that. It made you ... visible.

And the prince ... who knew what the prince would think, right? It was never bad to have a Comyn lord in your corner. It was never bad to...

Gods, I was such a liar, even to myself. I touched the white scar on my left hand. I hadn't had real friends at the orphanage. A kid who likes to read and who sneaks out to find books instead of beer isn't very popular. Jerrell had been my only companion, and Brother Hiram had ended that. But if you saved someone, they had to like you, right? They had to be your friend, right?

It was worth it to find out.

Eventually, the road opened into a clearing. I was expecting a run-down cottage, but what I found was a smaller version of the castle, suitable for entertaining no more than forty or fifty of your closest friends. It was still run-down, though. The wooden shutters and doors were warping, and I saw lots of broken windows. I peeped at the place from behind a tree. The horses were cropping grass in front of the main gate under bright red sunshine. I have to admit, it occurred to me that I could steal all six of them and be halfway to Neskaya before word of it got back to the castle. And on the heels of that thought, Brother Hiram's stony face burst into my head, waving a hot iron. *This is for the evil you produce!* I touched the white scar on my palm and thought no more about stealing horses.

But now what was I to do? I couldn't go in there, not with Lord Robard doing whatever it was he was doing. Were they hunting? No—the lodge was abandoned, and Robard was looking for someone. For me. I still didn't know why.

Just then, I heard shouts and yells from inside the lodge. All the men burst out of the lodge with Robard right behind them. Their faces were pale, their eyes wild. They leaped onto their horses, wheeled them about, and galloped away. Robard gave the lodge one last look over his shoulder before they all vanished into the woods. What the hell had gotten six grown men armed with pointy swords to run like that? I swallowed and listened. Birds called hesitantly. Insects buzzed. A rabbit-horn burst from the undergrowth near me and scampered away, nearly stopping my heart. I still listened, waiting for a ghostly wail or gibbering goblin. Nothing.

All right. I eased out of the trees and skittered across the small courtyard, half expecting an arrow through my chest or an icy hand on my shoulder. I hesitated at the main door of the lodge. The chilly shadows and smells of mold beyond told my very bones to leave. But thoughts of reward filled my courage. What was a little darkness compared to a pile of gold? Or some visibility?

"Hello?" I called, hesitantly stepping inside. "Anyone here? Aric?"

Silence. My footsteps echoed, and tiny bits of stone rattled down the short stairs I was climbing. The entire place had an oppressive feeling to it, tight as held breath. Shouting would bring punishment. Cobwebs teased at my hair, and I brushed them away. I ended up in a large room with a fireplace at one end. It looked recently used. Weird. Did ghosts light fires?

"Hello?" I made myself call again. "Aric?"

He must have been dead. Lady Marya's spell or *laran* or curse had killed him, and the rest of her magic had cursed this place, striking her blind and making everyone forget him. Any minute now I'd come across Aric's desiccated, animal-ravaged bones, and I'd have to decide whether or not to leave them there or bring back his skull as proof to Lady Marya that he was dead. Wouldn't that be delightful? Maybe he'd be wearing a Comyn ring I could take back instead, though the thought of sliding a ring off dead, bony fingers didn't delight me much, either.

A distant sound caught my ears. A *pock pock pock* of a rock bouncing down stone stairs. My bowels knotted up. Someone— something—else was in this place. Aric's ghost. Or worse, a vengeful spirit that wanted to rip the bones from my flesh and devour my soul.

"...hello?"

The voice was faint, distant. From the bottom of a grave. I wanted to run, but my feet were frozen to the floor. My breath came in tiny gasps.

"Hello?"

The voice was closer now, and more desperate. It sounded like a young man. I swallowed hard and found my voice.

"Aric?"

Silence. Then frantic scrambling. Footsteps clumped toward me from a hallway. I bolted for the entrance and the red sunlight beyond. Just as I reached the door, the voice called again.

"Wait! Please! You can hear me?"

He sounded more frightened than I was. That stopped me.

Whoever heard of a ghost that was scared?

"I'm ... I'm here," I said hoarsely. "Aric?"

The footsteps grew louder. I hovered in the door, ready to bolt. A young man shot into the room. He was maybe a year older than me, dressed in rags worse than my old ones. His hair flamed brighter than any ghost had a right to, and his green eyes put the forest leaves to shame.

"Zandru's hells!" Before I could react much more, he rushed at me, his arms wide, ready for an embrace. I ducked away, my heart pounding again. He pulled back.

"Sorry," he said. "Please don't run away! I'm just ... I'm so glad you're here!"

"I'm glad to see you, too," I said, backing away a little. "I mean ... who are you, exactly?"

"I'm Aric," he said. His eyes were bright. "You called my name!"

"Oh." I nodded. "Yes. You're Aric. My name is Kieron. Were you expecting me?"

Aric swiped at his eyes. "Sorry. I was expecting *anybody*. That was the awful part."

"Your uncle, Robard, was in here a minute ago," I said, trying to get handle on all this. "But he ran away."

"I know." Aric blew out a breath and sank to the stony floor. "I need to sit down. Can you sit down? Can you stay? You're real, right? You *can* see me, right?"

He was babbling. I sat down next to him. "Yeah, I'm real, and I can see you. Shouldn't I?"

Aric reached out to poke at my shoulder, and I pulled away again. "What are you doing?" I asked.

"Sorry," he said. "It's just ... I've been alone for so long. No one to talk to, no one to touch. I wondered if I even existed. You have no idea what it's like. Can I...?"

"Can you what?" I asked suspiciously.

"I just want to touch another person," he said. "So I can feel real. So I know *this* is real. Gods, please?"

All the water left my mouth and my heart raced at the back of my throat. Brother Hiram was shouting inside my head. *The evil you do! Zandru's own filth!* The scar in the center of my hand seemed to burn. I wanted to run away from Aric, leave him and his strange needs. But his face was so earnest, his pain so real. My hands shook.

"Go ahead," I said. "A little."

Aric ran his hand down the side of my face. It made me shiver. His fingers slipped down to my neck and rested lightly on my collar bone. Abruptly his forehead dropped against my shoulder and he was shaking. I didn't move.

"Gods." His voice was hoarse and shaky. "It's been more than a year."

"What has?" I said.

"Since anyone has seen me or talked to me or touched me," he blurted out. "Do you have any idea what that's like? You're my savior!"

Aric sat up and swiped at his eyes with his free hand again, though he kept his other hand on my neck. It seemed to burn, and I thought of Hiram's iron. But I didn't move away.

"I know a little about how that feels," I said. "What do you mean no one can see you? I can see you."

"You're the only one," he said, and his hand strayed back toward my face. He couldn't seem to help it, like his fingers were hungry. I swallowed but let it happen. "Any time someone comes in here, they look right through me. I shout and dance and wave my arms, but they act like they don't see or hear a thing. I've tried grabbing their arms, but they ... dodge away or slide aside without even seeming to realize what they're doing. I've shouted and thrown stuff and eventually they get scared and run away."

"How do you eat?" I asked.

"Hunting and stealing," he said. "The farms south of here all think there's a thief. I've walked right in and taken bread from the kitchen, and they didn't see me. I'll have to find a way to pay them back. At first it was kind of funny, but after a month, believe me— you'd do anything for someone to talk to you."

"So go home," I said.

"I've tried." Aric's hands were on my face again. He didn't even seem to notice. I ... still let him. He seemed to need it to bad and ... well, it felt nice to get a caress instead of a blow. Aric was looking at my features, studying them, as if I had been invisible all these months instead of him.

"Every time I headed home," he continued sadly, "I felt ... scared. I got an hour, maybe two, down the road before I had to turn back. This is the only place I felt safe. I can't explain it."

"Then how did you steal food from farms?"

"The farms are just over that hill. Close enough to grab something before the fear gets me, if I'm quick. And I set snares for rabbit-horns. Winter was the worst, in this ruin, all alone."

I nodded and gently took his wrist to pry his hand away from my cheek. His face flushed brighter than his hair.

"Sorry," he mumbled. "I just ... it's been so long. Right now, I'd touch a banshee-bird. And you're ... my savior."

I said, "It's okay. I'm not going anywhere. Here." I put his hand on my shoulder. "How about that?"

He was still flushing, but he nodded. His hand was warm, even through my new cloak and tunic.

"Is my mother all right?" he asked. "I haven't seen her since ... all this happened."

"She's still up at the castle," I evaded. "What happened last year?"

Aric inhaled hard and blew out a heavy sigh. "Mother and I got into an argument. Right here, in fact. It was a stupid. One minute we were talking, and then we were arguing, and then we were shouting, and then ... everything exploded all around us. I woke up with a bad headache, and everyone was gone."

His hand stayed on my shoulder. It was heavy. Now that I was calming down a little, I noticed other details- the way his hair was uncombed, the silver chain around his neck, his sharp cheekbones and long jaw. Brother Hiram screamed at me inside my head again.

"I tried to leave, go home, but I didn't get even halfway," Aric said. "Every time people came here to look for me, they saw straight through me. It didn't matter what I said or did, they didn't see me."

"Invisible," I murmured.

"Eventually all of them got scared of something and ran away," Aric finished. "Then they stopped coming altogether. Until Uncle Robard showed up today. And you. Why can you see me?"

I shrugged. "No idea. I grew up in Brother Hiram's orphanage, and if it wasn't in a book I could beg, borrow, or steal, I don't know about it."

He looked at me strangely. "Didn't he get you apprenticed? Or at least a menial job?"

"No. He brought work in to us. Mostly tailor stuff—sewing piecework—or making quilts and blankets. Brother Hiram said we had to earn our keep."

"What?" Aric looked outraged. "Every month my mother sends the orphanage one silver penny for each orphan. That's to cover food, clothes, and everything else, including apprenticeships."

I touched the scar on my palm. "Nope. Nothing like that. We didn't go out much. If we wanted to play outside, we went to the roof. I think a lot of the people didn't even know they lived by an orphanage."

"Hiram was keeping the money for himself!" Aric said in disbelief. "And if he made you work all day on piecework, he was probably collecting money for that as well."

"In the evenings he had us read lessons," I said.

"Avarra's tits!" Aric got up and paced. "It's still going on, isn't it? We have to do something!"

"What will we do?" I asked. The way he got angry about it made me feel good. "I'm just an orphan, and you're ... you."

Aric came back and slumped down next to me, leaning against me like an overly friendly dog. "We still don't know why you can see me."

"It probably has something to do with your mother," I said. "She couldn't see me at all."

"What do you mean?"

Oh, boy. I took a deep breath of my own. "Your mother's been blind since the ... accident. She finds her way around by sensing the minds of the people around her. But she couldn't sense my mind."

"Mother is *blind?*" Aric sat up. "Because of me? Because of what I did?"

"You don't know that," I said quickly. "It's okay. We'll figure it out. Come on." I got up and held out my hand to him. He took it and pulled himself upright.

"Where are we going?"

"Back home. Your home," I said. "The castle. We're going to

sort this out."

"I can't go that far," he said.

When you live in an orphanage, you make do with what you have. Right now, the only thing I had was a prince with two legs who thought he couldn't walk. I caught up my sack of food and walked out of the lodge.

"Wait!" Aric ran to follow. "Where are you going?"

I kept walking. "Back to the castle."

"You can't leave me!" he said. "I can't be alone again!"

"Sure, okay." But I kept on walking. Aric stopped a few paces outside the lodge. I could feel his uncertainty and desperation behind me, but I didn't look back. By the time I reached the road at the wood's edge, his frantic footsteps caught up with me.

"I'm coming," he said. "You're a *nedestro* bastard."

"Could be," I said. "I did grow up in an orphanage."

We walked for several minutes. Aric's face became a mask of fear, and I felt kind of sorry for him, but there wasn't anything I could do. "I think I know what's going on," I offered as a distraction. "Why you're invisible."

"Yeah?" He swallowed. "Why?"

"People don't see me, either," I said. "When I walked into the castle to look for work, people looked straight through me. I'm not really invisible like in a fairy tale or anything, but no one wants to see me because I'm poor and my clothes are bad and I don't have anything they want. The only person who saw me was your mother, and that was because I had something she needed—the power to find you."

"All right," Aric said doubtfully.

"*Laran* works all in your head, right? It changes the way you think, right?"

"Among other things."

"That's what happened, then. You and your mom are Comyn. You got into a fight, and you hit each other with *laran*, or something. It went bad. Now she can't see anything, and no one can see you. I mean, they *do* see you, but their minds don't let them notice you. Like they don't notice me. Just more powerful. And it's scary for them, seeing but not seeing at the same time, so they run away from you. The ... *laran* spell or whatever it is also makes you scared to leave the lodge."

"That ... makes a lot of sense," Aric said slowly. "But what do we do about it?"

I shrugged. "You're the Comyn lord, not me."

"There has to be more to it than this," he said, more to himself than me. "What would power a spell like that?"

"You still have that matrix thing, right?" Greatly daring, I reached for the long chain around his neck.

Aric drew back sharply. "Don't! You can't touch someone else's matrix. It's like touching their mind, and it hurts like you wouldn't believe."

"Oh. Can I see it?"

From under his filthy, ragged tunic, Aric pulled a locket wrapped in tattered silk. Carefully he opened it. Inside lay a small crystal the color of autumn water. Tiny lights flickered inside like fireflies. It was the most beautiful thing I'd ever seen.

"What's it do?" I asked.

"It amplifies and focuses *laran*," he said.

"What can you do with your *laran*?"

"Not much," he admitted. "I can sense what other people are feeling. If I concentrate really hard, I can sometimes make out thoughts."

"Can you tell what I'm feeling?" My gut grew tight, and I didn't know why.

Aric shook his head. "You're a blank to me. I can't even tell you're there." He nodded at the matrix in his hand. "My *laran* isn't powerful enough to make people's minds stop seeing me. Mother's is very powerful. So is Uncle Robard's. They can both work with feelings and thoughts. But I've never heard of them making anyone invisible."

I nodded and we kept walking. "So what did your uncle want just now? It's weird that he came down here just after your mother sent me."

"Yeah. I dunno." Aric rewrapped his matrix locket and dropped it back under his tunic. He was sweating a little. "He was calling my name, and the men looked like they thought he was crazy. I was shouting back like I always do when someone shows up, and then they ran away. And you came in."

"I think I can see you for the same reason your mother can't see me," I said. "My mind is immune to *laran*."

"Zandru! Don't spread that around!" Aric glanced about, as if someone might jump out of the bushes. "A Gift that makes someone immune to *laran*? The Comyn would want that suppressed, and fast. Any children of your line would be ... well, they wouldn't want you to have children, let's end it at that."

"I don't think we have to worry about that," I mumbled.

"Your hair is kind of red," Aric went on, and more sweat ran down his face. "You must have some distant Comyn ancestry that's showing up now as a wild Gift."

"My ancestors could be anyone," I said. "I was left on the orphanage doorstep, wrapped in a blanket. Are you all right?"

Aric took deep breaths. "Nervous. Scared. I should go back."

"It's all in your head," I told him. "There's nothing to be scared of. Have some food, and let's try walking fast to keep your mind of it."

The meat-filled rolls and apples in my sack were fantastic, the best food I'd ever eaten. Aric barely nibbled on them, though he'd been living on game and stolen food for more than a year and must have been dying for something from his home kitchen. I could see his nervousness increase. He started at every sound, like a rabbit-horn in wolf's den. I didn't like seeing him this way.

"I can't!" he burst out suddenly, and spun to run back.

I saw the reward running back to the lodge with him. Without thinking, I lunged for him and managed to grab his arm. The muscles moved under my hand. It was the first time *I* had deliberately touched someone else in the last year. Even Aric had only touched me, not the other way around.

"Don't!" I barked. "You have to stay!"

To my surprise, he did. Aric relaxed a little in my grip. His breathing eased and he turned wide green eyes on me.

"I'm better," he said. "When you touched me, I stopped being so scared."

In answer, I took my hand away. The terror returned to Aric's face, and he tried to bolt again. I shot forward and caught his arm again. He calmed.

"That's so strange," he said, turning red again. "Uh ... I guess it means...”

“Yeah.” I ran my free hand through my hair. Now *my* heart was pounding, and my mouth was dry, and I didn't know if it was because of Aric's arm in my hand or the memory of Brother Hiram standing over me.

Aric clasped my left hand. “All the way back?”

“Looks like,” I said in a hoarse voice.

Abruptly he opened my palm and ran a tapped my scar. “So what is this?”

I was ready to bolt myself, but his fingers on my hand weakened my knees and I couldn't have run from a mountain lion. “Uh ... it'll make you angry.”

Aric traced the scar with his fingertip. It sent a soft shiver all the way through me. This touch was more personal, more familiar than any touch in my life.

“You can't make me angry,” he said. “You're my savior.”

“My prince.” The words slipped out before I could stop them.

“What?” He looked at me with those impossibly green eyes.

Now I flushed. “I ... kind of imagined myself in a fairy tale, you know? The orphan who looks for work at the castle and end up saving the prince. It's stupid, I know.”

“No. It's not stupid. Never stupid.” His voice was quiet and even, like moonlight sliding over grass. “If you're my savior, I'm your prince. Or the son of a *domna,* anyway. But what made this scar?”

He touched it again, and I couldn't have kept quiet about it any more than a snowflake can stay frozen in a fireplace.

“Brother Hiram,” I said. “When my voice started to break, he took me to the cellar and beat me black and blue.”

“What in Zandru's name for?” Aric asked, shocked.

“He said to remind me never to ... touch myself for evil. He does that to all the boys.”

We were walking again, hand in hand. It was the strangest thing, holding hands with a male. I felt naked somehow, and I scanned the trees for some time before I remembered Brother Hiram was back in Haydentown and couldn't possibly see me. Could he?

“For that? All boys do that,” Aric said. “Men, too, if the way the hunters snicker among themselves is accurate.”

"But later I did it with someone else," I said in a rush. "Another boy. At the orphanage. His name was Jerrell. Brother Hiram found out and heated up a fireplace iron. That was a year ago."

"And you haven't touched anyone since," Aric finished. "Zandru's hells! And then I asked if I could touch you. I'm so sorry, Kieron."

I barked a laugh. "You spent the year cursed with invisibility, but *I'm* the one who gets the apology?"

"Just because I have problems doesn't mean you have none," he said, and squeezed my hand slightly. My breath caught in my chest. What did that squeeze mean? I both wanted to know and didn't want to know at the same time. I kept my eyes straight ahead and lengthened my stride. Aric hurried to keep up.

We reached the castle at about the same time the food in my sack gave out. This was the second time I'd climbed that stupid hill in two days, and I could see why no one would want to attack the castle—you'd be half dead by the time you got to the top. I started to pull my hand away before anyone saw, but Aric held it tighter.

"You were raised by a cruel *cristoforo* who rarely let you out of the orphanage," he said. "But out here, no one cares about two *bredu* clasping hands, Kieron. Men can love men, women can love women. It's not evil."

We were nearing the castle gate now. It seemed to jump and sway. The world was turning gently upside-down. In all my time with Brother Hiram, I had never questioned anything he said. Now...

"Everyone will think we're ... you know." I said, still not able to wrap my head around it. "Even though we're not."

"So?" he returned. "They won't care either way. Besides, I thought you were worried about being the invisible orphan. If they notice, you won't be invisible anymore."

I was getting nervous now. Fear twisted like a cold snake in my gut, and I wanted to run back to the lodge. Brother Hiram was waiting up there at the castle, talking to *Dom* Robard about me, I knew it, and he was heating an iron in the fire. My scar seemed to burn.

"If they don't care, I'll still be invisible," I said. "If they do care, I'll be visible in the worst way."

"Yeah." Aric squeezed again and flashed me a smile, the first one I'd seen from him. It was sunshine from behind a cloud. "You'll be visible clasping hands with a Comyn lord."

"We don't even know if they'll see you," I objected.

"Then it won't matter if we're holding hands." He raised a red eyebrow at me. Getting closer to the castle was raising his spirits now, even as it lowered mine. "Why does it matter to you what other people think?"

"Hot irons," I said promptly.

"You can march down to that orphanage this very day and kick Hiram in the balls, if you want," Aric said. "I won't stop you. You're not a child, Kieron. You've already saved me. Now you can save yourself. And I have one last question for you."

We were only a few paces from the gate, and I could see people going about their business in the courtyard beyond. "What?"

He looked me straight in the eye, and his gaze went straight to my heart. "Are we holding hands because we have to, or because we want to?"

I stopped then and stared at the ground. A war fought inside me, fast and furious. I was doing this for the reward, and for enough gold, I'd hold hands with a ya-man. It had nothing to do with how I felt. Nothing!

Except ... standing here with Aric felt right. It felt good. It was finding a home. To him, I was a savior. To him, I wasn't invisible.

But my scar still burned with painful memory.

"I don't hold hands with men," I said in a cold voice. "Once I get you to your mother, I'll collect the reward and head for Neskaya. That's the only reason I went down there, and the only reason I'm still here."

Aric's expression broke like an ale mug thrown into a fireplace, and my heart dropped cold into my shoes. I had to look away. This was the best way. It was the *only* way. I marched toward the castle gate, towing Aric behind so I wouldn't have to look at him. His hand turned chilly in mine.

The courtyard bustled with daily activity. Stable workers and a blacksmith and kitchen boys and serving maids made a small crowd. They hung out of windows and shouted across the stones. The hammer rang on the anvil. Horses neighed. Chickens squawked. It was a busy place.

No one gave us the slightest notice. At first, Aric's face lit up at being home, though he avoided looking at me, and he called out to people by name. Everyone ignored him. When we approached a pair of stable boys, they turned aside without seeming to realize what they were doing.

"They still can't see me," Aric said sadly.

"They don't see me, either," I said, and waved frantically at a passing maid. She continued on her way without acknowledging me. "Your curse is affecting me. What happens if I let go of your hand?"

Before he could answer, I pulled my hand away to find out.

Everything happened very fast. The maid and several other people near me screamed. "Demon!" "Ghost!" "Run!" The horses whinnied. Servants exploded in all directions, dropping what they held and fleeing.

Aric went dead white. Deep, gut-wrenching terror twisted his face. He froze for a tiny moment, then spun and bolted for the castle gate. It took me half a second to understand what was happening—the curse hadn't let him go far from the hunting lodge, but with my help he had gone much farther than the curse normally allowed. Several miles of terror had slammed into him all at once.

I sprinted after him, but Aric was pushed by panic.

"Aric!" I shouted. "No!"

He didn't hear me. I ran faster. Damn it! He couldn't get away, not now, not with the reward so close. I leaped and caught him in a flying tackle. We went down in a tangle on the cobblestones just inside the gate. People were still screaming and slamming doors and shutters. Aric twisted and fought like a drowning cat. I hauled him around on his back and scrambled on top of his chest so he had to look at me. His emerald eyes were wide with terror.

"It's okay." I put a hand on his cheek, skin on skin. "You have to calm down. It's all in your head."

"Let me go!" he howled. "Zandru's demons! Let me go! It'll get me!"

I didn't know what to do. Me touching him didn't seem to help now. And he was strong. I couldn't hold him for much longer.

"Let me go!" he yelled again.

I knew what Aric was feeling. Fear and terror were trousers and tunic that I pulled on every morning with my shoes. I also knew I didn't want him to feel so horrible, to feel so scared. I did the only thing I could think of—I leaned down and kissed him.

Aric's eyes widened, and he stiffened beneath me. But his screams stopped. His lips were warm on mine, and my left hand, the scarred one, was still on his face. It went on for a long time. Aric's body relaxed. His arm went around my neck, and he kissed me back. My soul paired with Aric's, and we soared to the skies, trailing silver light that filled the universe. The memory of Brother Hiram shattered into a thousand shards. At Aric's touch, I felt, for the first time, truly visible.

"I lied," I whispered to him. "It was because I wanted to."

"I know," he said. "My savior."

"My prince," I replied.

"My, my," said a new voice.

We looked up. *Dom* Robard was standing over us with his arms folded. A pang went through me. We were caught! We were—

"Looks like you found a way around the curse, Aric," he said. "True love's kiss, is it?"

Aric and I scrambled to our feet without letting go of our hands. "I'm back, Uncle," Aric said. "It's been a year, but I'm—"

"Wait," I interrupted. A terrible thought came over me. It slid together like clouds forming a thunderhead. A chill went down my spine. "He can see you, Aric. He can *see.*"

Aric stared. "You can, Uncle. Why is that?"

Before Robard could reply, I said, "Because he created the curse in the first place. You said he can work with feelings. Can he make them stronger? Can he, say, turn a small argument into a big fight?"

"And why would I do that?" Robard sneered.

"Lady Marya told me you're marrying that strumpet Nanna to solidify Rufus's claim as heir," I said. "But Aric was born first to your older sister. He's the real heir of Hayden. For Rufus to inherit, you needed to get Aric out of the way, and without a hint of scandal. How better than to make him just ... disappear?"

"You're an idiot, boy," Robard growled. "You make accusations against your betters, and you'll pay a heavy price for it."

"You damned bastard!" Lady Marya strode across the courtyard, her hair wild, her eyes blank, her expression furious. "All this time I thought I was the one who did away with Aric. The guilt wrecked me. But it was *you!*"

"Well, damn it." Robard dropped the pretense with a little chuckle. "To be fair, Marya, it was at least partly you, too. It was a fine bit of deception, you have to admit. The little smear of shit here whined and moped about how he didn't want to father an heir because boys were more interesting to him. And you got angry. And he got angry. It wasn't that big a fight, and you were dangerously close to working things out. So I ... nudged." He fingered the silver chain around his neck, and I caught a glimpse of a wrapped locket similar to Aric's at his breastbone. "Once things grew more heated, you didn't want to see him, and he didn't want to see you. You struck him with the family Gift, and I got behind you to push. Boom. No one could see anybody any more."

"Aric!" Lady Marya cast about. "Aric, are you there? I can't see you!"

"I'm here, Mother!" he said, but couldn't move far from me without letting go of my hand.

"Aric!" she cried again.

"You still can't sense him or hear him," Robard said. "Fantastic!" He glanced at Aric. "Thanks to that little tiff and a push from me, your own *laran* prevents people from seeing you, boy, and your own fear prevents you from leaving the lodge. Marya, you're in the same blind boat. Delightful! My older sister can't see a thing, and no one alive can see my nephew." He laughed. "I win. Rufus wins. Hells, even Nanna wins. The little strumpet."

"But now we know the truth," I said, and realized I was standing a little in front of Aric. "That means you've lost."

"Really?" The laughter left his voice and he drew his sword, shiny and sharp. "Let's take accounts. The only people who know anything are a ghost who can't be seen, a woman who can't see, and an invisible orphan boy. In just a moment, the woman will be dead, killed by the demon boy who appeared out of nowhere in my courtyard. I'll hold your heart over my head, demon, and be remembered a hero."

Lady Marya gasped. "You don't dare, Robard!"

"Let's find out." He drew back his blade to swing at Marya.

He wasn't looking at me, the invisible orphan beneath his notice. I didn't even think. I leaped forward and grabbed the chain around his neck. With a yank, I brought the locket—and his matrix—into the palm of my hand. The silk tore away and I felt hard silver.

Pain smashed through me. An explosion knocked me backward into Aric. I couldn't tell who was screaming more, Aric or me. The screaming went on and on. I heard Lady Marya's voice as well. A blue pillar of light blasted up into the sky. Aric was beneath my back, his skin hot against mine. Red pain tore through my muscles and raked my nerves. My throat was raw from the screaming. I would have gladly died to make it stop.

And then it did stop. I lay there, amazed at how wonderful a lack of pain could feel. Aric groaned under me and I rolled off him so I could get to my feet. I completely forgot to hold his hand, and a moment later, I lunged for him, expecting to have to catch him again, but he only sat up and rubbed his face.

"What happened?" he asked.

"Aric!" Lady Marya also got to her feet and flew across the courtyard. She snatched her son into a hard embrace. Tears ran down her face. "Oh, Aric! My son! It's so good to see you!"

"You can see me?" Aric said in her arms. "Mother! You can see me?"

She backed away and held him at arm's length. "I can! I can see you. I can see the castle. I can *see!* Blessed Cassilda!"

"Can you see Kieron?" Aric asked. "He's the one you need to thank."

Lady Marya turned to me, the tears still on her face. "I can damned well see you, too. And what a fine, handsome boy you are! You saved my son, and that makes you also my son." She embraced me, too.

Something inside me broke. I had always wondered what it was like to have a mother, someone who held you and kissed your wounds and called you nice names. Now I had that, and it made my eyes fill. I felt weak and small and big and strong all at once.

"You're welcome, *vai domna,*" I choked.

"Marya," she said. "Just Marya."

"Uncle," Aric said.

All three of us turned. Robard lay face-down on the cobblestones. Aric and I rolled him over. He was unconscious, and his ears were bleeding.

"What happened to him?" I asked.

"Overload," Marya said. "He was using his *laran* to keep mine and Aric's bound up. When you touched his matrix, your immunity created powerful feedback. It hit him hard. Good."

People were trickling back into the courtyard now, slipping out of doors and opening shutters to see what had happened.

"What will we do with him?" Aric asked.

"The Keeper at Neskaya will decide," Marya said. "His crimes were extensive, and his punishment will be as well."

"So you brought me back to the castle *and* broke the curse." Aric clapped me on the back. "You're not just my savior. You're everyone's savior!"

"Lord Aric?" An older man in blue bustled up. "Lord Aric! It's you! I can't believe ... we thought you were ... that is, I don't what remember what..."

"I know, Frederick," Aric said. "We'll explain everything to everyone, but first we need shackles for Uncle Robard."

"And who is this?" Frederick asked doubtfully, and I felt myself shrink a little under his hard gaze.

"This?" Aric took my hand. He turned to the crowd of people who had assembled in the courtyard. "This is my savior, my *bredu*." Aric lowered his voice. "Tell them your name."

I stared at all those eyes, a crowd of them staring back at me. For a moment, fear clutched at me, and I thought about fleeing back to the hunting lodge, or even the orphanage. But Aric had my hand, and I raised my head high.

"My name is Kieron," I said. "I found Aric Hayden, I broke his curse, and I made him my *bredu.*"

A cheer erupted from the crowd. Aric pulled me to him, and, to my surprise, kissed me hard. The world turned upside-down again. I wasn't an orphan, and I wasn't invisible.

"My savior," Aric whispered in my ear.

"My prince," I whispered back.

"Know what I want to do now?"

I was grinning like an idiot now. "What?"

"It would be great fun," he said, "to go down to that orphanage and kick Brother Hiram in the balls. Repeatedly. And then we'll put someone else in charge of the orphanage. And then we'll have to figure out why you're immune to *laran*."

I thought about that. "Can we have supper first?"

He laughed and kissed me again.

THE MOUNTAINS OF LIGHT

by Robin Wayne Bailey

Any place as long-settled as Darkover has acquired its share of myths and legends, some rooted in truth, others pure fabrication from the wilds of the human imagination. When a nonhuman race like the *chieri* are added, these stories can become even richer and more fantastic ... which makes human explorers even more dedicated to unraveling those mysteries. And where better to find them than in the majestic, glaciated Hellers Range, The Wall Around the World?

Robin Wayne Bailey is the author of numerous novels, including the *Dragonkin* trilogy and the *Frost* series, as well as *Shadowdance* and the Fritz Leiber-inspired *Swords Against the Shadowland.* His short fiction has appeared in many magazines and anthologies with numerous appearances in Marion Zimmer Bradley's *Sword And Sorceress* series and Deborah J. Ross's *Lace And Blade* volumes. Some of his stories have been collected in two volumes, *Turn Left to Tomorrow* and *The Fantastikon,* from Yard Dog Books. He's a former two-term president of the Science Fiction and Fantasy Writers of America and a founder of the Science Fiction Hall of Fame. He's the co-editor, along with Bryan Thomas Schmidt, of *Little Green Men— Attack!*

In heavy coats and fur cloaks, bound together by a stout rope, three weary figures trudged up the last snowy slope, their hooded eyes constantly shifting from their uncertain footing to the ancient observatory at the summit. Their boots were soaked, their toes near frozen, and their mittened hands fared no better. The light of two frosty moons, Idriel and Liriel, in a sea of bright stars lit their way, and three long shadows stretched out far before the climbers

"I knew it was real," Amira said through thick, woolen mufflers,

164

"but I didn't really believe it. Does that make any sense?"

In the lead, Micah stopped, leaned on a walking staff, and looked up at the rough-hewn structure. "Perfect sense, Amira," Micah answered in a deep voice. "When one is confronted with a mystery like this, something so far out of time, the mind may become a jumble. I dare say I feel the same."

The third figure, Jubal, stared back down the mountain, his eyes watchful, and suspicious. "We're still too exposed," he said as he adjusted his backpack. "We should hurry and get inside."

The two moons rose higher in the sky, and a third moon, Kyrrdis, sailed up over the eastern horizon. The light of three moons distorted and twisted their shadows, but it also set the snow ablaze with shimmering fire. The distant mountain peaks glowed like beacons.

"I've never seen anything like this!" Amira exclaimed. Her pale eyes shone with excitement above her mufflers as she brushed away the icicles that clung to her eyebrows and lashes.

Micah stopped again to look around and glanced upward. "There are so few times in our lives when we experience true awe," he allowed.

"If you don't keep moving," Jubal grumbled, "the only thing we're likely to experience is true death. If you don't mind, I'm freezing."

Despite the cold and discomfort, Amira smiled to herself. She missed the dry clothes and warm blankets they had left behind with their pack animals two days before, and they were perilously low on water and brandy, yet she had never felt so alive. Beneath the layers of snow, there probably lay a trail as old and forgotten as the observatory, overgrown perhaps, broken and barely visible to an ordinary eye, but right now she felt like an explorer, the first to ever walk this range. Certain at last of their destination, she gazed in all directions and marveled.

The *chieri* called this place *The Mountains of Light*. Most of Darkover considered them a myth. Only a very small handful knew that the mountains really existed; fewer still where they really were. Not even the Terrans with their advanced technology and space surveying capabilities knew of these mountains. That was another mystery.

A flight of snow-covered steps led up toward a set of immense doors so tarnished and corroded by time that they had turned black. They looked like an uninviting maw in the face of the domed structure.

"Are we supposed to knock?" Jubal grumbled as he shifted his backpack again. Forgetting the rope that bound them together, he walked forward, and brought up suddenly short, slipped on ice and sat down roughly.

"No need to knock," Amira answered, trying not to laugh. "They know we're here, and they're coming." She touched Micah's arm as she gazed up toward the top of the dome. "How old is this?" she whispered.

"As near as we can estimate, it pre-dates Landfall by some millennia," he answered in a quiet voice. "It might be the best evidence yet for your theory that the *chieri* are not native to this planet, either." He helped Jubal up and then untied the rope that bound them together.

Amira hugged herself inside her cloaks. It wasn't the cold that made her shiver, though. She could hear the starstones inside the observatory, hear them singing their strange, inaudible songs in the dark vaults below. She felt them calling to her. Neither Micah or Jubal heard. They didn't have *laran*.

With a scraping of metal hinges, a smaller portal opened at the base of one of the immense doors. A beam of amber light spread across the snow, and a thin shadow appeared. An old man surveyed the three from the entrance.

"Well, invite us in!" Jubal snapped. "Can't you see it's snowing?"

The old man looked at Amira, and his gaze lingered. "You may come in," he said finally. To Micah he said, "I may admit you later, but only if his temper improves."

Jubal sputtered. Amira looked at both of her companions. At a nod from Micah, she walked toward the door and inside. The old man closed the door again. She felt warmth on her face. She had thought her face would never feel warm again.

You can hear me, child?

Amira jerked around as her host spoke to her telepathically. Instinctively, she pushed him out of her mind. Then, noting the sudden pinched look around the old man's gray eyes, she regretted her defensiveness. "My apology," she said aloud. "I've learned to guard myself."

"That is a smart thing," her host acknowledged before entering her thoughts again, *when you have such strong* laran *and belong to no Comyn family.*

"Your name is Olin," she answered, demonstrating that she could enter his thoughts, as well. *You belong to no Comyn family, either.*

Olin's eyes twinkled suddenly as he grinned. *Delightful!* he said in her mind. *Your thoughts are not just your thoughts—they invoke the taste of violets! You are synesthetic, as well as telepathic!*

Amira frowned. She was aware of her strange defect. She was also aware that Olin was holding something back. "My friends," she said pointedly, "are freezing outside."

"Your friends," Olin answered back, "are not who they appear to be. One of them poses a serious threat to us. I asked you inside first because I wanted you to be aware of this, if you are not already."

"That's ridiculous," Amira said. "I've just traveled halfway around the world by aircar and pack animal with Micah and Jubal. I think I know them pretty well by now."

Olin regarded her for a long moment, and Amira felt him probing at the edges of her mind. She kicked him in the shins. "That's rude," she warned him. "Don't do it again without permission. Now bring them in out of the cold."

"Did you really think we would leave them to freeze? They are already inside safe and warm. You are invited guests, after all."

Amira frowned as Olin led the way deeper into the observatory. As she followed the old man through winding corridors under dim illumination panels, she probed ahead with her mind and telepathically sensed the others who were waiting, among them Micah and Jubal. As Olin had said, they were safe and warm, and she felt bad for kicking him.

At the end of the winding corridor another portal opened. As Amira followed Olin inside, she caught her breath.

The observatory's central chamber was a vast complex of computers filled with pale glowing monitors and arrays of mysterious blinking colored lights. However, all the modern technology faded into insignificance in the presence of the towering old-style telescope. Amira stared, wide-eyed. "Does that work?" she whispered.

Olin shook his head. "The great mirrors are cracked, and the dome was long ago frozen shut." Her host stared upward, too, then shrugged. "We could repair the mechanisms, I suppose."

"But who built it?"

"We have no idea," Olin answered.

Micah and Jubal stood on the far side of the chamber in conversation with four other men. All looked toward Amira, and she felt their thoughts. She recoiled, thinking that she had inadvertently breached good manners. She had spent her young life learning not to invade the thoughts of others. Indeed, she had struggled to conceal the fact that she even had such ability. She rubbed her temples, feeling strange, and frowned again.

Micah smiled when he saw her. He broke off the conversation, and strode across the chamber with a brisk stride. Jubal followed Micah. Both had shed their cloaks and coats. The other four came along, as well. They had the look, like Olin, of men who had been here a long time.

The four introduced themselves. The tallest was Steven Glencallow, then a man who called himself only Cadmus. He looked liked the oldest among them. The third named himself as Kennard Ardais. An Ardais! A member of the Great Families here!

The fourth figure proved to be no man at all. She pushed back a thin hood to reveal close-cropped hair, hard features, and bright, wise eyes. "Call me Camilla," she said, extending a hand to Amira. "I have read all your papers on the archeology of Darkover. Your work is very insightful."

"Inspiring," Glencallow added.

Like Olin, Camilla was also strongly telepathic. Amira sensed the old woman's curiosity and scrutiny like soft hammer blows at the back of her head. Amira pushed back against it, but Camilla remained gently in the background.

"You've all had a hard journey," Olin interrupted. We have food ready and rooms for each of you. After you've rested, we'll talk some more and explain the purpose for which we've invited you."

Amira slept uneasily on a hard bed that was really little more than a cot. Her body ached from the long journey through the mountains and, wrapping herself in her blanket, she got up several times to stumble and pace around her small room, hoping to work the cramps out of her legs. In the dim light of a single lamp, she studied the bare stone walls and the low ceiling, and felt strangely claustrophobic. Her head ached, as well, and that was the worst of it, the dull hum behind her temples and at the base of her skull.

She blamed the mountainous altitude. Now that the initial awe was passed, she was more aware of the thinner air and the faster beat of her heart. She couldn't seem to draw a complete breath, nor could she quite get warm. She lay back down on her bed, drew the covers up to her neck and wondered why she had ever left the lowlands of Thendara.

But then, even through her discomfort, she remembered the day Micah had shown up at Thendara University, how he had appeared in her office doorway and spoken her name. Her breath had caught then, too, as she regarded him like a wide-eyed school girl, recognizing him at once by bearing and appearance as a Terran officer, retired as it turned out.

A gentle knock interrupted her thoughts, and she rose from bed again. When she opened the door, Camilla stood there. She wore a look of concern. "Are you all right?" she inquired in a soft voice.

Amira looked puzzled to see the taller woman so late. "Why do you ask?"

Camilla put a fingertip to her temple. "You're broadcasting," she answered.

Puzzlement turned to shock. "I'm so sorry!" Amira beckoned for Camilla to enter and brightened the lamp. "I don't know what's wrong with me! I'm usually much more guarded, but this headache...!"

Camilla smiled sympathetically. "Does Micah know how you feel about him?"

"Good heavens, no," Amira answered. Then she sighed. "At least, I hope not."

"A silly hope," the taller woman answered as she settled into the room's only comfortable chair. "Such things shouldn't go unspoken. Do you know your thoughts smell like roses? It's quite nice, actually."

Amira sat down on her bed as she picked up a stray thought from Camilla. She had known Micah for a long time. "Olin said that one of us poses a threat. Is it Micah because he's a Terran?"

Camilla laughed lightly. "Olin is an old fool sometimes," she answered. Then she leaned forward, serious. "If anyone is a threat right now, it's you, Amira. You're so young, so talented, and not yet fully comfortable with your abilities because you've been hiding them from others for so long."

Amira looked down at the floor for a long moment. "I never wanted the Comyn to know. They would have taken me away from my parents, and I don't, well, I don't trust them. I don't trust any of the Families."

Camilla nodded. "So you hid in plain sight and eventually established yourself as an archeologist and anthropologist at the new university in Thendara. That's a rare occupation. You see, we know quite a lot about you, Amira. We've been observing you."

Amira leaned forward and clutched her hands together. "But why? Why me?"

Camilla also leaned forward and caught Amira's hands between her own. "Because you have a role to play, child," she said, "and more *laran* than you know." Releasing Amira's hands with a soft pat, she rose to her feet and backed toward the door. "Try to get some sleep, dear."

When Amira was alone again, she got up, dimmed the lamp once more and crawled back into bed with the covers drawn high. In the darkness, she tried to calm her chaotic thoughts and the pounding of her heart through meditation and breathing. With a measure of success, she sank into her pillow.

Yet, in the background her head still ached, and there was something else, the singing of soft, dark voices. Not the songs of the starstones—she still heard their faint music, too—but something else, unusual and alien, harmonic, yet soothing and reassuring. The music eased her headache. She closed her eyes and slept.

Amira woke to an intense quiet, completely rested and relaxed. For a few moments, she lay still in bed, clinging to the edges of fading dreams. She wondered where Micah was, and Jubal, too. As she sat up, she looked around her room. She hadn't been alone for a very long time, and these few moments of silence felt like a luxury.

Good morning, Amira. She shot a look toward the door before realizing that Olin was speaking directly into her head.

Where are you? she asked, not bothering to conceal her irritation.

In the commissary, he answered. *We're all here having some breakfast. I sensed you were awake and thought you might like to join us.*

She perked up, surprised to discover that she was famished. She dressed quickly. All the living rooms were on the same ground level, but the corridors were maze-like. She made her way through them with a surety, but she wondered if she was remembering the way on her own or if Olin had subtly implanted the route in her memory. Telepathy was such a tricky art.

Before she reached her destination, the smells of cooking tickled her nose, and her stomach rumbled. She picked up her pace and pushed open the commissary doors. Everyone was there, including Micah and Jubal. Micah rose from his seat at table, indicated another seat at his right-hand side, and held it for Amira. "Good morning," he said, smiling. Jubal just stared at his plate with a troubled look on his face.

"I hope you slept well, Amira." Kennard Ardais rose from his seat and executed a slight bow. "I'm afraid our quarters are not lavish."

Amira laughed. "I've been sleeping on the ground for the better part of two months! The beds here are paradise." She sniffed as she sat down and gazed over the table. "I haven't seen so much food, either!"

"Your arrival is cause for celebration," Camilla said.

Glencallow also rose to bow, and then sat back down. "After breakfast, I'll give you a better tour of the observatory, the computers and equipment." He nodded toward Micah. "The good major is the real expert, of course. I'm sure he'll come along with us."

"I want to go outside," Jubal declared without looking up from his plate. He seemed sullen, uneasy, but then, he often was that way. Amira resisted the urge to probe him and learn what was wrong. She glanced at Micah, who just shrugged, and in that small, seemingly innocent gesture, she briefly thought she saw something else, something he was hiding from her. But she recoiled suddenly, knocking over a water glass, at the ease with which she had penetrated his mind.

"Oh, I'm so sorry!" she said, reaching for the spill with her napkin. Micah beat her to it with his own and refilled her glass from a pitcher.

"I want to go outside!" Jubal slammed his fists on the table, startling everyone. Half out of his chair, he began to shake and tremble. "Amira!" he cried, his gaze seemingly fixed on a far wall. His fingers curled around a table knife. "They're waiting for me!"

Olin appeared in the commissary entrance. "Calm him!" he shouted, and Glencallow lunged out of his chair to seize Jubal's arms. "Gently, man!"

Shocked, Amira pushed into her friend's mind and found utter chaos, a storm of confusion and terror. "Jubal!" she shouted. She shot an accusatory look at Olin. "What have you done to him?"

While Glencallow held Jubal, Kennard Ardais pried the table knife from his grip. Jubal calmed a little, but his gaze darted everywhere and, pale-faced, he continued to shiver. Amira pushed back her chair and stood, uncertain and angry. Micah rose also and laid a gentle hand on her right shoulder. Camilla was suddenly on her left.

"Am I to be restrained, too?"

Micah jerked his hand away with a hurt look. Camilla merely picked up a breakfast roll, broke it in half, and offered a piece to Amira. "Nobody is restraining anybody," she said. "Jubal is upset and confused and needs some care. I calmed him telepathically, and Kennard will see him safely to his room. That's all. Now eat something."

"Are you calming me, too?" Amira shot back.

Camilla continued to hold out the bit of bread, but her face hardened. "Do you feel me in your mind?"

Amira had to admit that she did not. But her headache was back. So were those incomprehensible songs. She squeezed her eyes shut and rubbed her temples, trying to make it all go away. When she opened her eyes again, Jubal and Kennard Ardais were already gone. Ever since arriving at the observatory, things were going awry. *What's happening to me?*

THE MOUNTAINS OF LIGHT

Everything will be explained soon, Olin answered.

Camilla entered her thoughts, as well. *Sooner is better than later. We've underestimated their sensitivities."*

Amira pushed them both out of her mind. "I'm not your damned telepathic switchboard," she admonished. "We're all in the same room, and you can speak to me like normal people."

Steven Glencallow put on a smile. "But my dear, none of us here are exactly *normal people.* Not even the estimable Major Micah Johns." His smile broadened. "Although in most ways he comes closest."

"Not even close," Micah countered.

Amira recognized that they were trying to lighten the mood in the room, but she couldn't dismiss her concern for Jubal. She hadn't known him well before the start of their journey—an historian new to the faculty at Thendara University, somewhat older, crusty—but he had become her friend. Still, she finally accepted the piece of bread Camilla still held out and took a bite.

One by one, those who remained sat down to breakfast. When Kennard Ardais returned, he took a quick look around, said, "He's sleeping," and also began to eat. Amira resisted the urge to scan their thoughts. Without asking, it would have been rude. Instead, she concentrated on her meal, and when she finished, muttering a quick thanks, she got up and left the commissary.

She made her way back to the main observing chamber. In solitude, she stood for a long while in the presence of the awesome, ancient telescope. She ignored the flickering array of computers with their graphs and numbers and columns. The long tube, standing in the gloom, held her attention. Its cracked mirror, frozen gears, and the dome that refused to open anymore struck her as a metaphor. If only she could say for what. Time?

For Darkover itself?

Micah had told her the great mystery of the scope, that it predated even the *chieri,* who were considered aboriginal. She walked slowly around it, noting the dusty chair where once an observer would have sat. It was large for a human, even for a *chieri.* Who then? She wondered.

Jubal had told her once on the trip that humans had now been on Darkover so long that they had forgotten their own history.

That saddened him, and he sometimes questioned if those who dwelled here now were human at all.

She had only scientific answers for him when he sought philosophical ones.

Amira touched her temples again and wished the headache would go away.

Olin was suddenly beside her. She had not heard him enter the chamber and had no idea how long he had been there. "You are broadcasting your thoughts and emotions to everyone," he said. "I thought you would like to know."

Amira looked up at the taller man, horrified and embarrassed.

"Even your embarrassment," he added, folding his arms over his chest. He wasn't scolding or chiding, just matter-of-fact, as he also looked up at the telescope. Without looking at her, he continued. "You hear them, don't you? The starstones calling to you."

She touched her head again. Behind the pain, there was music, a chorus of indecipherable voices from deep in the vaults beneath the observatory. And yes, they sang to her specifically.

Not just from the vaults, but from the mountains all around. This is the Secret of the chieri, *why these mountains are sacred and hidden. These frozen peaks and valleys are repositories of matrix crystals larger and more numerous than the Comyn can ever know.* Olin turned to her finally, and his old, gray eyes locked with hers. "The *chieri* have chosen to share this with you, Amira."

She swallowed as she processed his words. "And Jubal and Micah?"

"Micah has known for some time," Olin informed her. "He is a rarity, a brilliant man with no *laran* potential at all. He can't be tempted by the starstones' power. I met him a long time ago and saw in him someone I could trust. It was one of the smartest decisions I've ever made. He has been helpful to our common cause." He gestured to the computers.

"What about Jubal?" Amira demanded. "What happened to him this morning? Micah recruited him, too, just as he recruited me from the university. That's the right word, isn't it? Recruited?"

Olin didn't look away. "Yes, it is the right word. We saw immense potential in Jubal. What I didn't see was the undisciplined curiosity he concealed even from you. Last night, instead of sleeping, he crept down into the vaults alone."

Amira's eyes widened; she put a hand to her mouth. "To the starstones? He touched one of them?"

"Without a keying ceremony or any guidance at all," Olin explained. "Now his *laran* Gift is awakening, and we don't know yet what that Gift is. He isn't like you."

Amira understood. Her modest telepathy was rooted in her genetics. It had always been a part of her, and though she had concealed it, she had trained herself and learned control. She could only guess what Jubal, an older adult, might be experiencing, and she couldn't guess at all which *laran* gift he might now possess—or which might now possess him.

"Can he be helped?" Amira asked. "Guided?"

"Kennard Ardais is trying to do that," Olin said. "But you saw yourself. He may be mad."

"I won't accept that," Amira answered. "We'll find a way. You brought us here for a reason, and to come so far, it must be a very good reason." She looked up at him sharply. "What reason?"

Camilla spoke as she walked into the chamber. Micah came behind her, then Kennard Ardais and Steven Glencallow. Camilla paused beneath the great scope. "We call ourselves *The Observers*," she said as the gathering formed a ring around Amira and Olin.

"Well, the scope doesn't work," Amira noted, "so what do you observe?"

Camilla put on a subtle smile and indicated her companions in the room. "Together, we are the scope," she explained. "We observe the Great Families, the Comyn, their Towers, and all their activities."

Steven Glencallow inclined his head ever so slightly and Amira felt herself telekinetically lifted inches off the floor and gently set down again. "In the centuries after Landfall, the Great Families were our protectors and guardians," he said, "but power corrupts, especially *laran* power. They brought about the Ages of Chaos, all the storm queens and thunder lords, and the nearly constant warfare that has too often ravaged Darkover's ecology and engulfed our world in bloody conflict."

Kennard Ardais took over the narrative. "The Comyn built

Darkover into a feudal culture with themselves at the top of the food chain. Even after the Rediscovery, they never relinquished their positions or their power."

"Nor are they willing to share that power with the rest of Darkover," Micah added. "They hoard the starstones to themselves and seize any new ones when they are found. God help any Terran that tries to take one off-planet."

"So you do what?" Amira pushed. "Plot revolution?"

"For now, we observe and record," Olin answered. "Our vaults below contain more than starstones. We have the true records and histories of thousands of years. We know families and lineages that have long since been forgotten."

"Secrets hidden since the Crash."

Amira's head hurt. It all sounded incredulous, conspiratorial. How could any small group stand against the powers of the Comyn? She had no love of the Great Families, no faith or trust in them to serve anyone but themselves, but what could a small group of Observers ever hope to accomplish?

And why did they want her to be a part?

She thought of Jubal, supposedly asleep in his quarters, and inadvertently, she reached out to him, crept into his mind as softly as she could.

And she screamed. The sound of it echoed in the chamber, and the others closed around her, clutched at her. Micah wrapped her in his arms as she started to collapse. Amira was no longer aware of any of it. Jubal's mind sucked her in and swept her up in a relentless maelstrom of precognitive possibilities—all possibilities! She saw Micah's love for her, then his distrust and his hatred. She saw the collapse of the Towers and the Great Families and centuries of turmoil. She saw a thriving Darkover at peace, a people who prospered and advanced. She saw Darkover destroyed and Darkover at the center of the universe.

But she didn't see Jubal. Her friend was lost in his own cascading visions.

She was nearly lost with him. Only the telepathic hands of Olin and Camilla saved her. *Together, they pulled her consciousness from Jubal's mind and gave her back herself. For long* moments, she gasped and cried in Micah's arms.

Unlike her morning dreams, these visions did not fade, nor would they ever.

Amira finally knew her path. She knew all her paths, and they began here. "Take me into the vaults," she said. "The starstones are calling to me. It's time I answered."

"Are you sure you're ready?" Camilla asked, worried.

Amira didn't answer as she got to her feet. She didn't need Micah to steady her now, only to love and support her. In time, she would need him for more, but not today. Nor did she really need the others to guide her. The starstones were her guides now.

She left the chamber, walked into the corridors and navigated the maze with her companions following. Rough-cut stone stairs led down into darkness, but illumination panels flared with each descending step.

The songs in her head grew louder—and more clear.

She reached a pair of tall doors. Without assistance, she pushed them open.

Three starstones, each larger than her hand, set perched upon a stone pedestal in the center of the room. Amira had never heard of stones so large. Two shone with blue-white fire. The third also shone, but its light flickered slightly. That was the one Jubal had foolishly touched.

The others held back at the threshold, and Amira entered the vault alone. She felt Olin and Camilla in her head, ready to assist and support her, but never so confident of her own ability, she gently pushed them away and faced the stones.

They were living creatures!

Amira greeted them like new friends. These were the true aboriginals of Darkover, not the *chieri*, but these crystals. All through the difficult trek up the mountainside, she had heard them in her head, singing, calling, welcoming her. Now, in her mind, she sang back to them.

It all begins here, she told the crystals. *It begins here now.*

Amira touched the centermost starstone, and its song soared inside her mind. All the music she had heard in her head for days, it came from this stone, and from its companions, and from all the other matrix crystals in the caves and hidden places of these mountains. They all welcomed her. She hadn't understood it at first. Sometimes it felt like pain, but that was passed. Now she felt only joy, and she reveled in that.

Yet, wisely, she clung to a slender thread of awareness and began the delicate work of sorting her consciousness from all the consciousnesses around her.

I am Amira.

After a time, the simple statement proved enough. She took her hands away from the starstone, and it dimmed ever so slightly. Its light, however, continued to shine in her eyes.

"Are you all right?" Micah called from the threshold. The others had to hold him back to prevent him from rushing in.

Amira considered how to answer. Then she smiled. "I can hear the thoughts of an entire planet," she said, "and yet, I know who I am." She said goodbye to the crystals and thanked them, then walked into the corridor and closed the vault doors. The crystals preferred the dark places.

She went to Olin. The old man had seen her potential and invited her here. She rose on tiptoe and kissed his cheek and telepathically shared with him just an instant of what she felt until he began to weep. She kissed each of them in turn.

To Kennard Ardais and Steven Glencallow she said, "Wake Jubal and bring him outside." Jubal had tried to tell her earlier. *They are waiting!* She knew now what he had meant.

When they were upstairs again and bundled in winter coats and cloaks, Olin opened the same door through which she had first come. The cold winds blasted inside, but she welcomed the brisk air on her face. A moment more, and Glencallow appeared, leading Jubal by the hand.

Jubal looked at her with child's eyes and a child's hurt expression as he transferred his hand from Glencallow's into hers. "You will be better soon," she promised him, "and you will work wonders."

With her companions at her back, she led her friend down the icy flight of stairs. A semi-circle of seven tall figures waited, cloaked and silent. "Go with them," she told Jubal. One of the seven figures stepped forward, and took Jubal's arm in a six-fingered hand.

"*Chieri!*" Micah whispered. He had never seen one before.

"They will sort his consciousness and help him find himself," Amira said as the eight figures moved away and vanished into the snow. "In time, he may return to us, and we will celebrate."

For a long time, Amira stood staring. Gradually, the snow stopped and the clouds broke up. The moons of Darkover strove valiantly to shine, but their light was not nearly as bright as the light in her eyes.

The others went back inside. Only Micah remained with her. He put her hand in hers, and she could feel the love in his heart. They would make a good pair.

Yet, he looked at her with uncertainty. "What are you now, Amira?" he asked softly.

She laughed and turned her gaze upward toward the rounded dome of the old observatory and to the stars breaking through above.

"Just an Observer," she answered. "For now."

BONE OF MY BONE

by Marella Sands

During the Ages of Chaos, *laran* was used to create terrible weapons, some of the worst of which included mind-shattering spells, napalm-like clingfire, and bonewater dust, akin to radioactive fallout, which left the very land itself poisoned for generations. With compassion and unflinching clarity, Marella Sands presents us with this tale of the consequences for ordinary people.

Marella was born in a greenhouse surrounded by smug hothouse roses, but they made her sneeze so much, she left the greenhouse for different pastures and now lives in a fairy hut by the shores of a beautiful blue lake where she is sung to sleep every night by tree frogs. Or, at least that's what it says in her bio.

Marella's latest works are a series of novellas about a bartender who must cope with the discovery of a supernatural world just beyond our own that wants her for its own purposes. *Through a Keyhole, Darkly*, the first of the *Tales of the Angels' Share* series, was published in September 2016.

I shivered as I gathered wood to make a fire. *If* I could make a fire; the wood was so damp I was doubtful it would do more than smolder.

Rella was trying to help, but she was having difficulty focusing on any task and her breathing was shallow and noisy. Perhaps that was due to the exposure to bonedust: that dry, flaky, evil substance that travelers whispered about. I had heard it was made with sorcery by the *laranzu'in* in Towers, and given to the lords of the Hundred Kingdoms to fling at each other, and at the people who wanted nothing more than to exist in peace with their land and their families.

Everyone said it was deadly. But so far Rella was still alive, so maybe they were wrong. What we needed to do right now, though, was get warm. The waters of the Kadarin were swift and icy cold, having just tumbled down the unpassable ravines and deep gorges of the Hellers to rush their way toward the sea. We were both soaked to the skin and needed to squeeze the chill of the Hellers out of our veins. Quickly. Or it wouldn't be bonedust that did us in.

My shaky hands finally grasped a few pieces of wood tightly enough to carry back to our makeshift camp, and I made a fire while Rella collapsed onto the hard ground. Although I had managed to grab a few supplies as I'd run from the house, Rella had not had time to take anything. And now the river had stolen everything except one blanket and the tinder box.

The men from Storn had stopped their pursuit at the river, possibly because of the stories of the trailmen who lived on the other side. I wasn't sure that the stories were true, and didn't care. All I wanted was to stop shaking and see how Rella was doing. Everything else could wait.

Rella was curled up on the ground. The blanket, which I had carried over my shoulders when we crossed the river, so that it was still partially dry, was spread on the ground beneath her. She lay as close to the fire as she dared. Fire was always a problem in the forest in summertime, but with a flame this meager, and wood this damp, I was more worried the tiny fire wouldn't last the night than that it might get out of control.

In the back of my head was the faint heartbeat of my sister, a constant song in my mind since birth, perhaps before. An ever-present reminder that I was not alone. The people of our village weren't sorcerers like the Hasturs and their kin, but many of us had small flashes of odd abilities. Feeling each other's heartbeats was all my sister and I could do, but that was something I had been grateful for every day of my life. I couldn't bear the thought that, if the stories were right, Rella would die, and I would never hear my sister's heart again.

All because of the lordlings and their stupid wars. And their cowardly weapons that killed over long distances and across time. Travelers to our village had spread stories that bonedust poisoned everything, even the soil. When people walked over that soil, and inhaled the dust their feet stirred up, even if decades had gone by since the original attack, they would still get sick. Whether exposed at once, or years later, bonedust would make people nauseated and feverish, cause their hair to fall out, and make them progressively weaker while they broke out in unhealing sores. Eventually they died. No one knew of a way to stop the symptoms once they started. Death was the inevitable result.

Rella was not yet retching, which I counted as a good sign. But I had no food to give her, and no thick blankets to tuck around her aching body. The fire was weak and smoky, and the blanket thin and threadbare. Rella would not heal out here like this. We had to find better shelter, and food, tomorrow.

"Liana?" Her voice was weak. "Am I going to die?"

"Of course not," I said as I settled in behind her, heart bursting with fear and dread. If I could only hold those thoughts away from her! She was bone of my bone and flesh of my flesh in a way no one else could ever be. She was my twin, my second self. I couldn't lose her and stay myself. Who would I be without her? I had never had to find out. Even when our parents died, when our friends moved to other villages to marry, when grandmother had passed away, we had had each other. We had always had each other.

I looked up into the trees above us and squealed. Two red eyes looked back at me, and blinked. Then two more eyes, and two more. Other eyes seemed to be hundreds of feet above us, while a few had come down quite close, maybe only twenty feet away. We were being watched by a horde of forest dwellers.

"Rella," I said quietly. "There are people in the trees."

"No one lives here," she said weakly. "Except..."

"Except the trailmen." We had heard stories of them, of course, strange creatures who lived in the top of the forest and sang to the moon. People talked about their cities hundreds of feet up in the towering crowns of magnificent trees, and how the trailmen never came to the ground. Some people said they could speak the languages of the forest animals, to lure them into their traps. Others said that was nonsense, and that they weren't intelligent enough to have a language at all, and that, if they sang, it was no more than bird song: pretty but meaningless.

I had no idea what to expect, but my heart was beating so fast and hard against my ribs I was sure Rella could feel it. In the back of my head, I heard her heart doing the same.

"Greetings," I said as politely as I could, considering I was lying on the ground with my arms wrapped round my sister. "My sister is ill. We have no weapons. Please let us be."

The pairs of eyes continued staring, with one pair, then another, blinking languidly. I did not get the impression that the trailmen were worried about us at all. Well, we were hardly a threat, as cold and helpless as we were.

A strange high-pitch twittering, which I realized I had been hearing for some time, but dismissing as unimportant, came from the trees above. One phrase kept repeating.

"I think they're asking us something," I said to Rella. "But what?"

"If it were me, I'd be asking, *Who are you and what are you doing here?*" said Rella.

"It's a start," I said. I waved one hand in what I hoped was a friendly gesture. "I am Liana, and this is Rella. Our village was destroyed. We're running away from the fighting. Everyone we know is either scattered or dead." I couldn't believe how calm I sounded when I said that, when my heart was twisting in grief and my eyes burning with unshed tears.

More twittering. A slashing sound came from above and a knife zipped by our heads to impale the dirt near our fire. Rella startled and gasped. "What?" She stared at the knife, which appeared to be made of bone, in horror.

"I don't think they're attacking," I said with a shaky voice. "At that range, they surely could hit whatever they wanted to. It must be a warning."

"I don't think they want us here," she said, her voice even shakier and weaker than mine.

"Should I take it?" I asked. "Maybe the Storns will send men after us in the morning. We could be armed."

Rella shuddered. "Don't touch it. Leave it be. If the trailmen want it, they can get it back when we leave." A sob caught in her throat. "Leave! But for where? We have nowhere to go! Everything is gone."

Rella began weeping, which turned into the feared retching, and I spent the rest of the night trying to soothe both her nausea and her fever, with nothing more than gentle words and a supporting arm around her shoulders. We heard no more chattering and no one came to collect the knife or do more to deliver whatever message had been intended to go with it.

Damn the Storns. Damn all of the Hastur-kin to Zandru's ninth hell. Damn every single one of them. None of them was worth a single hair on my sister's head.

By dawn, Rella had stopped retching, at least temporarily, and I was taking that as a good sign. We doused our fire and I wrapped Rella in the blanket. Neither of us was warm, and my toes were numb from the prolonged chill, but that would change once we got moving again.

We did not have the strength to cross the Kadarin again, whether or not we wanted to. Our only option was to head into the forest and pray to Evanda that the trailmen would leave us alone. I didn't even dare hope they might help. The best the stories offered was the possibility of walking through their territory unmolested.

Rella leaned on me as we went, her auburn hair dull and tangled, her hazel eyes closed as she trusted me to lead. I kept watching her face: the red lashes that almost seemed to glow in the crimson sunlight at midsummer; the pattern of freckles across her nose that I had memorized in the cradle; the slightly upturned nose that our grandmother had loved to pinch. I had imagined this face, identical to my own, beside me for the rest of my life. Rella and I had sworn an oath that, if marriage was to be our fate, we would marry the same man and thus never be parted. We would make a house together, have a lover together, raise our children together, and die old women together. I did not want to live in a world without my twin. Such a world was too alien and empty for me to contemplate.

The forest was dense and only animal trails available for us to tread. If we could have climbed to the treetops, perhaps we would have found the road of the trailmen, but Rella was too weak to even try.

The way was difficult and steep, with no options for turning aside or backtracking. We were hopelessly far from any familiar landmarks and moving forward our only choice. I kept my misgivings to myself, only too aware how miserable Rella was, and how little attention she had for the direction we went and where we would end up. She simply put one foot in front of another as long as I urged her forward. As soon as I stopped, I was sure she would collapse and I would not get her up again.

"Rella, it's all right," I said until the words lost all meaning. "We just need to keep going. It will be all right. Just keep on."

Our second night in the forest was worse than the first. Rella started retching again, and of course, since she'd had nothing to eat or drink, she had nothing to bring up. Her vision had become blurry and her hands trembled. Clumps of her hair began to fall out. Worst of all, a headache had built up behind her eyes and radiated around her head and down her neck, a headache the likes of which neither of us had ever experienced. It was so strong, I felt the echoes of it in my own head through our bond. If what I felt was only a fraction of what Rella endured, the pain was frightful indeed.

By dawn, she was barely conscious, and a small trickle of blood leaked almost continuously from her nose. Her scalp was visible through the thinned and shedding hair. I shook her awake, but she pushed me away. "I'm too tired," she said.

Desperate to get her on her feet, I glanced around the dimly lit forest floor for something—anything—that looked edible. Even if I poisoned her, I couldn't make the situation any worse. "I'll find something for you to eat."

"I'm not hungry," she said weakly. "Don't leave me."

I ignored her plea and spent several minutes searching through the undergrowth but couldn't find a single thing that looked like food. No fruits, no berries, no thick tuber-like roots. But there were plenty of unforgiving thorns on woody shrubs that bit my hands and scratched my face.

Defeated, I went back to my sister and drew her into my arms, aware now that we had come all this way just to die, alone and unmourned, in the middle of a dense, hostile forest. Two more victims in the wars of the Hundred Kingdoms; wars that had nothing to do with us, but which had killed everyone we knew and loved.

I rocked Rella and hummed the nursery song that our mother and grandmother had always sung to us when we were ill. I couldn't remember the words, but the tune was something comforting and familiar in this terrifying dark place.

Night fell and the dense forest floor was shrouded in a darkness so deep, I had never experienced anything like it before. I could see nothing at all; no stars, no moons, no friendly flicker of a fire nearby. I might as well have been blind.

Rella moaned and I held her close. Her skin was dry and hot; I had the despairing notion that this fever was never going to break. I tried to stay awake but I was so exhausted I slipped into a stupor, still humming the old nursery song.

I woke up being jostled about like a sack of laundry slung over someone's shoulder. I lifted my head and exclaimed "Ow!" as I smacked the back of my head into a tree limb.

The hairy body holding me shook me slightly and twittering came from all around. Dismay filled my heart as I realized I was being carried by a trailman. Great Avarra, what had happened to Rella?

"My sister! Where's my sister!" I tried to twist around, to see something, but even though a slight shimmer of moonlight streamed through the branches above, it was still too dim for me to distinguish the forms around me.

I was shaken again, this time more forcefully. Clearly, I was being ordered to be still. I complied and tried to keep the tears from coming. I wouldn't know anything until we stopped, and being dropped through the tree branches onto the ground, which had to be dozens, or if the stories were true, hundreds of feet below, was not an attractive proposition. Rella's heartbeat still resonated in my head, so I knew she lived. At some point, the trailmen would put us down and I would go to her. We would be together again. I had to believe that. I had to be calm. I had to keep my wits about me.

I couldn't tell how much time had passed, but eventually the trailman holding me stopped and put me down. More moonlight filtered through the trees now and I could see my captor was one of several. I looked around wildly but my attention was snared by the silhouette of a woman standing over me.

"Who are you?" she demanded in an odd highly-pitched voice.

"Where's my sister?" I asked as I looked around, my worry for Rella outweighing my shock at being addressed by a human woman in my own language.

"She's here," said the woman. "Now tell me who you are. Both of you."

"I'm Liana. My sister is Rella. We're from a small village in Storn lands. Our village was destroyed and we ran away."

A pause. The woman muttered, "Damn Storns." She walked away.

"Wait!" I called after her, but she did not respond. Well, she'd said Rella was here, so I looked around and saw several forms kneeling around something lying on the ... well, not *ground*, but what served as a walking surface here in the treetops. It felt like tree branches woven together and covered with vines and soft leaves. It smelled spicy and green, much like our grandmother's herbal stores, and made me frightfully homesick for a brief painful moment.

But this was not our grandmother's house. We were far from anything familiar, with no one around us who cared. We had each other, and that was all.

I didn't trust my footing on the intertwined branches. I crawled over to the others. The crouching figures—trailmen, of course—backed off as I neared. I had no attention to spare for them.

"Rella?"

She didn't respond, but I heard the raspiness of her breathing with my ears while the rapidity of her faint heartbeat echoed in my mind. I gave a silent prayer of thanks to Evanda. She lived. My sister lived.

I picked up her hand and squeezed it gently, but she moaned and pulled away. "Hurts," she whispered.

Trailmen approached with woven containers containing glowing insects. The greenish light turned Rella's skin a garish sickly pale color, but by that light I could see the oozing sores that had opened up on her face and her hands. My heart nearly stopped. Could anyone recover from something like this? How could the Storns—and all the lordlings of the Hundred Kingdoms—get away with such cruelty? Dropping dust on harmless people from the sky? Our grandmother had been worried something like that might happen. When Rella had laughed and said we were no danger to the Storns or their enemies, grandmother had shaken her head and said that we were. Because we grew food. And soldiers needed to eat. Cut off the food supply, harm your enemy. We had been killed for a strategic advantage and nothing more. To the petty kings and their soldiers, we were nothing. Perhaps not even pawns. Just something to be swept from the board.

I was so bitter I could barely breathe around my anger and grief.

"Here, have some food," said a woman's voice. I jumped. I had been so focused on Rella and our plight that I had forgotten my surroundings.

The woman thrust some strange mushrooms and unidentifiable bits of meat at me. I ate them without tasting; I couldn't even remember the last time I'd eaten something. Two days ago? Three now? A bowl of water was given to me and I slurped that down as quickly as I could. The food was oddly satisfying but sat like a lump of rock in my gut. Or maybe that was merely dread of my sister's fate.

The woman sat down next to me. "The Old One of this nest wants to know if you've brought disease here. I said I didn't think so, but I couldn't tell him what this was. I've never seen a sickness like it."

"It's what happens when you breathe in bonedust," I said. "They make it in the Towers, or so we were told. It's dropped onto the land and it poisons everything—the crops, the animals, the people, even the very soil." My voice broke as I thought about our green valley in the foothills and how no one would be able to go back there for generations. The people were gone, our animals were gone, our crops ... nothing would be salvaged, not until our grandchildren's grandchildren's time. Or maybe not even then. I was so angry at the injustice of it all, I couldn't speak any more.

The woman seemed to sense that, and filled the silence. "I'm Ysabet," she said. "I came from a small village, too. But that was years ago and I don't remember much. I was chased by those-who-may-not-enter-cities until some people from this nest found me."

I took a deep breath and found my voice, though it was thinner and weaker than I could recall hearing it before. Still, I could feel strength coming from the food. With a few more meals and some rest, I would be strong again. But my sister...?

"Why didn't you go home?" I asked.

"The Sky People aren't in the habit of letting captives go," said Ysabet. "I'm useful to them. I was adopted into a family and help with their work. And, on occasion, I can act as a translator."

"Sky People?"

"That's what they call themselves."

"Why would they need a translator?"

"Sometimes the Sky People trade with a few trusted people in certain villages; those humans are allowed to come into the forest to make deals, but it's still painful for the Sky People to be at such a low altitude. They're used to the thin air up here on the high slopes. Lower down, they don't do so well. I'm taken along to facilitate things and make sure they can get back up here to the higher slopes quickly with as few miscommunications as possible."

"But don't you want to go back?"

In the weird green light of the glowing insects, Ysabet's face looked lined and careworn. She could have been anything from twenty to fifty years old, but I would bet she was on the younger end and had aged beyond her years. "Go back to what? My village was destroyed, too. I lived near Caer Donn. We woke up one morning to see fire shooting from the sky, lighting up the forest, and the men of Aldaran swooping down on us with their aircars. I escaped by diving into the river, but no one else, as far as I could ever find out, survived. At least here, I'm away from the fighting of petty lords and their murderous soldiers and *laranzu'in*."

Rella moaned and I turned to her quickly. "Rella?"

"I'm sorry," said Ysabet. "But it doesn't look good. I'm not familiar with bonedust, but anything the Towers produce has to be deadly."

"No," I whispered. "No, she's my sister. She has to live."

"She'll die," said Ysabet baldly. "And you'll be adopted into a family so you can serve them the rest of your days. It's not so bad. At least the Sky People aren't interested in us as wives, just servants. And they're better to their servants than the lords of the Hundred Kingdoms."

Tears rolled down my cheeks as Ysabet rose from the intertwined branches and expertly walked away on the springy surface. This was to be my life now? To lose my sister and serve a trailman family forever? To have Ysabet as the only other person around whom I could talk to? This couldn't be.

Rella thrashed around but I didn't dare touch her. Two trailmen approached, their thickly-furred bodies oddly human and oddly not, their limbs spindlier than a human's, their faces wider and chinless. But the compassion in their pale eyes was enough to keep me from protesting their presence. One of them had a basket of leaves and gestured toward Rella. I could only guess that he wanted to dress the weeping sores that were opening up on her skin.

"Yes, thank you," I said, stung by the thought that these people—inhuman as they were—could still be more human than my own kind.

The two trailmen carefully tended Rella's wounds and dripped some water into her mouth. But it was clear she was not going to be able to swallow anything more. After they left, I laid next to her and, despite my desire to listen to her every breath, I fell asleep almost instantly.

When I woke, Ysabet was back with a gray-furred trailman. The quality of the light filtering through the trees told me it was morning. Panicked, I looked over at Rella, but she seemed about the same. A glimmer of hope bloomed in my chest. Perhaps she could hold on. Perhaps she had not been exposed to enough bonedust to be killed by it. Surely, the longer she held out, the longer she fought it, the better the chance she could recover.

I sat up. Ysabet nodded to the gray-furred trailman beside her. "This is the Old One of this nest. He wanted to see the two of you for himself."

The Old One crouched beside Rella and sniffed her breath, touched her forehead. He looked at me and made more of the twittering sounds I'd heard in the forest.

"He says they might be able to treat this, but they might not. His people are willing to try, anyway."

"Please," I said to him, while Ysabet made high-pitched noises in translation, "Please help my sister. I'd do anything for you, for the rest of my life, if you could save her."

The Old One said something in a low voice, and Ysabet said, "You'll do whatever they want you to, anyway, because you're a captive."

"But this way I'd have sworn to do it. Surely a willing captive, bound by her word, is better than an unwilling one."

The Old One pondered this a moment. Finally, he said something, and Ysabet said, "And what if she dies? Will you still swear?"

"To be a captive?" I frowned. "No. I'd swear revenge against the men of Storn."

"Revenge is of no interest to the Old One," said Ysabet after a brief period of exchanging vocalizations with the trailman. "If you're not to be a captive, you will be driven out, to become one of those-who-may-not-enter-cities."

"*Those who* ... what?"

Ysabet said something briefly, the Old One responded, and she nodded. "He says I can explain it to you. At puberty, the young females of the Sky People are driven out. They live on the lower slopes, even though it can be difficult and painful for them. But there's no place up here in the high reaches where they're welcome. Only when they are claimed by a male as his mate can they return to a nest."

I thought back to the first night Rella and I had spent in the forest, nearly frozen from the icy river water, curled up near our tiny fire that barely put out heat.

"So that was who we met at the river's edge?" I said out loud. "They threw a knife at us."

"Threw a knife?" For the first time, Ysabet seemed shocked. "That's unusual. That's an invitation to a duel. If you'd taken it, they would have assumed you wanted to join their band. You would have had to fight for a place."

"Good thing I didn't touch it, then," I said, glad to know we'd avoided that fate. How easily we could have been sucked into a fight without even knowing how we'd gotten ourselves mixed up in such a thing!

I looked at Rella, whose sores were worse. The brief hope that she would get better crumbled into ash. She was failing. I couldn't help her. But I knew what I had to do; I had to at least *try*. She was my sister, bone of my bone. My twin, my second self.

"If they save Rella, I'll swear allegiance to whatever family takes me in. I'll be their lifelong servant, willingly. If Rella dies, I won't make the same vow."

In moments, trailmen had come forward with more leaves and bowls of some foul-smelling liquid. Others brought me more food, which I ate without thinking. I watched the ones tending Rella bathe her wounds and bind them with leaves. Despite the reek of the medicine, Rella did seem more calm and able to rest once they were through. I was even able to hold her hand without her pulling away.

"My sister," I whispered to her. "Don't leave me. Stay with me."

I don't think she heard.

Suddenly, a dozen or more trailmen descended onto the surface of the city and chattered anxiously. Ysabet sat up straighter.

"What?" I asked. "What's happening?"

She waved me to silence while she listened. Finally, she spoke with the Old One, and then turned to me. "Two air cars have crashed in the forest on this side of the Kadarin. Most of the men inside survived and are chasing each other through the forest, fighting with weapons of light and fire. The forest burns!"

Fear twisted my stomach so badly I thought I might vomit. "Will we burn here? What about Rella?"

Ysabet shook her head. "I think we're safe here. But the Sky People will lose part of their nest if the fire gets much closer."

"I want to go there," I said, even as that wrenched my heart in two. I wanted to stay with Rella, and yet I could do nothing for her. But I could perhaps get even with the Storns for what their men did to our village. Then I could tell Rella our friends and neighbors were avenged.

More twittering. Finally, the Old One shook his head and walked away. Ysabet said, "He says you can go, and if your sister lives, he will take your oath personally and choose a good family for you. But if your sister dies, you may not return. You will be considered one of those-who-may-not-enter-cities."

I nodded. "Good."

Ysabet looked unconvinced. "It's better to live here in the nest than out there in the forest. Those-who-may-not-enter-cities aren't friendly toward outsiders. You'll have to win a place among them. Here, you can be adopted and treated well."

I kissed my sister's hot forehead one last time. The pulsing of her life was faint, but I could still feel it in the back of my head, where it had been since I could remember. Since we were born. Since before that, even. I had never been without that intimate sense of Rella's life singing within my own head.

"I'll know if she dies," I said. "And I won't come back. I'll make a place with those-who-may-not-enter-cities or I will die trying."

"Death," said Ysabet bitterly. "Is that all you can think of?"

I looked at my sister longingly. I would see her face forever in my dreams, I knew. "What else is there?"

Several trailmen took me toward the crash site, but I didn't need their help finding the burning forest; black smoke hung thickly over the place where the soldiers were fighting. On occasion, I could see the thin silver ribbon of the River Kadarin in the distance, and the hills beyond were familiar. From here, I could have found my way home, if I'd a home left to go to.

As we approached the burning forest and the elevation got lower, the trailmen traveled more slowly. Finally, they waved me forward, blinking at the light, hands trembling and lungs struggling. I nodded to them, and said "thank you," and they crept back into the forest.

The fire was pushing its way toward the river and now I could see aircars hovering overhead, pouring something on the flames. More bonedust? But no, it was water.

I moved closer. Of course the fire crews would try to put out a fire this close to the river, when it could easily spread to the farmlands and villages on the other side. Embers could travel a long way on a strong breeze, and summer was always a dangerous time when it came to fire.

In the distance, I heard an odd punctuated sound and the crimson sky was speared by blue shafts of light. Someone screamed. The soldiers! They were still fighting amongst themselves. I found a solid fallen tree branch and hefted it. Not too heavy to carry, but good enough to hit someone without breaking.

The soldiers no doubt had cowardly weapons that killed at a distance, and maybe even matrix stones that could kill with sorcery. But for me, a branch would do.

I headed back upslope a short ways until the undergrowth of the forest thinned out a little. I had noticed it got thicker near the river. But here, I could move among the trees and force my way through the underbrush with minimal effort.

Ahead, I heard arguing. I slowed, and got closer.

"...damn stupid of you, Kyril. Those men were from Serrais. They're our allies!"

"Allied only through trickery. We are best rid of them. Our lord is the rightful ruler of Serrais and we are beholden to *him*, not that upstart who sits on the throne of Serrais now."

"Our lord is master of Caer Donn, and no more than that. Talk sense."

I stopped listening. Petty lordlings, and their soldiers, arguing over land, was all anyone cared about, all anyone knew. For generations, no one had managed to rule more than one small area at a time, or unite with their neighbors for more than a season or two. Our village headman said it had always been that way, and would always be that way, and it was best for us to keep our heads down, grow our crops, and mind our own business. That we could ignore the wars and the warlords, and they would ignore us.

That policy had not worked so well.

I got closer. The two men were rummaging through a third man's pack while the third may lay dead between them. They didn't see me. A high-pitched call sounded from the branches above and the second man suddenly hit the ground with a knife sticking out of his back. He thrashed a moment, then lay still.

The other looked up in alarm as his companion crumpled to the ground. "What...?"

In my mind, I imagined myself running toward the man, branch cracking down on his skull, but the shocked look on the man's face and the blood running from his companion's back held me in place. The attack on our village had brought death, but not streams of blood. In my mind, I had imagined a glorious revenge, but it had been bloodless. Now I was facing death in its gory reality.

Ashamed, I lowered the branch. I couldn't do it. No matter how justified I was, I couldn't. There had been too much death already. Ysabet had been right to scorn me.

The man glanced up and saw me, confusion in his face. "What did you do to Kyril?" he asked. "You killed him!" He raised a weapon toward me, but I still couldn't move. Was this what it was like to die? To be helpless? Unable to turn aside the fate Zandru had in store for you?

"Who are you?" he demanded. "What are you doing here?"

My tongue began to loosen. "Are you Storn's men?" I asked.

"Who are you?" he demanded again.

"I am no one," I spat at him. "My village is dead. Men in aircars destroyed it."

"Ah," said the man. "That village the other day. That was a sight to see from the air. We flew by just after it happened."

"Just ... after? You're not from Storn?"

"Caer Donn," he said. "But we would have gotten your village if Storn hadn't." He must have decided I was powerless, because instead of shooting me, he made an expansive gesture with his hands as if dropping things over the side of a boat. Or an aircar. "A few packages of bonedust, and poof! All gone. Problem solved."

Anger rose again in my chest, pushing the shock and paralysis with it. "You mean all the people, gone. You *killed* us. Even the children. Even the animals! What harm had they ever done to you?"

He shrugged. "Nobody harmed me. But if it hadn't been Storn, it would have been me and my crew, or someone else would have seen to your village. You peasants have to be shown that being loyal to your lord is important. No one can stand aside and be neutral. If you won't be loyal to Caer Donn, or Storn, or Serrais, you can die."

"And your friend? He can just die, too?" In our village, anyone who was injured would have been assisted immediately, but this man had barely given his companion a glance after seeing him collapse.

"Kyril was an idiot. He's better this way."

Suddenly, the heartbeat at the back of my skull stopped. The silence was overwhelming.

"Rella!" I screamed and I fell against the solid bulk of a forest tree. Without that support, I would have collapsed to the ground.

My sister is dead. The words had no meaning. The silence in my mind, though, could not be ignored. Until now, I had never realized how *loud* the beating of my sister's heart had been, how it had accompanied my dreams, threaded through my thoughts, occupied my entire being with life and warmth. Not until it was gone.

Now I truly had no place. I couldn't go home. I couldn't go to the trailmen. I was alone in the world, more alone than I had ever been. *My sister is dead.*

Twittering came from above us. The man glanced up, just briefly, but it was enough. Rage and grief plunged through my mind, my body, as wildly as the surging ice-cold Kadarin poured itself through the ravines of the Hellers. I yelled and rushed forward, lashed out with my branch, and hit the man full across the face. He went down with a grunt. I struck him again and again until his face was nothing but a bloody mess.

I panted in exhaustion and shock, and stared at the ruin of the face and skull of the man I'd beaten to death. Blood was everywhere—on him, on me, pooled on the ground. I threw away the branch, stumbled into the forest, and heaved under a tree. But I had eaten so little, and it had been so many hours ago, that I brought nothing up. I'd killed someone. With my own hands.

I had thought revenge would feel better than this. Instead, I felt crippled inside, grief-stricken and angry, shocked and shamed, all at the same time. A man had died at my hands. Instead of elation, I just felt sick. Nor could it bring Rella back. The emptiness in my head would never go away. I was still alone. I would always be alone.

I slid to the ground and wept bitterly. The trailmen had not been able to save my sister, just as I had not been able to save her—or anyone else. Death was all the warlords knew, and their soldiers were the same. Death was inevitable.

I heard twittering overhead and waited for those-who-may-not-enter-cities to kill me. Surely they would. Then I would be free of this madness and pain. I would be able to put down my grief and anger in Avarra's arms, just as my sister had.

The absence of that beloved heartbeat was the largest and most horrific abyss I had ever faced, and nothing I could have imagined or prepared for. I spent the night on the edge of that abyss, waiting to tumble in, to die along with Rella, to go to Avarra and have my rest.

But I didn't. Morning found me under the tree, the dim crimson locks of sunlight weaving their way through the branches of the forest. I stared ahead, uncomprehending for a time. But as the daylight grew thicker, the silence became more than absence. It became a companion. As if the Rella-shaped hole in my mind became a second sister, a dark sister. And suddenly I understood the relationship between Avarra and Evanda, the dark and the light. By evening, I felt clean, washed-out, born anew, and no longer alone. My new sister might have no heartbeat, but she was with me now, and would never leave.

Sunset came, the first of my new life. I had no name, no home, just the dark sister filling the back of my mind. I strode forward and pulled the bone knife out of the dead man's back and lifted it toward the branches overhead. I would climb to the treetops and take my place among those-who-may-not-enter-cities. I would learn their language and their ways. And since I would never be claimed as mate by a trailman, I would live my life in the forest. Woe to any armed men who disturbed this side of the Kadarin's wild tumbling course now. They would find me here. They would find death.

My sister and I could still have our revenge. She was, after all, bone of my bone.

"WHERE YOU'RE PLANTED"

by Rebecca Fox

The earliest tales of Darkover (*The Bloody Sun, Star of Danger, The Spell Sword*) began with a Terran arriving on Darkover and having subsequent adventures and self-discoveries. Among other things, this technique invited the reader, also a newcomer, to explore this marvelous world and its inhabitants. Not only that, but the juxtaposition of the two worlds highlighted assumptions and cultural differences, as well as harmonies. Very much in the vein of "a stranger coming home" is Rebecca Fox's tale of a woman spacer and the luck that rides with her.

Rebecca ("Becky") started writing stories when she was seven years old and hasn't stopped since. She lives in Lexington, Kentucky with three parrots, a big gray goof of a gelding, and a Jack Russell terrier who is not-so-secretly an evil canine genius, but no flamingos, pink or otherwise. In her other life, she's a professional biologist with an interest in bird behavior.

Rumor had it that Cat McCreary had a truly uncanny knack for being in exactly the right place at just the right time. The reputation might have helped her win berths on a couple of very fine ships, but Cat herself had always been pretty sure it wasn't anything more than a case of spacer superstition and selective memory. And even if she'd ever given serious thought to believing her own legend, the mess she was in right now would be more than enough to put paid to it.

The dreams, which were weirder than hell, began even before they—meaning *Wilhelmina* and her crew—had hotfooted it to Grayson IV to make an emergency delivery of vaccines. The dreams had stopped, then—for a while. But now they were back with a vengeance: dreams where Cat wandered around on the shoreline of a lake made of fog, searching desperately for someone or something she couldn't find. Sometimes she glimpsed other people along the shore. An old man with silver hair and golden eyes. A woman who might have been her long-dead mama. Others, too far away and too wrapped in fog for her to get a good look.

That was creepy enough, but it wasn't the worst of it.

Swimming through the fog, as if they were perfectly ordinary fish in a perfectly ordinary lake, were the shadows of creatures out of her worst nightmares. They crowded along the shoreline like they were just waiting for her to stumble a little too close.

By the time *Wilhelmina* blew one of her main power conduits after leaving the Grayson system, it had been a solid week since Cat had managed to sleep more than two or three hours a night, and by then she'd added a constant low-grade headache—plus dizzy spells and nausea—to the mix. When Captain Fisher announced the news of their trouble, Cat's first thought was that at least once she was dead she'd be able to *get some sleep*.

The ship had been scheduled for maintenance on Tollywocket when Grayson's distress signal reached the nearest Spaceforce station. *Wilhelmina* had been the closest ship, and each hour of delay would cost lives.

It looked as if delivering the medicine would cost lives anyway: they'd resumed their flight to Tollywocket by the shortest route, and that meant crossing between the upper and lower spiral arms.

Without that conduit, they had just about 72 hours (if they were lucky, but no one said that out loud) before they lost power and became a galactic derelict.

Hours of searching the charts for somewhere to put down before they wound up as space junk had yielded three habitable possibilities: two were completely unsurveyed and might well contain toxic flora, aggressive fauna, unstable geology, deadly pathogens or some truly delightful combination of the above. The third was Cottman IV.

Jan Brenner, their First Pilot, had said that the entry for Cottman IV said the climate sucked. That turned out to be a pretty tame description of the actual weather there. From orbit, all they could see was a storm that looked like it covered most of the continent, but they had no time to wait it out and hope the weather would clear.

So *Wilhelmina* put down.

Or, as a less generous observer might put it, and in spite of all that Jan could do, *crashed*—but (as Captain Fisher said) at least he hit the Spaceport. When the storm finally diminished to the point it was possible to walk upright through it, a couple of people from the Port came out to meet them.

The gust of wind-driven snow that preceded the welcoming committee was so cold it took Cat's breath away, even though she was still running that miserable fever. It had felt good for maybe half a second, but now all she could do was shiver. Fortunately, their two visitors didn't seem inclined to dawdle in the doorway.

"You folks sure picked a fine time to pay a visit to balmy Cottman IV," the shorter of the two said dryly, removing several layers of cold-weather gear. "Name's Thorsten Kenwick. I'm Portmaster here. Young fellow with me is Rodrigo, assistant to the Legate. Welcome to Darkover."

Captain Fisher offered him her hand. "Captain Maida Fisher. We're sorry to just drop in on you unannounced like this, Portmaster, but we blew a conduit and we're in pretty dire need of repairs." Rodrigo bowed to each of the four crewmembers in turn. When Rodrigo got to Cat, he looked startled, as if he wasn't expecting to see her here. (Which was ridiculous, because she'd never seen either of them before in her life.)

"If we've got what you need on hand, we should be able to get you up and flying in a month or so," Kenwick said, smiling affably. "Otherwise I'm afraid you're stuck enjoying our hospitality until winter's over, and Maintenance can order the equipment."

"How long is that?" Captain Fisher asked warily. When they weren't flying, they weren't earning, and if *Wilhelmina* was grounded for any length of time, what should have been a nice big Federation bonus for their mercy trip would have to keep them solvent until they could lift.

"About three standard months," Kenwick said apologetically. "But look: I'm pretty sure you're covered by the 'distressed traveler' clause in our charter, and that means you're entitled to free room and board. Why don't I send a team over to talk to your engineer, and you folks can bring your things over to the Port and get settled in. The accommodations aren't exactly up to Vainwal standards, but they're warm and we've got beer."

Rodrigo and Kenwick waited until they were ready to go, and then walked them back to the main building for check-through. Kenwick bore Captain Fisher off for a short meeting with the Legate, while Rodrigo (who apparently didn't have a last name) saw the rest of them through Customs: two clerks scanning credentials and ignoring personal baggage. Either Darkover didn't get smugglers (given the weather, Cat wouldn't really blame them for giving the place a wide berth), or no one here cared.

When the clerk got to Cat, it was the usual call and response. She'd done this so many times on so many worlds that she could pretty much recite both the questions and the answers in her sleep.

Back when she actually slept.

Yes, she was Cass McCreary; yes, she was Third Mate on *Wilhelmina*; yes, her license was paid up; yes, she'd had all her inoculations; no, she had not come to *Insert Name of Planet Here* to engage in subversive activity against the Federation or the local government.

She was expecting the clerk to ask for her last port of call next, but instead he said, "Where were your folks from, if you don't mind me asking?"

By now, the adrenaline high of the landing had worn off, and Cat's feverish headache had come back in full force. All she could do was stare (and tell herself firmly she would *not* throw up on the scanner).

"Beg pardon, but Murray here thinks you look like one of the *Comyn*—the local nobility, you know," Rodrigo said apologetically. "Red hair and gray eyes—that's how you tell them apart from everybody else. Not that most of them would ever consider setting one foot off Darkover."

Murray gave him a dour look. "But some do. Remember that— oh, I forget her name, she was a ward of old *Dom* Felix, eloped with a Terran..."

"Whereas my mother didn't elope anywhere, and married *Dom*

Felix's paxman," Rodrigo said, shutting the conversation down thoroughly. "C'mon, Murray. I need to get these people settled in. You can bother them later."

Murray mumbled an apology as he handed back Cat's docs, and Cat barely had enough wits about her to reassure Murray that she hadn't minded and everything was fine, really.

Not that she could have answered the questions even if she'd wanted to. Her mama had died when she was all of nine years old, and her father had forbidden Cat to ever mention her again.

Rodrigo-call-me-Rodi's definition of getting folks settled in was apparently taking the entire crew out for a drink. ("Gods know you all could probably use one after that landing.")

Rodi was also the sort of person who could inspire ship's captains to spend a fat sum in order to recruit him as their First Mate: affable, charming, good-humored, and firm. So even though all Cat wanted to do was get her head down and possibly *die*, all she could really do was go along helplessly as he herded the lot of them into one of the recreation rooms and ordered beer ("Not that *Terranan* swill, but *real* beer!").

The only reason Cat stayed as long as she did was because the Darkovan brew met with her stomach's approval and even seemed to ease the damned headache a bit. But when some of Rodi's friends showed up to join the party—and party it was by that point, loud and boisterous in the way only a room full of spacers on shore leave could be—Cat mumbled some excuses and went back to her temporary quarters.

Or rather, staggered dizzily. The walk back from the rec room seemed easily three times as long as the walk over, but she eventually made it back to the chilly, overlit little cubie with its rock-hard mattress.

Maybe I'll actually sleep tonight, mattress or no mattress. Fortune knows I'm tired enough. She pulled off her boots and tossed them into a corner, then fell backwards into bed without bothering to finish undressing.

In the dream, Cat could feel the clammy fog beading on her skin as she walked hopelessly along the shoreline. It seemed utterly unfair that she be sick in her dreams as well as awake, but her stomach was twisting queasily and her body was running with sweat. She couldn't remember what she was looking for, only that it was desperately important that she find it.

Suddenly, the man she'd seen in her other dreams was standing before her. He looked startled.

"Miralys?" he whispered, voice trembling.

But Miralys was mama's name. How do you know it?

"I'm not—" she said.

The creatures in the fog swam closer, circling eagerly. And then one of them wrapped a slimy tendril around her ankle and she woke with a scream, her heart and head pounding in time with each other.

So much for sleep.

She forced herself out of bed by sheer bloody-mindedness when her chrono went off, and then stood in the 'fresher for so long the thing offered to send for a medical team. When she finally opened her message queue, there was one from Captain Fisher giving a time—0900—and a place—Commissary Three North—for Captain's Mast. She dragged on last night's clothes as fast as she could and ran.

The look on Captain Fisher's face when Cat slid into a seat at precisely 0905 told Cat all she needed to know about how things stood with *Wilhelmina.*

"Better make yourself comfortable, my darlings," Captain Fisher said, "because it looks like we're going to be enjoying Darkover's hospitality until spring. The replacement power conduit and a few other things are going to have to come in from off-world—how far off-world nobody knows yet. Meanwhile, we fix what we can, and since we put off our scheduled refit to run the Federation's errand, they're going to be footing the bill for all this."

There was quiet cheering from *Wilhelmina's* crew, which Cat joined in on a beat or two late.

Captain Fisher caught her eye as she stood to leave with the rest of the crew. Cat was sure she was about to catch hell for being late, but all Captain Fisher did was pour out another cup of whatever it was they'd been drinking at breakfast and offer the pitcher to Cat. "You feeling okay, McCreary?"

Cat shrugged. "Depends on what you mean by 'okay', Skipper. Haven't been sleeping real well. But I don't think I'm likely to drop dead anytime soon, if that's what you're asking." *Though it might be nice if I was.* Breakfast wasn't sitting well and the headache was a steady drumming in her skull. She hoped she didn't *look* anything like as bad as she *felt.*

"Well, it looks like you're going to have a few months to catch up on all that sleep you've been missing." The captain's voice was dry but her eyes were somber.

"You didn't keep me after to ask if I was coming down with something." It was days like this that made Cat glad she wasn't the one sitting at the top of the chain of command.

Captain Fisher's mouth twisted wryly. "I could wish you didn't know me quite so well. No, I didn't, though I'd like you to see Port Medical sooner than later." She sighed and stared into her cup like it might offer some answers. "I didn't want to say this during the Captain's Mast because morale's in the toilet right now as it is, but we're almost certainly going to be grounded here for two local months after traffic is moving again."

Cat did some mental calculations and whistled softly. She was foggy enough that she wasn't sure her numbers were quite accurate, but they didn't need to be. The answer wasn't good regardless. "Making payroll's going to be all kinds of fun."

"Yeah. And I can't ask good people to spend months freezing their asses off for nothing more than an IOU. I hate to do it, but I'm going to release anyone who wants it from their contracts—at least they can get the hell off this ice ball and get back to earning a paycheck once the storms clear."

"I'll draw the paperwork up, but I bet we're going to keep more people than you expect." Maida Fisher was the kind of captain who inspired loyalty, partly because she was willing to do exactly what she'd just done. "And Skipper—for what it's worth, I'm sorry I used up all that luck I've supposedly got at a really inopportune time."

The captain's laugh was genuine. "Well, we're not a hunk of floating space trash right now, so I'd say you used up that luck to good purpose. And McCreary? Medical. This morning. I mean it."

"Yes ma'am. As the Skipper wishes." Cat tossed off the jauntiest salute she could manage under the circumstances.

All Port Medical could do for Cat was run tests (inconclusive), give her a bottle of aspirin and some sleeping pills, and tell her to check back with them if the symptoms persisted.

The symptoms not only persisted, but got worse, but she didn't go back. All she needed was to get her license pulled for an *Unidentified Disease Of Unknown Origin*. So she gritted her teeth, did her work, and tried not to throw up or pass out anywhere there were witnesses.

"You look like our twenty-eight hour days are agreeing with you about as well as they do with most people used to the good old Terran standard twenty-four." Portmaster Kenwick said.

Cat shrugged and forced a smile. "Nothing I'm not used to. I think it's this damned weather. Every time I get my head down I wonder if I'm going to wake up buried in a snowdrift." It was a lie, but what was she supposed to say? That she was having bad dreams and might be going crazy?

When she glanced up from the sheaf of documents she was checking, Kenwick gave her a sympathetic look and poured her a mug of tea from the carafe on his desk. She took a sip. Whatever it was, it was pungent and spicy and put paid, at least temporarily, to her mental fog.

It seemed as if the more time the Dockyard maintenance crew spent going over *Wilhelmina*, the more they found wrong with her. And every time they found something else wrong, Cat got to put on ten layers of cold-weather gear and hike out to the Portmaster's office to sign things.

At this rate *Wilhelmina* was going to be here until *next* winter.

He grinned ruefully. "I promise it'll stop snowing eventually. Of course, by eventually, I mean maybe in a couple of months."

Cat flipped through a few more pages. She would have tossed some of these work orders out as low priority, but if the Federation felt like paying for them, she sure wasn't going to argue. "Right up until I set foot on Darkover, I would have said a few months' unplanned shore leave sounded great," she said when she looked up again. "I take it back." She couldn't imagine what had possessed Rodi's mother, who had once been a quartermaster on one of the Big Ships, to *stay* here.

"Darkover grows on you," Kenwick said with a faint smile. "You'd be surprised."

"I'll believe it when I see it." She went back to the stack of flimsies. When she looked up a few minutes later, rubbing her temples, Kenwick was studying her with a bemused expression.

"You know, you really *do* look like you could be one of them."

"The Comyn, you mean? What's the big deal with them anyway? Half the First Expansion colonies we've stopped at had some kind of ruling nobility."

"Yeah, well. The Comyn aren't your ordinary lords and ladies," Kenwick said. "At least not if you believe what the locals say about them."

"What about you?" Cat asked. "What do you think?" *Have you seen a lake of mist filled with weird fish and golden-eyed men?*

He spread his hands. "Jury's still out. I've been here in Thendara a long time, but I'm a skeptical old Terran in my soul and half that stuff sounds like fairy tales. Sorceresses in towers. Stones inhabited by the spirits of the gods. Varzil the Good turning Lake Hali into mist, and okay, the mist part is apparently true..."

Cat set down her cup very carefully. "A lake of mist?" she asked, struggling to keep her voice steady. "There's really a lake of mist here?"

"So the planetary survey report says. I'd like to see it for myself, but the place is sacred to the Comyn and they don't allow tourists. Even anthropologists, although they're fine with Cultural Reconciliation going just about everywhere else. Anyway, the Comyn supposedly have 'abilities'—clairvoyance, telepathy, precognition, that kind of stuff."

Invading other people's dreams?

Luck?

(Miralys, *the golden-eyed man from her dream whispered.*)

Now she was sure she had to be losing her grip on reality. But if mama was from Darkover, that would mean...

What?

Nothing, she told herself firmly. *Just that she was smart enough to leave this frozen hellhole.* "So ... I guess Cultural Reconciliation has written a lot of stuff about Darkover? Do you think I could read some of it? I mean ... it would be something to do..."

And maybe there'd be something in there about turning off weird dreams.

Kenwick didn't seem to think the request was too out of line, though. "The Legate will have to approve it," he said. "But I don't see why not. It's harmless enough."

Cat put off sleeping for as long as she could, hoping she'd tire herself out so much she wouldn't dream. But it seemed that the moment she put her head on the pillow she was back beside the lake of mists.

Lake Hali. The Darkovans call it Lake Hali. It's only a few hours' ride from Thendara...

Just as always, her body walked into the lake despite everything she could do to stop it. The mist seethed with half-seen horrors, and Cat was sure this was the time she wouldn't wake up.

But suddenly the golden-eyed man was there, standing between her and the awful things cruising through the fog.

It shouldn't have been comforting, but it was.

"I'm not Miralys," she said, as he turned to face her. "Miralys was my mother."

The man cupped her face between his hands, gazing at her with a mixture of wonder and grief. *"Cassilda,"* he said in a low, wondering voice. "But how?"

"My mother called me that," she said. "Only my mother."

She felt a wrenching grief, as if her mother had died hours ago and not years. She drew a deep breath, wanting to ask the man to help her ... (*If he was real. If any of this was real. If she wasn't just losing her mind.*)

Then she woke up.

As was far too usual these days, Cat opened her eyes, rolled to the edge of the bed, and vomited. Then she staggered into the 'fresher for a towel, wiped the floor, and went back to take a long shower. (The 'fresher unit had stopped asking if she needed help a couple of weeks ago.) By the time she lurched out again, she was in good enough shape to check her tablet for anything she needed to do today, but the only new thing on it was a link to the Cultural Reconciliation open database.

The thought of reading anything right now made her stomach lurch.

But what if mama's name is in here?

So what if it was? All that would mean was that she now knew what planet her mother had been born on—information that she could not imagine would be of any actual use. It wouldn't bring her mother back from the dead. It wouldn't reconcile her with her father. It wouldn't make her *belong* anywhere. And it sure as hell wouldn't cure whatever was wrong with her.

But the sense of unsolved mystery nagged at her, so once she was dressed, she took the tablet with her when she headed for the Commercial Lounge. It was just as depressing as her cubie, but at least it had windows.

Rodi had said the Commercial Lounge was the most revolting establishment on all of Darkover. Cat didn't care about the dingy walls and stained rug, both in shades of orange, magenta, and green. What she cared about was the fact that it was usually completely empty, and today was no exception.

She drew herself a mug of beer from the dispenser and settled down on the couch facing the windows. Today the sun was out, and she could see a good deal of the Port, which was a nice change.

You're putting it off, you know.

With a sigh, she picked up her tablet. A short argument with the database's archaic searchable index got her a long boring monograph on Darkovan naming customs. It was written in academic jargon so dense that she understood maybe one word out of every three.

But it had appendices, and one of them contained an alphabetical list of known Darkovan given names. She paged through quickly, not knowing whether she hoped or feared that the name was there.

Melora—Merinna—Mhari—Millea—

Miralys.

Maybe Miralys is a common name on a lot of worlds. It might not mean anything at all.

Her heart pounding, Cat scrolled back up to the Cs.

Camilla—Carise—Catriona—

Cassilda.

There was a cross-reference: *(see Hastur and Cassilda, Ballad of).*

She opened the linked file. It contained lyrics, a translation of them into Standard, and a sound file of the song being performed. She didn't need to click on the song file, because her mama had sung the same song to her when she was a little girl.

("The silver wheels of night had swung/where bright Avarra's sickle hung...")

Cat threw her tablet at the wall and strode out of the room without a thought for where she was going.

Rodi tapped on her cubie door a few hours later. When she opened it, he offered up her tablet. "Found this in the Commercial Lounge. It's not broken," he said encouragingly.

It's the only thing here that isn't, Cat muttered to herself. She'd been alternating between staring at the ceiling and watching an old vid-drama on the wall screen. It was a late Empire gem called *I Survived Mandragora,* and seemed to consist of equal parts Imperial propaganda, crowds of extras screaming and running, and on-screen sex. It was pretty bad, but at least watching the two leads exchange faux-passionate kisses in front of an erupting volcano kept her mind off whatever the hell was going on right here in reality.

"You look like you've already had a full day," Rodi said, stepping through the door. "Penny for your thoughts?"

She tried not to glare. "You don't want them. Besides, if I told you I'd probably owe you reparations for emotional damage." *I'm sure as hell not going to tell you what I found out today. Or what's been happening to me. It sounds crazy, and I'm the one living it.*

"That bad, huh?" He gave her a sympathetic smile. "Well, it's not going to get any better sitting in here watching this garbage—or even drinking the worst beer on Darkover. Which the stuff in Commercial Lounge is. Officially, I mean. The Legate's staff had a taste test last winter. Anyway, meteorology says the next storm isn't due for a couple of days. Why not come into Thendara with me and get some fresh air? We can stop at The Cask and Chervine for lunch."

The thought of lunch made her stomach lurch again, but she thought of the tea she'd had in Kenwick's office. Maybe she could find a place to buy more.

The Cask and Chervine was Rodi's parents' inn on the outskirts of Thendara, nestled right smack between the city itself and the spaceport. "Beloved of *Terranan* tourists and Darkovans come to gawk at the tourists alike," Rodi said with a grin. They made their way there after stopping at Cultural Reconciliation to borrow some outdoor gear for her, since Rodi said it would be better if she didn't waltz into Thendara looking like an advertisement for *Terranan* cold-weather gear. From the way the guy at CR acted, this was business as usual, and the jacket and boots Rodi found for her were enough warmer than what she'd been wearing that Cat decided she wasn't going to think too hard about what they were made of (even though they were clearly of native manufacture and might be lined with actual fur from actual animals). Her head was pounding too hard for her to do much thinking anyway.

The inn itself was a solid little building constructed of some local stone. The common room was warm, inviting, and packed—as promised—with a mind-boggling assortment of overwintering spacers, natives, and staff from the Port and Legation. Rodi said the place had been a wedding gift from the mysterious *Dom* Felix, who people (even people at the Port) spoke of in awed tones but whose name meant absolutely nothing to Cat.

"I hope I'm not being offensive, but who exactly is this *Dom* Felix person?"

"The man who's advised two and a half Hasturs—they're the ruling family of the Comyn," Rodi said affably. "He has the Old Blood and I don't think anyone'll be surprised if he lives long enough to advise a couple more."

"Old Blood?"

"Six fingers, golden eyes, the whole bit," Rodi said. "And that's Da calling. We'd better go in to lunch. I'll give you a history lesson later."

Golden eyes. Like the man in my dream. The thought stayed with her all the way through lunch with Rodi's parents. Not that she could eat much. Her stomach lurched at the smell of all that heavy, heavily-spiced food and her fever-fogged brain could barely parse all the questions—mostly about life aboard ship these days—that Rodi's mother Beatrix kept tossing at her. Cat was sure that Beatrix was just trying to make conversation but it mostly just made her head hurt.

And Rodi's *father*, Daniskar (who was older than she'd expected, not that it mattered), kept looking at Cat with a knowing sort of concern, like he thought he knew exactly what was wrong with her and just wasn't saying.

Eventually it got to be too much to stand, like some intolerable pressure squeezing all the air out of her lungs.

She staggered to her feet. "I—I'm sorry. It's late. I can't stay. I have to go."

She half-fell down the short flight of steps into the common room and stumbled outside. When the cold slammed into her she realized she'd left her jacket, but going back for it would mean going back in *there*.

She ran into the street, narrowly missing colliding with a man carrying an armful of parcels. He yelled at her in a language she couldn't understand. Behind her, she could hear Rodi and his father shouting her name.

She ran, slipping and sliding on the ice, and numb with cold. *I hear freezing to death isn't such a bad way to die.*

When she stopped to lose what little lunch she'd eaten in an alleyway, she realized that wherever the hell she'd been running, it wasn't back to the Port. And she had no idea whatsoever where she was.

Shit.

And then she saw *him*. Silver-haired, wrapped in a fine cloak with silver embroidery. He was standing across the cobblestoned street beside a wagon piled high with barrels, scanning his surroundings.

And then, as if Fortune herself had dropped the information into Cat's mind, Cat knew two things: the man was *Dom* Felix, and he was searching for *her*. Suddenly, she knew one other thing too:

that the rope securing the barrels on that wagon was about to give way.

Somehow Cat McCreary always manages to be in the right place at just the right time.

"*Dom* Felix!" she screamed. "Watch out!" She charged across the street.

Somewhere in the distance, Rodi screamed her name.

Then the world tilted sideways and the ground rose up to meet her.

After that, there was a long period where nothing made much sense. She alternately sweated and froze. She cried out when people touched her, and cringed away in terror from monsters no one else could see. Once, she opened her eyes and thought she stood atop a high tower looking out over a city she didn't recognize. Once a woman scolded her in stilted Standard and made her drink something that tasted horrible and made her cough. Once she heard Captain Fisher shouting at someone.

Finally, blessedly, she slept deeply and without dreams.

When Cat woke again, she felt like she'd just lost a cage match with someone at least twice her size. She was lying on a soft mattress in a room she didn't recognize. There was an oil lamp burning on the bedside table, and an old Darkovan man—*Dom* Felix—dozed in an overstuffed chair on the other side of the bed.

Her movement must have roused him, because he came awake immediately. "Be easy, child. You're at Comyn Castle, and among friends."

She blinked at him. "You *are* real." It was an idiotic thing to say, but it was too late to take it back.

He smiled gently. "As real as you. But let me introduce myself properly, since we've only really ever met in a dream, as it were. I am Felix Javier Hermes-Reuel Aillard y Elhalyn. Your mother, Miralys, was my ward. She eloped with a *Terranan* named Jameson MacRorie—your father—and I have been seeking them ever since. Do you feel up to sitting?" At her nod, he gestured, and a woman Cat hadn't seen before came from her place beside the door to help her upright.

"My father's name is James McCreary," Cat said irritably, "And I'd love to know exactly what the hell is going on here." Things had been intolerably weird since before the run to Grayson IV and she just wanted it all to *stop*.

"Then he is still alive?" Dom Felix sounded eager. "I will send for him as soon as winter is over. As for you, I would venture to guess that you have been suffering from threshold sickness for some time now. I'm afraid I was a bit slow to put things together; it wasn't until the last time we stumbled across one another in the Overworld that I realized you must be the woman at the Port young Rodrigo had been telling me about."

"Threshold sickness? The Overworld?" Dom Felix didn't seem to think she was going crazy, at least. She wasn't sure whether that was reassuring or not. He was a *Comyn*, after all. "What about my father?"

"Threshold sickness often occurs when one's *laran* begins to awaken." *Dom* Felix seemed to be perfectly capable of not hearing questions he didn't want to answer. "As yours clearly has. I suppose I needn't have worried about your mother falling in love with a *Terranan* after all."

"But that's crazy," she protested. "I don't have magic powers!"

"Don't you?" His smile was teasing, but his eyes were solemn. "Then I suppose it's someone else to whom I owe my life."

Remembering that moment in the street brought her bolt upright. "The barrels!" she said.

"It's *lucky* you were there to warn me, don't you think?" *Dom* Felix asked blandly.

A few weeks later, Cat (she didn't think she was *ever* going to learn to answer to "Cassilda" even if she lived as long as *Dom* Felix) was sitting in the common room of Rodi's parents' inn, nursing a mug of hot mulled wine and contemplating the fire. Her recovery had progressed to the point she could be irritated by her convalescence, but not far enough for her to be able to actually do much.

Dom Felix had wanted her to stay at Comyn Castle while she recovered, Captain Fisher had wanted her back at the spaceport. Rodi had come up with the compromise—The Cask and Chervine straddled both worlds. (Cat was thinking she was going to have to get used to doing some straddling herself.)

Of course Rodi appeared almost instantly. Without him she would've been completely lost, but apparently Rodi's work for the Legate involved explaining Darkover to wandering *Terranan*.

"Winter's almost over," Rodi said, favoring her with his charmingly lopsided smile. "The parts for *Wilhelmina* should be part of one of the first cargoes landed. Have you decided what you're going to do?"

Are you going to stay or are you going to leave? That's what Rodi was really asking. When Captain Fisher had found out Cat was half-Darkovan, she'd offered to buy out Cat's stake in *Wilhelmina* if she decided to stay. She knew the Legate had already sent a farcomm to the Old Man back on Scrimshaw where Cat'd grown up. She wondered if he'd come. She wondered if she wanted him to. She really hated questions she couldn't answer.

"*Dom* Felix wants me to spend some time with him—once I'm fully recovered in everybody's opinion—to make sure this *laran* thing is under control. After that, I'm not really sure."

"Well, regardless of what you decide you'll always have a home on Darkover."

"*Home*," Cat said. "I've been spacing since I was seventeen. I'm not sure I even know what that word means."

Home. She thought about the gossamer strand of fate that had led her to this out-of-the-way world where her mama had been born, and from there to *Dom* Felix, the man who was practically her grandfather. She thought about Rodi's mother, a spacer who had left the Big Ships behind to marry *Dom* Felix's paxman. She thought about her own mama, who had abandoned her pampered life on Darkover to follow the man she loved to the other side of the Federation. She thought about the Old Man, who had loved her mama so much he couldn't bear to hear her name spoken aloud after she died. Cat wondered if she'd ever know their story.

She didn't know what Rodi read in her expression, but he reached out and squeezed her hand. "Home," he said firmly. "And I promise it will never be too late to find out."

BELIEVING

by Leslie Roy Carter and Margaret L. Carter

Margaret L. Carter specializes in vampires, having been marked for life by reading *Dracula* at the age of twelve. Her vampire novel *Dark Changeling* won an Eppie Award in the horror category in 2000. She's the author of *Different Blood: The Vampire as Alien, Passion in the Blood* (a vampire romance), *Sealing the Dark Portal* (a paranormal romance), and "Crossing the Border" (horror erotic romance novella with Lovecraftian elements). She and Les Carter attended the College of William and Mary together as a married couple and earned their bachelors' degrees there. Les later received an MS in Electronics Engineering from the Naval Postgraduate School. He retired from the U.S. Navy as a Captain after thirty years of service.

"Believing" is related to "The Mountains of Light" by Robin Wayne Bailey, in that both involve a search, a treasure hunt of sorts, that turns out quite differently from its original goal. When Darkover is concerned, this should come as no surprise.

Lucia noticed the frown on the face of the young security officer sitting before her and sighed. *They always expect an answer from the library even if it is not about the question they asked.* "There is no proof in the database that a sapient life form existed on Cottman IV before the arrival of the Lost Ship from the Earth Expedition Force. Our records don't even have the name of the ship and who was on board as crew or cargo. All we have is what our planetary historians have gotten from the Darkovans themselves, which includes their myths and legends."

Frustration evident in his voice, David said. "Your point would be valid if I could call up the records of the Earth Expedition Force to show a direct tie between the ships sent to the Coronis

Colony and Cottman IV. I can't. I've searched the entire database. There are records that go all the way back to early space flights from Earth and before. I can find the weapons loadout King Henry V had when he landed in France before the battle of Agincourt. There are records of that."

Lucia busied herself at her keyboard, tapped a final instruction, and turned the monitor to David. "There it is. It also tells the pay they received and their food ration. The point is we can call it up because it was written down and other people recorded it for posterity. It has been researched and verified. No one has done the same on Cottman IV, either the Darkovans themselves or our staff. It is not that we haven't tried, but the Darkovans are so close-minded."

"Not all Darkovans," David said, glancing at the head of Information Services. "One of our newest hires, a kid name Eddard something something Ridenow. I helped rescue him four or five years back, and he decided to join the Search and Rescue service."

Lucia queried the name from records and looked up from her screen. "Eddard Hastur Ridenow, one of the ruling class? You couldn't have found a more likely representative of close-mindedness then that."

"Yeah, I know his relatives include the Hastur, but he is so far from the throne that he actually has to work for a living like the rest of the Darkovans. The kid has shown real potential and he has done it all without 'outside influence.' Inquisitive as hell and unwilling to accept the lore of his people as the answer to all his questions." David reached for his cup of coffee and took a sip. It had cooled, and he grimaced at the taste.

Lucia took it from his hand and asked, "Refresh that for you?"

David nodded. "They don't mind his working with us but have drawn the line at his being sent off-planet for training. They are afraid we will indoc him so badly that he will cast off their culture for ours. Not much chance of that; he is in every way a Darkovan. He reads a lot and has gotten pretty adept at working the system, but he is searching for something, and I can't help him."

Handing him the steaming cup, the head of research shook her head. "If he is searching for the proof of gods or the ultimate intelligence, he will just have to join the rest of us in our frustrations with the quest. You can't find something that doesn't exist."

David looked away from the screen and sighed. "My expertise is in search and rescue. There are a plethora of ships lost in space exploration, and finding them usually begins with showing that a ship actually existed in the first place. We have managed to find a majority of the Lost Ships by starting with the premise that Ship X was last seen on Planet Y at such and such a location and time. We then search outward from that point. The area of search could be infinite, but since the ship existed, it has to be somewhere."

Lucia grinned at David. "But you don't have that problem here, Lieutenant. We can prove a ship was once located here on Cottmann IV. The Darkovans are genetically of Terran stock. They for the most part don't agree with that, but then they don't believe in most of our science, anyway. There are other life forms that originate from Cottman IV, if they weren't planted by some beneficent intelligent beings. Those banshee birds are not from Terra; the Lost Ship didn't bring them."

"The problem, Doctor, is just that. We know a ship landed here, but we have no way of knowing what ship from where. The Darkovans have names traceable back to Terra only if one believes their stories. They can't be verified because we don't have anything to cross-check."

A strong believer in provable, accurate research herself, Lucia understood David's reluctance to simply accept what was handed to him as fact. "What difference does it make if we believe the Darkovans or not? Our Empire trading rights to the planet stand on finding it in the first place. That, and it had no advanced sapient life forms except for humans of provable Terran stock. Sure, I know some people count the catmen and trailmen as having intelligence, but no more than Terra's dolphins and chimps. Since we have chosen not to conquer Cottman IV and waste time defending it from our Empire 'allies,' we are willing to go along to get along."

She glanced out the window at the barren landscape that surrounded the spaceport. She envied the lieutenant his ability to get away from the sterile environment of the base and walk in the forest and mountains she had seen in the vidcast. "When Cottman IV was discovered, or rediscovered counting the first landfall as successful, it was described as a Class M planet of little or no deviation from the norm. We convinced ourselves the inhabitants were Terran, but they have regressed very far from their roots."

David stood and joined her at the window. "They couldn't fix their ship because they could not find the resources to do so. The decision must have been made to cannibalize their ship and use its resources to survive."

Returning to her desk, she started punching buttons. "A colonization expedition would have the experts on hand to find those resources. Why couldn't they?" Lucia pulled up the latest satellite geological survey. "Cottman IV is quite low on the scale of typical Class M accumulations of iron and heavy metals. Disturbingly so, in fact."

Stepping over to her desk, David studied the survey displayed up on Lucia's monitor. Excitedly, he pointed to the mass spectrometer projections. "The Darkovans have managed to deplete an already understocked planet of useful metals—without visible mines. How?" Holding up a warding hand, David said, "Don't answer that, their answer always contains their word *laran*. So they stripped the ship of anything useful."

"Your point, Lieutenant?"

"What happened to the atomics? Early Terran ships were powered by fusion or fission rockets. Remains of the power sources have to be somewhere."

The director queried the report on the screen. "There is a mention in here that atomics have been found scattered over sizable areas, making them too risky to salvage. The Darkovans claimed their ancestors used *laran* to pull up atomic material and made it into weapons to kill. The survivors of that conflict said that the dispersion was done to prevent their use again—that the gods forbid their use."

Reading the displayed material, David pointed to a table. "All the material is a collection of unstable heavy metals, mostly refined uranium. It is not fission or fusion byproducts. Core material from a star drive would contain byproducts."

Lucia sank heavily into her chair. "We don't put much faith in the claim that the Darkovans pulled it from the ground with *laran*. It is also hard to believe their non-industrial culture could refine uranium. There is a theory that Cottman IV experienced collateral damage between warring space factions. An unlucky wayward round or two. The radiation fields are not that extensive."

David grimaced. "I've heard of that theory but know from the spectrometer readings that the material scattered over the surface was not exploded atomics. They tried to explain that data away as Cottman IV having been used as a dump site. In any case, we need to survey those sites directly."

"All our attempts to send an expedition to find out what is really in those fields are strenuously opposed by the Darkovans. That request for research is out of my department, Lieutenant. I can't help you."

"This is a classified operation. We do not have permission from the Darkovans. Use covert tactics and avoid detection by anyone, I repeat, anyone at all costs. Employ stealth. Use an unarmed scout flyer, and do not engage anyone with personal weaponry under any circumstances. This is a two-man operation. If you are discovered, we will state you were conducting a training flight for our latest recruit, Scout Eddard Ridenow. To avoid their psionic inquisition, no one other than me knows anything about what you are doing out there. That includes Scout Ridenow. Am I clear, Lieutenant?"

David acknowledged with a firm, "Yes, sir!" He looked at the drawn face of Legate Rystov. The stakes were pretty high for what Rystov was risking and the likely return of little real value to him politically. "Sir, I think the earliest humans had help. That help came from advanced sapient beings who originated from this world, depleted its resources, and then journeyed into space to keep their people alive. Time passed, and their race dispersed among the stars. As with all species, there are those who believed in purity of race and stayed home and covered their tracks so the spacefarers would not be traced back to Cottman IV. It is just that we can't find them." David pointed at the legate's office window. "They have to be out there!"

"You have this one shot to prove that, David, and not a lot of time. Return to us. If you don't come back, it doesn't prove they exist. Dismissed."

The scout flyer hovered close to ground while David checked the flight path for the umpteenth time. Eddard sat quietly in the co-pilot's seat and traced with a finger the glowing line on the navigation screen. "Your records of our population dispersement are amazingly accurate. There are families plotted on the map that are mostly legend to us."

"The data is a compilation of what your people have told us, Eddard. We have just gathered it from many more sources than those you have had access to. Your people come from a narrow gene pool and have been breeding among a relatively select few families."

Holding up his hand, Eddard wiggled his six fingers. "I barely understand 'gene pool,' but I take it is the cause of some of us having an extra finger. My people believe it is because of the *chieri*."

David taped a correction into the navigator and glanced at Eddard. "It may also have been due to radiation from your wars, or constant exposure to Darkover's sun, or something in the water. We have on Terra legends of creatures that have walked our planet..."

"Oh, yes. I read about the 'yeti' and 'bigfoot.' I don't remember there being offspring from these creatures."

"But they were derived from 'Neanderthals,' Scout Eddard. They were mutations that occurred naturally on our planet—from radiation, sun, water, etc."

"Good point, sir. You have found their 'DNA' and verified these things?"

"No, no more than we have found anything special from *chieri* in yours. That is why we are out here today, Scout Eddard. Your research, combined with ours, gives a probable location where the ship landed." Pointing at the screen, David said, "Here. It is near a radiation field. We are going in to make a quick survey. Are you ready, Eddard?"

"Ready and willing, sir!"

The scout flyer ghosted along a meter above the river's surface at a speed well over two hundred kilometers per hour. Its passage was marked only by a wave of water pushed below the narrow black hull, which rapidly and noiselessly dispersed on the surface. The craft darted ashore to avoid villages that lay along the rare fords where roads crossed the river, then returned to its former course. In the deep of night there was little activity on the water and almost none on the roads. They were making good progress.

"Why aren't we rising above the clouds?" Eddard asked, staring at the shifting video image. He found it highly unusual to follow their actual flight through the air without actual visual reference to the ground. For all he knew, he was watching a movie of their flight.

"We're being graded on this exercise for being undetected. This includes our own people. We are emitting no energy sources, and allowing no reflections, including those coming from our windows. Ours are using radar—you've read about radar?"

Eddard nodded. "I don't understand how it works, something about light we can't see bouncing off the flyer and reflecting back to sensors that can see it."

"Close enough. We're approaching the mountains surrounding the area we want to search. It is here on the navigation screen."

Eddard glanced at the screen, then at the lieutenant's face. "You look worried, sir. Is something wrong?"

David touched a screen below the navigator panel. "We had perfect weather en route and into the mountains. Now, from our captured readings of weather sensors, there are storm clouds building up rapidly all around our area. These were not predicted at all for the next twelve hours. It looks like we are going to run into some violent winds and heavy rain."

"Shouldn't we should seek shelter, sir? I remember that storm the day I ran away from Saint Valentine's, and it kept every air car and flyer grounded. It almost killed my cousin Mikhail and you trying to get to the monastery."

David grinned. "This scout flyer is a different bird of wing than most of the ones you are familiar with. It is built to handle this weather. It may be a rough ride, but that shouldn't stop us."

"If you say so, sir, but the mountains we are trying to reach are higher and more rugged than those around Nevarsin. It was with good reason my ancestors fled to the surrounding valleys."

The first gusts began hitting the flyer, and David programmed their flight path to a higher altitude. Watching his sensors record the air mass activity around the flyer, David told the now-worried scout they had to risk climbing above the mountain ridges in search of air that was not churned up by winds pouring over and around the mountains. Higher up, the winds were very strong and had the effect of pushing them away from their intended landing point. Their ground speed rapidly dropped to a snail's crawl.

"We're going to have to risk the shaking and buffeting at a lower altitude, Scout Eddard. We're not making any progress to the landing zone you picked out. Make sure you're strapped in tight. We are..."

The loud blaring of a klaxon cut off his words. His eyes swiveled to the rapidly blinking red light on the flight control panel. He swore an oath that the young scout had never heard translated before. "It's the intruder alert. Someone is trying to hack into the flight control computer. Push that button next to the flashing light."

Eddard reacted quickly. The klaxon stopped wailing, but the displays on the console all blinked out. The window shields snapped open so that Eddard was able to see outside for the first time that night. What he saw was the heavily forested side of a mountain rushing toward him, and he gasped out, "We're going to crash!"

The lieutenant calmly said, "No, we are not. Help me search for a spot to land. Your eyes are better than mine on this planet."

Eddard pointed off to the right of the window, at a clearing of trees that looked like a cut for a road. David turned his gaze in that direction. After a precious few seconds, he said, "Got it," and mashed a button on the flight stick, which had popped out of a recess in the console directly in front of him.

A visible laser lanced from the nose of the flyer and lit up the center of the clearing. To Eddard's eyes the craft was flying down a string of light connecting it to a spot on the ground of the clearing. They were moving too fast, and he found himself pushing back into his chair to avoid what he was sure would be the ground crashing through the windscreen.

"Try to relax, Eddard. The Inertial Navigator has us well in hand. Keep an eye out for anyone or anything watching us. I have to reset the Believe circuit." With that, the lieutenant unstrapped himself from his seat and made his way to the core computer. Eddard found himself staring after David, then, suddenly remembering his orders, frantically looked back at the approaching clearing.

His stomach told him before his vision verified that the clearing abruptly slowed and halted its approach. His scream died in his throat, and he stared open-mouthed at the small, furred creature returning his stunned expression.

"Zandru's hell, it's a *kyrri*, sir!"

The snap of a relay closing presaged the revival of the console screens and the furious blinking of a highlighted image of an actual animal with glowing green eyes staring at them through the windscreen. David took his seat and returned the creature's stare. "I've heard of them. Can you speak to it? My *cahuenga* is terrible, my *casta* worse." Hitting a button on the console, David gestured for Eddard to speak.

"Ah, aah!"

Barely suppressing a chuckle, David said, "Scout Eddard, I can do better than that." In crude *cahuenga*, the lieutenant said, "Can you speaky me?"

The *kyrri* just stared back wide-eyed.

"Sir, as far as I know they can only communicate with *leroni* using *laran*."

"Damn it, psionics again." David sat back in his chair. Eddard noticed the lieutenant's finger hovering over a button on the console.

"Don't kill him, Lieutenant! He may be in communication with his own people, if not linked to a tower."

Moving his hand away and into his lap, David sighed, "You're right, the whole planet probably now knows we're out here." Staring at the *kyrri*, he wondered, "You don't suppose he/she/it is in shock? I would be if a flyer suddenly appeared in my face out of the night sky."

"I think it is a male. From the expression in his eyes, I'd say he has been badly frightened. Still, he hasn't run away. Let me try something, Lieutenant." Eddard raised his right hand and spread his fingers to show he was unarmed, saying, "Peace be with you" in *cahuenga*.

The *kyrri* blinked, and his eyes narrowed, focusing on the six fingers. He slowly waved them to follow him.

While the *kyrri* waited at the edge of the forest, David pulled out two sets of trail gear and handed one to Eddard. The gear clipped to an A-frame harness and carried a week's worth of supplies necessary to survive in Cottman IV's environment with its often rapid changes. David holstered a standard-issue laser pistol to his utility belt but did not hand one to Eddard. As part of their contracts, native scouts were not allowed to carry weapons except for their own Darkovan blades.

After a quick equipment check, the two headed for the exit hatch. From a storage locker next to the exit, David took out two recording sensors and handed one to Eddard.

"We were close to the radiation fields just before we got hacked. We're going to need these. They will let us know if we encounter radiation."

Turning the instrument around in his hand, Eddard asked, "How does it work?"

David sighed at the delay his explanation was going to take. "Listen, unstable material is radioactive because the atoms that make up the materials want to be stable. They are unstable because they have too much energy. The atom throws out the excess energy..."

"Sir, the question I meant to ask is how do you turn it on?"

"Slide the cover off the probe—there. Then push that button—here. The measurement shows on the screen below the 'on' button. If the radiation level starts to become life-threatening, you'll hear a buzzing. Got it?"

"Yes, sir."

Searching the clearing's edge, David saw the *kyrri* beckoning to them. "You lead out, I'll follow. Let's go."

The *kyrri* led them at a pace that was fast for him but was a good ground-eating walk for them. Trying to talk to the gray-furred humanoid had proven of no value, with their questions answered only by blank stares. After an hour of marching through the trees, Eddard obviously lost interest in the never-changing terrain and started asking the lieutenant questions.

"Sir, you said you had to reboot the Believe circuit. What does it do?"

Taking a sip from his water bottle, David thought of the easiest answer that he could offer to explain stealth technology. "There are two ways you can actually know where any object is. First, you can bounce energy off it and then get the range and direction of the reflected energy. We use many types of sensors—like sound and all of the forms of light you can imagine. The other way you can detect an object is to track the energy that comes off the object. The noise it makes..." glancing at the *kyrri* ahead "...or doesn't make. Body heat—like the banshee birds. Radar that the object is using to look for you. To make yourself invisible, you must not radiate any energy yourself and not reflect any energy being sent to highlight yourself."

Eddard nodded. "That seems clear enough to me, but what does the believing have to do with it?"

"We can't always stop energy from radiating away from us or emitting it ourselves. When we have to use energy to locate objects we don't want to hit, for example. A blind person who knows where everything is in a room can walk quite easily. But if you move an object out of its proper place, that person will be forced to relocate it by some means, often with a cane."

David reached out and touched Eddard's shoulder, pointing to their guide. The *kyrri* had stopped and was staring off toward the right. He seemed to be more listening than staring. David followed the humanoid's example.

"Sir, I don't hear anything. You?"

The guide seemed to nod at something and silently started off again. David followed after him. "Nada. Maybe he was talking with his psionics. Your cousin Mikhail once told me *leroni* used animals to see and hear for them."

"I am not privy to such knowledge. I have been tested and told I am, as the expression is called, head-blind."

"Too bad, it would come in real handy right now."

Eddard shrugged. "There exists a fear with my people that *laran* could be used to control or trick a person into doing something they normally wouldn't do."

"Interesting that you should say that. That is what the Believe circuit is for. That part of the computer constantly monitors the data coming from the sensors. If the data coming from one sensor starts changing and does not correlate with what other sensors are saying the object is doing, it disbelieves all sensor data and switches to the Inertial Navigator. It knows where you are in space and shuts off all external forces driving the craft, and your path becomes ballistic. Someone or thing got into our sensors, was sensed, and tripped the circuit."

"Hence we were flying blind, right, sir?"

"Correct. The computer knew where point A was, it needed a point B it could trust. We provided that with the input from flight stick. Once the flyer was safe, I reset the Believe circuit."

"But who got into our sensors, sir?"

David pointed ahead to a crowd of *kyrri* advancing to meet them. "I was hoping we would find the answer when we reached wherever our guide was taking us."

A white-furred, ancient female *kyrri* took over the job of leading the party, and the remaining humanoids formed up around David and Eddard as a sort of escort guard. A short hike later they found themselves led to a cave. Only the old *kyrri* ushered them inside. The rest of the humanoids squatted down outside the cave facing the entrance tunnel.

She made her way through the tunnel without the benefit of any light, but David and Eddard were forced to rely on hand lanterns with red lenses on them. The lieutenant quipped to his scout, "Do you have ghosts on Darkover? I could easily believe in them after watching her up ahead of us."

"I and my fellow students at St. Valentine's believed the monastery was haunted. I never really saw one."

The ancient *kyrri* stepped into a large opening and stood pointing at a pool of water in the center of the cavern. The pool glowed with a strange blue light.

David pointed his detector at it and crept slowly toward the edge of the pool. "There's something down there. I'm picking up gamma radiation." He switched the lens cover from red to clear and set the lantern on high intensity, then shined the beam into the pool. "That's a control rod from a ship's reactor. What the hell is it doing in there?"

The scout was not looking into the pool. His eyes had alighted on a tall, ghostly white, six-fingered humanoid man with one finger to his lips.

Eddard stared in awe. *Then they have not died out as we feared.*

The *chieri's* thought entered Eddard's mind. *So we wished you to believe. Neither you nor David will remember what really happened this day, but because you are one of my people, I need to explain why we did what we are going to do.*

Did we do something wrong? Eddard asked in his head.

David is becoming a threat to our people. We have to distract him from his real mission, which is to uncover the existence of the chieri.

Eddard shook his head. *No, he is just trying to find proof of the existence of a Terran ship.*

He believes that someone may be tampering with historical records. It is true, we have. Now we will do so again. It is necessary we make an adjustment to our plan. No one need die if we succeed in this deception. Here is what are going to do.

Eddard understood and approved, just before he crumpled to the ground next to the supine David.

Lucia raised her coffee mug in a salute to David. "Congratulations on your find, Lieutenant—so sorry, I should have said, Captain."

David made a small bow in acknowledgement. "My mission was a complete success. We sortied into the area of highest probability for the detection of a ship's reactor core. We got a reading for a control rod and, on landing after a day-long search, found it lying in a deep pond. We safely recovered it. The name of the manufacturer and their control number stamped into the rod will allow us to identify the reactor it belongs to, which in turn, will give us the name of the ship. We now have a traceable link."

"This calls for something stronger." Lucia said, pulling out a bottle of Scotch from her desk drawer.

Passing his mug over to be filled, David winked at the Director of Research. "Now about my other project..."

THE PRICE OF STARS

by India Edghill

Our revelry concludes with a tale that involves both an unusual form of *laran* (two, actually, but only one that plays a crucial role in the plot) and a journey. On Darkover as everywhere, the conflict between the demands of duty and the longing for freedom can lead to unexpected resolutions.

A writer of historical novels (so far, mostly set in Ancient Israel) and fantasy short stories (set everywhen from India to Darkover to Imperial Russia), India's love of history has resulted in the acquisition of far too many books on far too many subjects. A former resident of the beautiful Mid-Hudson Valley, New York, India and her Cavalier King Charles Spaniels now live in the beautiful Willamette Valley in Oregon.

Don't expect to get any of the real names in this tale from *me*. If the future falls out as I think it will, the names will eventually become all too obvious. I hope I'll have lived a long life and be long dead by the time that happens. On the other hand, my luck has never been that good.

And don't think you can read them from me, either. While I possess what is usually the most worthless Gift in all the Domains—no one, absolutely *no one,* can Read me—in this case, it's actually valuable. Usually, it's just another reason for my family to regard me as useless. Come to that, it's proved useful on one other very important occasion. But it's my twin sister who's the shining star in our family, which is why I was surprised to be summoned by my father the day all this started.

"You're going to the Dry Towns," Father told me. Even for Father, this was outrageous; while I was gaping at him, he rushed through his explanation for why my presence there was vitally necessary. The Dry Towns, you see, contained within its barbarous borders a very valuable gem indeed: a maiden whose *laran* was so strong she'd attracted the attention of the Keeper of a certain powerful Tower. And since my twin sister was working in that Tower, it was inevitable that she—and I—would be seen as the perfect pawns to collect the priceless young lady and escort her to—

"The Tower," I said, using my best Bored Young Lord voice.

"Here," my father said. "You and Darissa will bring her here, until it's decided what's best to do with her."

"You want me to take Darissa to the Dry Towns?" Taking a Comynara to the Dry Towns and expecting to bring her back again—well, perhaps Father planned to trade Darissa for the Dry Towns girl. If that were his plan, I really would have to object....

"Why not?"

"Why not? Really, Father—"

"Darissa rides better than you do, Dario."

That was hardly the point, but I abandoned that argument and started a new one. "Darissa will want to take her back to the Tower," I pointed out. Since Darissa hoped to one day be Keeper in a Tower herself—Sharra Alone knows why—I thought it would be more likely she would fall in with her Tower's wishes than her father's. However, our father was a hopeless optimist.

"Darissa will do as she is told, as a woman should." My father glared at me as if I'd contradict him again. I didn't—but if Darissa did as she was told, it would be the first time she ever had.

"As you say, Father. But why am *I* going?"

The answer staggered me; I hadn't thought my father given to outrageous humor. "Why, to ask for the girl's hand in marriage."

"I'm going to *what?*" Last I'd heard, I was going to marry Camilla—well, as I've said, no real names, so I won't mention that family's name, but it's a good one—unless my father discovered a better catch before our wedding day.

"Well, we need some way to get the girl out of the Dry Towns. What better way than a marriage proposal?"

I managed to not offer any suggestions. Instead, I said, "But what about little Camilla? You *do* remember I'm betrothed to her? And isn't she about ready for marriage by now?" I knew perfectly well that Camilla had only just turned thirteen; I'd given her a copper butterfly clasp to celebrate her nameday.

"Don't be ridiculous, of course you're not actually going to marry a Dry Towns girl.... Although she is very gifted.... You know, that might not be a bad idea..." My father looked thoughtful. "You know, Dario, perhaps you have a brain after all—"

"Oh, I don't think so," I said hastily. "And we can't disappoint that family, you know. They're counting on me marrying Camilla."

"Betrothals were made to be broken."

I dropped the subject before the notion of marrying me to a Dry Towns girl took serious possession of Father's mind. Instead, I asked precisely how and why I had become enamored of this unknown girl a thousand miles from my father's castle.

"Oh, ask your sister. She'll come up with something."

This wasn't as encouraging as Father probably meant it to sound.

When I applied to Darissa for more information than our father had chosen to divulge, I wished I hadn't. For of course, inevitably, little Lady Jelisaveth dwelt in Shainsa, the grimmest, most rigidly unfriendly of all the collection of dust-heaps known as the Dry Towns. It was also about as far from the Domains as it could be while still being on the same planet. I tried, tactfully, to point this out to Darissa.

"*Shainsa?* Now *really,* Darissa—"

"Blessed Cassilda, stop whining, Dario!" Darissa's my older sister—older by exactly thirteen minutes. Add in that she's got *laran* and I have the single most useless Gift *ever,* and you see why she's the bossy one. "You know perfectly well that Jelisaveth's family won't just hand her over—"

"I am not whining, I am simply pointing out that Shainsa's apt to be—"

"—to a Comynara, especially if they think she's of value, assuming a Dry Towns brute can manage to think a mere female of any value to anyone."

"—even more dangerous than the average Dry Town, and it's so far away it might as well be on—on Terra!"

"So you asking for her will make sense to her father—especially since you're so besotted you'll do anything to marry her."

"Oh, and I became besotted with this paragon of rare delight exactly *how*, sister dear? Father said you'd come up with something to explain why I'm panting to wed this girl."

"He did?" This made even Darissa pause for a moment. Then she waved the problem aside. "I'm sure I can think of a plausible story."

"And the bride-price? Or do you expect her father to hand her over for nothing?"

"The Tower will pay it. Anyway, none of that matters. What matters is Jelisaveth. We must rescue her."

Rescue her? As far as I'd heard, the girl was in the bosom of her family, perfectly safe. "Why did I let myself get talked into this madness?"

"Because it's your duty as a Comyn. We can *not* leave a child with that much untrained power in the clutches of the Dry Towns." Darissa glared at me meaningfully.

As everyone knows, an untrained telepath is a danger to themself and others. "But—"

"But nothing. We have to get her out."

I stopped talking. Once Darissa gets that *I'm older and wiser* tone in her voice, no possible good ever comes of arguing with her.

We rode down out of the Kilghard Hills with an impressive entourage—I still couldn't imagine how Father thought he'd profit from this affair, but I assumed he'd thought of *something*. As I wasn't paying for it, I didn't care, save that I knew we'd at least be comfortable. I should have remembered that nothing my father plots is ever pleasant or comfortable for anyone else.

Darissa did indeed "come up with something" to explain our journey of a thousand miles so I could propose marriage to a Dry Town girl I'd never met. Something absolutely preposterous, but what else but something outrageous would be, well, believable in an affair like this?

Of course, she didn't confide the details to me until we were well on the road to Carthon—probably for fear I'd turn my horse around and ride straight back home. That just showed she didn't know me very well, really. I would have turned my horse around and ridden straight to Camilla's father and asked to marry Camilla *di catenas* immediately.

"You saw her in a dream."

"I *what?*"

"You're a poet. They dream a lot."

"Not like that we don't." One epic poem and half-a-dozen sonnets, none of them worth reciting twice, but they'd marked me for life as "The Poet." I was better at writing music, actually, and longed to be a bard—but the jokes about my poetry were bad enough. Almost as bad as the poems, actually. "How do you come up with these things, Darissa?"

Darissa ignored my perfectly reasonable question. "Just remember, you're mad to marry her."

"And I knew how to find this veiled, secluded Dry Towns girl that I saw in a dream *how?*" I fell in love with *a girl in a dream. I ask* you. "Well, sister dear? How about something this girl's father—"

"You know perfectly well that her name is Jelisaveth, and she's—"

"I don't care if she's Camilla and the Blessed Cassilda combined. I don't want her undoubtedly murderous barbarian father taking a sword to my neck the second I start talking about marrying his damn daughter."

Darissa considered the matter for less than a minute, which gives you some idea of how important she thought the explanation was. "Just act like a besotted poetical idiot. That shouldn't be too hard for you."

I sighed. Loudly. "I *am* already betrothed, you know."

"That only adds verisimilitude to your wild passionate love. You'll throw aside all obstacles, and all—"

And all common sense. I could hardly believe my levelheaded sister was spouting this nonsense.

"—objections," Darissa finished, adding, as I stared at her, "Besides, your little Camilla's dreadfully boring, isn't she?"

"Not that boring." True, Camilla was a docile, well-mannered girl—well, what could you expect when she, like me, is the younger twin, and her slightly older sister is named Cassilda? "And not that little, actually—"

"It *doesn't matter.* You're not actually marrying Jelisaveth!"

Darissa sighed, even more loudly than I had. "Do *try* to keep that in mind."

I kept that in mind. I just wished everyone else involved in this escapade would.

I gazed upon Thendara, if only from the hills as we circled the city. The clear autumn air let us clearly see the *Terranan* spaceport lurking outside Thendara. A monstrous wall surrounded the alien space, and vast machines hulked behind that wall. The *Terranan* had come to Darkover, and their spaceport looked very, very permanent. For a moment I wondered what Darkover possessed that a space-faring people could possibly want, then shrugged. It was certainly nothing to do with me.

Or so I thought then.

I didn't bother to mention my thoughts on the *Terranan* spaceport to my sister. Her expression clearly indicated she had no interest in *Terranan* and less than no interest in their spaceport. I had to admit it looked less than attractive. Or was that the point? Keeping people in, or keeping them out...?

"What are you staring at, Dario? Move your horse!"

Honestly, you'd think Shainsa was just the other side of the hill and we were late for an urgent meeting. I considered asking Darissa what we'd do if we got to Shainsa and Jelisaveth had been married off to a Dry Town lord the day before we arrived—but then decided I didn't want to hear her answer. It would probably involve another clever plan that couldn't possibly fail. Until it inevitably did, and guess who would wind up blamed for the disaster? Me, that's who.

Since we knew Jelisaveth lived in Shainsa, I'd thought we'd avoid the other desert cities, but instead we rode straight into Carthon, where Darissa insisted I ask where I might find the Lady Jelisaveth. As Darissa was a mere female, none of the Dry Town men would talk to her, so she'd had to put on a veil *and* wrist chains and make do with me as her voice. As you can imagine, this didn't improve her temper much.

"If I fell in love with her in a dream, why didn't I dream about where she lived, too?"

"Why are we even having this conversation?"

"I just think it's odd I don't know where I'm going to find this girl when I know her name, that's all."

"It adds verisimilitude to—"

"A pathetically inadequate explanation?"

"Oh, stop being difficult and go ask that spice merchant! You might even suggest Shainsa as a place she can be found, if you can do it subtly."

I looked at the spice merchant, and then decided to ask the man standing by the booth instead. He wore a lot of heavy copper-etched iron ornaments, and seemed to me far more likely to know where a well-born Dry Towns lady might be found. He regarded me with about as much delight as Darissa had when she saw me ignore her choice in favor of my own. But I'd been right; the man had heard of Jelisaveth—or, as he put it, he had heard of her father, Lord Wolfran—and to my absolute amazement, he seemed relieved to tell me everything I wanted to know, and by the time I returned to Darissa's side, he was gone.

Almost as if he'd been waiting for me to get there and ask—

It was a fleeting thought, banished by my enjoyment of the look on Darissa's face when I said, "Guess what? The Lady Jelisaveth's father lives in Shainsa. Why don't we just ride straight there now?"

Jelisaveth's father turned out to own a considerable part of Shainsa, and his fortress truly inspired wonder. I wondered, for example, how Darissa and I were going to leave the place if Jelisaveth's father decided he wanted to keep us. I wondered, too, what Darissa would say if I brought up this very minor point, but I suspected this concern, too, would come under the catchall heading of *worrying about every little detail.*

Rather to my surprise, we were admitted to Lord Wolfran's fortress without argument and without delay. Very much to my surprise, Lord Wolfran greeted us happily. Of course, he ignored Darissa and politely stared straight at me.

"Greetings to you, Comyn. You're here for my daughter?"

What made him say that? How did he know? Still, since he'd brought up the subject, and since he was smiling, agreeing that I was here for his daughter didn't seem too risky. "I've heard so much about her, I feel as if I know her well already," I added hopefully.

"Who can truly know a woman well?" Lord Wolfran asked. "But once she's your wife, Comyn, you may know her as well as you choose."

Is that a joke? If it was, it was in rather poor taste.

"I vow I will treat your daughter—" I hesitated, considering the best promise to make. *As well as he would himself? No, I think not.* "—I will treat her as well as she deserves," I finished. That seemed safe enough.

"Of course. She will be a fine wife to any man. Have no fear of that. Now you may see her." Lord Wolfran sounded eager to hand her over. Too eager? How could I know? I'd never met a *Dry Towner* for more than five minutes before.

"Perhaps you wonder how and why I—"

But Lord Wolfran didn't let me get well-started on the nonsensical explanation for my presence in his home. He turned and beckoned, and a girl walked forward from the shadows behind his chair. At first I thought I knew why he was eager to marry her off to anyone who'd have her, for Jelisaveth certainly was no great beauty. She was as thin as a stray cat and pale as winter milk, though her hair was a true burning copper rarely seen even among the Comyn. Her eyes—well, I couldn't see her eyes. She stared down at the chains wound through her long thin fingers.

"You may speak to her," her father announced.

For a moment words actually failed me. Finally I said, "How old are you, my lady Jelisaveth?" Feeble as an opening gambit, I know, but really, she barely looked twelve, and I wasn't going to pretend to be in love with a child no matter what *anyone* said.

"In fourteen days I will be fourteen." She never looked up, as if the chains on her hands also chained her eyes. Then she slanted a fleeting glance at me through her long fire-bright lashes. Her lashes so veiled her eyes that I wasn't even sure if her eyes were dark or light—not that it mattered of course, any more than what she looked like mattered. All that mattered was her Gift.

Poor girl, I thought, and smiled at her encouragingly. To my surprise, I received the shadow of a smile in return. An enchanting smile; it transformed her face, let me see the beauty hidden behind her shyness.

Lord Wolfran nodded, and Jelisaveth walked over to the long table and poured a goblet full of wine from a truly over-elaborate jug. With great care, she carried the goblet to me and offered it. *She's so graceful. Graceful as a cat—no, that's too trite. Graceful as—as—*

"My lord?" she whispered, and lifted the goblet a fraction of an inch.

I took the wine goblet, and I received that shadow-smile once again. *Such a lovely girl. So sweet, and so—* The only word that came to mind was *chained.* Well, soon she'd be all mine and those chains would fall away....

"So, you like her?" Lord Wolfran asked.

Based on my extensive knowledge of her? I resisted the temptation to ask that aloud. Instead, I said, "How could I not?"

Lord Wolfran looked relieved. "Good, good. Now we'll send the women where they belong, and drink like men."

As opposed to drinking like what? However, I merely nodded and smiled as if sending the women away was the best idea I'd heard recently.

Lord Wolfran waved his hand, and Jelisaveth held her hand out to Darissa. To my surprise, Darissa didn't argue, but walked off hand in hand with Jelisaveth to wherever women belonged in Lord Wolfran's fortress. The great hall seemed empty without Jelisaveth—but at least I wouldn't have my sister glaring at me while I drank like a man.

Fortunately, Lord Wolfran didn't seem to notice that he drained his third goblet while I still toyed with my first. I had no intention of getting blind drunk while in the clutches of a Dry Town barbarian, no matter *how* enticing his daughter was.

Far, far too long a time later, I managed to suggest I needed to sleep after the rigors of my journey. Lord Wolfran and I agreed we'd discuss bride price in the morning, and then he ordered a servant to show me to my room—don't ask me how the man managed to give a coherent order after the amount he'd drunk. Even only pretending to keep up with my host's drinking, I still stumbled slightly as I walked. All I wanted now was to fling myself very gently upon a bed and lie there contemplating Jelisaveth's infinite charms. Which I did in peace for precisely three minutes before Darissa burst in.

"Oh, Dario, she is so much more than I dared hope!" Darissa was almost laughing. "Oh, untrained and unskilled as yet—but she is so strong, and so dedicated to learning to control her *laran*—she's rather afraid of it, you know, but that's only natural. And she's delightful—such a sweet girl—"

"You sound as if you're in love with her." I frowned, suddenly jealous. Jelisaveth was mine, promised to me. She counted on me to get her away from Shainsa, to safety—

"Don't be ridiculous." Darissa glared at me. "And get that look off of your face."

"I do not have a 'look' on my—"

"Jelisaveth belongs to the Tower and you know it."

No, she doesn't. She belongs—I frowned. To me? To herself? I was sure of one thing: she didn't belong to Darissa.

"Just tell me one thing, Darissa: what color are her eyes?"

"What do you mean?"

"I mean what color are her eyes?"

"Why, blue. Blue as matrix crystal. Really, even you must have noticed that color."

Whatever color Jelisaveth's eyes were, they certainly weren't matrix crystal blue. Clearly Darissa couldn't see the girl at all. She probably thought Jelisaveth a mere pawn in *Leroni* games, rather than a brilliant chained jewel—

A faint memory nagged at me; when I first saw Jelisaveth, hadn't I thought her too thin, too plain? *I must have been dust-blind.* Jelisaveth's beauty shone bright as her copper-fire hair. And her eyes—yes, her eyes were that rarest of colors, copper. Red; red as High Summer's sun. I was sure of it. And she was to be mine. My wife, no matter what my father plotted, and I would keep her safe.

"Honestly, Dario, didn't you pay any attention to Jelisaveth *at all?*"

This from a woman who hadn't even noticed that Jelisaveth's eyes were copper-red! I promptly decided Darissa didn't need to know everything I thought; even I could make sure she didn't read my thoughts! This should have struck me as very, very odd, but all I can say is that it didn't ... at that time.

"Oh, I paid as much attention to her as I needed to. Now, when can we leave? And don't sigh at me, Elder Sister, because you don't want to stay here either."

"Well, that's true enough. What a *horrible* place! I'm sure poor Jelisaveth looks forward to being freed of it and those ghastly chains she's forced to wear."

"I think they're rather attractive. Of course, not every woman can wear them well, but she does, don't you think?"

Darissa managed to refrain from calling me disgusting. "You're drunk," she announced. "I'm going to bed."

"Say goodnight to Jelisaveth for me."

I won't bother to repeat what Darissa said. If you have an older sibling, you probably have a pretty good idea of what it was.

The next morning I wished very much that I'd drunk like a young girl or like a pack pony instead of "like a man", because my head felt as if someone had dropped a rock on it. Someone had left a jug of wine and a goblet beside my bed, which seemed cruel, but I was thirsty enough to drink some, and I have to admit I felt slightly better after I did. I dressed and waited for Lord Wolfran to summon me to discuss the finer points of acquiring his daughter. When he did, the discussion that followed took less time than I'd thought it would, and the terms seemed almost too generous.

Almost as if he's pushing her out the door and into my arms. Now, I wonder why?

However, I simply agreed with everything he said, and when negotiations concluded—and the copper ingots transferred from my pack to his vaults—he slapped me on the back and told me I was welcome in his hall any time. I interpreted this as "go away and stay away forever," which suited me perfectly. I just wanted to take Jelisaveth and Darissa and get out of the Dry Towns before this entire farce collapsed from the sheer weight of accumulated absurdity.

First, however, I had to marry the girl. Yes, despite the myriad assurances I'd received that I *wasn't actually marrying Jelisaveth*, I was. Because her father wouldn't let her set foot past the door of his fortress without the key to her chains being in the proper hands. Mine.

I summoned Darissa to explain this appalling development to her. Naturally, my objections fell into the extremely large category of *worrying about every little detail.* In fact, and to my absolute astonishment, Darissa announced that this was actually a *good* thing.

"Because it will make it all so much easier," Darissa told me.

"My marrying Jelisaveth will make *what* so much easier, Darissa?"

"Don't take that tone with me, Dario! Really, even you should see that if you're already married, she'll have to stay with m— with us."

This staggered me. "What about the Tower? What about the fact that it wants Jelisaveth and will undoubtedly strongly object if we don't hand her over?"

"Oh, Dario, will you stop arguing about—"

"Every little thing," I said in chorus with her. So Darissa glared at me and stomped off. And I sat there and wondered what in the Seven Hells had happened to make Darissa shrug off the claims of a powerful Tower and forget her lifelong ambitions just to keep a little Dry Towns girl with us.

The wedding ceremony took place in the gateway between the men's portion of the fortress and the women's quarters, and like everything else there, it all seemed to take place very fast. I could almost taste the sense of haste in the air—odd, because what would "haste" taste like, anyway?—and still found myself wishing Lord Wolfran would hurry matters along so we could get out of here. I frowned, wondering why I was in quite such a rush to leave what was, after all, a rather comfortable place to rest for a week or two. I mean, I'd never seen Shainsa before, and probably never would again. Why wasn't I more curious about the place?

Come to that, why Darissa smiling on this insane ceremony—?

Then Jelisaveth's father set the key in my hand and I stopped thinking at all. Jelisaveth was clever, all right, but she wasn't even quite fourteen yet, after all. It takes life to bring wisdom, and she hadn't lived much of hers yet.

Anyway, my so-called bride held out her chained hands to me. She held them palm up, as if to accept an offering, and I almost laid that ridiculous, evil key right into those waiting fingers. Even then, I couldn't really see her eyes—*so modest*—but something made me hesitate even as I held the key out.

Hand her the key, and she ruled her own chains. Darissa had told me that not a day before, during one of our increasingly furious arguments about the girl's future. But why would a demure, modest, proper Dry Towns girl desire that? *Come to that, why would she want to go to a Tower? Why—*

The chaotic emotions vanished; I was merely standing in a Dry Town lord's hall staring at a Dry Towns girl I'd just married. I only hoped that no one in the Domains would consider this a binding marriage, or that if they did, it could be *un*bound. And that's when I realized what should have been obvious to me the first time I thought Jelisaveth was the most desirable creature under the moons.

She's playing us. She's playing us all.

But the key had been—nearly been—a mistake. Jelisaveth was desperate to leave Shainsa, as why wouldn't she be? *But this is too much haste. Far too much. She needs more patience. And I need to get us all out of here. Alive.*

If I handed Jelisaveth the key, or even unlocked her chains, I was pretty sure Lord Wolfran would object. Strongly. *Wait,* I thought as hard as I could. I didn't know if even Jelisaveth could read me, but I did my best to think very, very loudly. *Patience. It's a virtue. Trust me. Just WAIT.*

I looked questioningly at Jelisaveth, and she slanted a glance at me through the veil. Her eyes glinted in the torchlight, just as the copper key did. I thought her hands shook a bit, but then she drew a deep breath, and I found myself able to relax, and smile, and put the key's chain around my neck just as if nothing at all out of the ordinary were taking place here.

"I thank you for entrusting your daughter to my care," I said, and Lord Wolfran smiled. Rather uncertainly, but still, he did smile. I wondered if Jelisaveth had released all of us from her thrall; how much did using such power cost her? *She must be exhausted, poor girl.* I heard Jelisaveth's chains chime softly as she lowered her hands. Now she stood meek and submissive. The perfect Dry Towns bride.

But I knew better. I had solved a riddle no one else even knew existed. For now I knew what Jelisaveth's Gift was: to project her desires into the minds of others and make them take those desires for their own. Even I was not immune.

I thought of confiding this to Darissa, and realized in the same moment that should I do so, I would condemn both of us to death. To control another's will by *laran* was anathema in the Domains, as every child of the Comyn knew—and what Darissa knew, Jelisaveth also now knew. If I was certain of nothing else, I was certain of this. In my silence lay our only hope of safety.

I could only mouth humble yet pompous platitudes to Lord Wolfran, vow I would take as much care of my false bride as her father had—no, I'd take much, much better care of her—and explain that really, we simply *must* leave now, no matter how enticing his hospitality, because my father expected...

Here I trailed off into an embarrassed shrug, which Lord Wolfran, a father himself, accepted as adequate justification for our swift leave-taking. I didn't dare look at Jelisaveth, but I suspected she had something to do with her father's amiability. But there really wasn't anything I could do but bid farewell to beautiful exotic Shainsa. I hoisted my alleged bride onto a horse—I hoped her powers gave her the ability to ride, as it was unlikely she'd ever been on a horse in her life—mounted my horse, and began the long ride home to the Domains, with Jelisaveth riding beside me, prim-mouthed and outwardly docile.

You'd think heading for home would be calming and comforting—and it might have been, if I hadn't been trying to keep both Darissa and Jelisaveth from noticing how uneasy I was. Fortunately, the grueling journey gave me an excuse to put off our wedding night. I wasn't at all sure I wanted to be alone with Jelisaveth; I also was pretty sure Darissa didn't want me to be alone with Jelisaveth either.

The more I thought about Jelisaveth and what I suspected about her Gift, the more I yearned for her to be safely ensconced in the Tower ... and the less I believed she'd actually be content to remain there.

But what *would* satisfy her?

And how did she intend to gain what she desired?

Once again we circled high around Thendara. Just before the road curved north, Jelisaveth's horse stumbled—she'd learned to ride astonishingly quickly—and immediately she was out of the saddle. She ran her hand down the horse's leg, then slowly straightened and stood with her hand on its neck, staring down at—not Thendara city itself, but at the Terranan spaceport.

"How ... astonishing," she said at last.

I looked down, trying to see the spaceport with her eyes. It still looked ominous to me, and the electric lights the Terranan used created a ghastly glare even in full daylight. But it entranced Jelisaveth.

"Such ugly things." Darissa turned away, but Jelisaveth remained still.

"I think they ... could be beautiful." As Jelisaveth stared down at the spaceport, I suddenly knew what color her eyes were. They were black as the depths of space and silver flashed in those depths. Silver bright as stars. Silver bright as the metal of the machines waiting on the flat artificial plain of Thendara Spaceport.

Starships shone in Jelisaveth's space-black eyes.

No marriage for her, and no Tower either. No planet will ever hold her. And I'm not even going to suggest someone ought to try.

A wave of sheer relief swept over me as I realized Jelisaveth didn't want me. She had used me, that was all. I couldn't blame her for that. She'd only been rescued from the Dry Towns because the Tower had uses for her and her power.

And thanks to Jelisaveth, I'd developed a new appreciation for my docile little Camilla. Life with her might be boring—but there were far worse fates than a placid wife and a boring life. No—a peaceful life. Yes, peaceful. I would, I thought, make sure I never went within a hundred miles of the Drylands again—or of Thendara spaceport either.

I watched Darissa gazing adoringly at Jelisaveth. I thought of my father's plans, and of the Tower's plans. I watched Jelisaveth gaze down at the ships that she so desired. And I realized Jelisaveth cared for no plans but her own.

And why should she? Who has cared for what she wishes? No one, ever. If the Terranan ever learned of her Gift, they too would seek to turn her to their own use. *Good luck,* I thought, unsure to whom I sent that silent wish.

I only hoped my Gift would keep Jelisaveth from knowing just how much I'd guessed about her. And I twice hoped Jelisaveth never found any more uses for me.

As for the mighty, cocksure *Terranan* ... I suspected they were in for a salutary shock in a few years.

ABOUT THE EDITOR

Deborah J. Ross is an award-nominated author of fantasy and science fiction. She's written a dozen traditionally published novels and somewhere around six dozen pieces of short fiction. After her first sale in 1983 to Marion Zimmer Bradley's *Sword & Sorceress*, her short fiction has appeared in *F & SF, Asimov's, Star Wars: Tales from Jabba's Palace, Realms of Fantasy, Sisters of the Night, MZB's Fantasy Magazine,* and many other anthologies and magazines. Her recent books include Darkover novels *Thunderlord* and *The Children of Kings* (with Marion Zimmer Bradley); *Collaborators,* a Lambda Literary Award Finalist/James Tiptree, Jr. Award recommended list (as Deborah Wheeler); and *The Seven-Petaled Shield,* an epic fantasy trilogy based on her "Azkhantian Tales" in the *Sword and Sorceress* series. Deborah made her editorial debut in 2008 with *Lace and Blade,* followed by *Lace and Blade 2, Stars of Darkover* (with Elisabeth Waters), *Gifts of Darkover, Realms of Darkover,* and a number of other anthologies.

THE DARKOVER® ANTHOLOGIES

THE KEEPER'S PRICE, 1980
SWORD OF CHAOS, 1982
FREE AMAZONS OF DARKOVER, 1985
OTHER SIDE OF THE MIRROR, 1987
RED SUN OF DARKOVER, 1987
FOUR MOONS OF DARKOVER, 1988
DOMAINS OF DARKOVER, 1990
RENUNCIATES OF DARKOVER, 1991
LERONI OF DARKOVER, 1991
TOWERS OF DARKOVER, 1993
MARION ZIMMER BRADLEY'S DARKOVER, 1993
SNOWS OF DARKOVER, 1994
MUSIC OF DARKOVER, 2013
STARS OF DARKOVER, 2014
GIFTS OF DARKOVER, 2015
REALMS OF DARKOVER, 2016
MASQUES OF DARKOVER, 2017

CPSIA information can be obtained
at www.ICGtesting.com
Printed in the USA
LVOW10s2349161117
556633LV00008B/165/P